The Poor Singer of an Empty Day

Robert John Goddard

DEDICATION

This book is dedicated to all the boys and girls I played with at Thames Ditton Primary School from 1958 until 1960. Wishing you all the very, very best.

ACKNOWLEDGMENTS

Having an idea for a novel and turning it into a cover picture design is hard. I want to thank Andrea for creating a wonderful cover for *The Poor Singer of an Empty Day.*
andrea.price.concept

1

Journal of Julian Everet - 28 November 1968

Midnight. God help me to sleep. Keep these diaries safe after what I've just seen and done. I can't believe what's happened. I'm ashamed and I'm frightened at what I've become. He hit you in the face. I did nothing about it. I could have helped you. Some hero! I've rescued you a thousand times in my dreams. A hero would've run to your side. I just ran away. I've done a terrible thing. God help me find peace.

Can't sleep. Don't understand. The evening was just like the others. It wasn't a wild and stormy night, full of foreboding. It was just another autumnal evening with a hint of mist hanging low over the streets, and the hedges were damp, bare and forlorn. In other words, it was no different from all the other countless and wonderful evenings when I've followed you home. I was behind you as usual. This time I was clutching a bouquet of red roses to my chest. I'd written on a little card: "Dear Kathy." It was a beginning and an end. I had and I have nothing else to say.

The cars were whooshing past, and the pavement was wet and glistening but splashed with shimmering pools of lamplight. Your shoes clippety-clopped on the paving. Half-obscured in the darkness and the mist, you were lit up in a car headlight at full beam. I lowered my head in case you should turn and see me. You were walking faster than usual, and there was something about your back that said you were worried and tense. I wanted to approach you. I wanted to put my arms around you to comfort you and ask what was on your mind.

If only I'd summoned up the courage to approach you, it would've saved you that slap in the face. But I wasn't braver. I simply followed you at a distance as usual. When you turned into your street, I held back and I watched you fading away into the mist. You always need time to settle in. I know you always check the post before taking off your coat and turning on the heating.

He must've been in the driveway, but I didn't see him. If I hadn't been so respectful, I might've seen him there. But I am respectful of your privacy and I didn't hurry.

So, I waited for some minutes before moving forward. I kept to the edge of the pavement. I forced myself into the deepest shadows and felt the touch of moisture on my cheeks when my shoulder brushed the dripping foliage. I stopped at the hedge and parted it with my hands. There was silence except for the sound of my breathing and the rise and fall of my chest as I peered at your flat. I jumped at the sudden clackety-clack of a distant train rushing through the night.

Light bulbs burned and glimmered yellow in the autumnal evening. I can't remember whether there were other lights, and was there a car - his car - in the driveway? It's difficult to say. The mist was developing into a real fog.

You were suddenly at the window. Your arms were

spread out as if in crucifixion, and then you tugged at the curtains to shut out the night. Before turning away, you did a strange thing. You stood square at the window and you raised your hand as if signalling to someone. I turned to see if anyone else were close to me. There was nobody, and when I looked back at the window, you were gone. Why did you make that strange sign?

You had switched on a light, and it threw your shadow upon the wall. There was another shadow in the room, and it tapered upwards to break over the ceiling. The two shapes danced lightly; a ghastly shadow show played out to the music of air hissing through my nostrils. One of the shapes moved forward. A hand was raised. It chopped downwards like a guillotine. The other shadow - your shadow - crumpled out of sight.

It was awful. I was paralysed, and my mouth hung open stupidly. The next thing I heard was the song of Davy Cohen. A window was opened, and his words burst from your flat like a cork exploding from a champagne bottle: *"Goodbye Mary dear...,"* and the rat-a-tat-tat of the snare drum beating urgently into my temples.

Then, despite the thickening fog, I saw him. He was at the window, his head poking through. His face peered from right to left before withdrawing. The window clumped shut. The words of Davy Cohen were truncated whilst in full flow: *"It's time we began to live again, to laugh again, to be...,"* and then silence. But he must've forgotten to pull the catch. After a second or two, the window opened again, and Davy Cohen's words emerged once more: *"There was a time when we were not alone..."*

Could you have fallen? Did you smash your head on the radiator? There was no time to act immediately because a dog barked, and the old cow strode towards me with her arm raised. She really meant business.

3

Worst of all she remembered me from before.

"You again," she said. "There's a law against perverts like you."

I didn't wait to argue with the old bag. I saw the light go out in your flat. I heard a door slam shut, and I took to my heels and ran. Now I need to sleep. Sleep is as far away as I can get from perverts like me.

30 November

God, where is she? I can't accept the fact that you've gone. I don't believe that my eyes will never again rest upon you. Where are you? I turned up today at our usual place in the Aldwych. Waited for 90 minutes before realising you weren't going to come. Not to worry. On my way back to the Hall, I stopped in a call box near Russell Square and I phoned you. Oh, how much better I felt. How wonderful to hear the tone. That purring in my ear was actually ringing inside your flat. I knew you wouldn't be there - no matter. I was close to your presence.

1 December

Dreary and miserable evening. Pavements glistening damp, and the tops of the big buildings in the Strand disappeared into a grey cloud. The dampness worked its way through my clothes and touched my skin. I think the sky itself was crying too. No sign of her. Where are you? You didn't come, so I shadowed your usual footsteps. Dream lover, where are you? I've lived with you for so long it was easy to imagine you walking across the bridge in front of me as normal.

So, the day was already several minutes shorter than when I last saw you, and it was a little colder. I actually crossed to the embankment-side of the river as you usually do. I took the time to look at the Houses of Parliament and Big Ben. Somehow, you've left a piece

4

of yourself in these buildings. You must've done. I felt your presence in the gentle breeze that breathed up from the water. You caressed my cheeks.

Waterloo was crowded, and the usual commuters jostled around the departures board. These were faces that you saw every day, and they seemed special to me now. Part of you is in them. I was so sad when the Kingston train pulled away. The whistles followed me out of the station. Somehow, these sounds were desperate and forlorn. Please, please, please, I don't want to play this game anymore. Come out, come out! Please come out, come out, wherever you are.

Cutting from the Kingston Gazette. 19.12.1968

Appeal for Information about Missing Woman.

> *Three weeks on from her disappearance, police are reiterating appeals for any information regarding the whereabouts of a 20-year-old woman from Kingston. Kathleen McCullagh was last seen by colleagues at work on the evening of 28 November. She has not been seen since. Kathleen is white, 5ft 3ins tall, slim build, with dark shoulder-length hair and brown eyes.*
>
> *Kathleen was wearing jewellery, including a matching necklace with a shamrock-shaped pendant. When last seen Kathleen was wearing a green three-quarter-length leather coat and knee-length boots.*
>
> *Kathleen lives alone in Riverside Road, Kingston. She took no belongings or money with her and has not been in contact with*

her friends or family since. She has missed appointments and outings that she had arranged and has not been in contact on important family occasions.

DCI Robert McKinley from the Kingston Incident Room said: "Because of the length of time that Kathleen has been missing without any sightings or contact, I am very concerned about what might have happened to her. I would urge anyone who has information about her disappearance to contact police immediately. We are particularly concerned as Kathleen had complained to police that person or persons unknown were following her and making threatening calls to her flat. We are also anxious to interview a young man who was seen in the vicinity of Kathleen's flat on the evening of her disappearance. There is no evidence to suggest that Kathleen could have been harmed by the man, but this is one line of inquiry I would like resolved."

If you have any information that could assist the police with their inquiry, please contact the incident room at Kingston Police Station.

2

It was the afternoon of 3 September when Kathy came back into Julian Everet's life. Her arrival was shocking and unwelcome. She arrived from nowhere and nose-dived at his feet while he was strolling on the cliffs and watching the ferries appear and disappear in the mist. She rolled a couple of times, stopped again and stared at him.

He stared back, unsure whether to kick the face away or to hold it gently in his hands. He took a reluctant step forward and hesitated. He muttered excuses to voices telling him to run away from the guilt and shame that arrived with the face. He thought he had buried these old companions here in England but they had not gone away. They had been waiting in the air, in the grass and in the trees for almost thirty years. Now they had jumped at him with a force that stopped the world and knocked the air from his lungs.

Bending forward, regaining his breath, he warned himself that if surprises came in threes, he had better watch out. The day had started with a bizarre incident. Focused on the immediate difficulty of keeping to the left-hand side of the road, he had successfully negotiated the first roundabout. He was still keeping left when, at the next roundabout, he decided to turn right. This manoeuvre was followed by a screeching of tyres and hooting from behind. Glaring into the rear-view mirror, he snarled an obscenity. He shook his fist. His finger stabbed at the air. These were normal reactions in Italy, the gestures and behaviour of day-to-day life on the road. But he was back in England. He ducked when a beefy and tattooed arm emerged from the window of the XR2. When the fist shook, he flinched violently and knocked his temple hard against the side window.

"Oi, John," the driver shouted through his teeth, "you're in fucking England now."

The aggression that tightened the driver's eyes and thinned his lips prompted a surge of adrenaline, prepared Julian for a violent confrontation. He was relieved when the fist withdrew through the window. The driver put his foot down, and his car sped onto the one-way system and roared away into the traffic.

He was still rubbing his temple when he parked the car. He was not thinking of the past while he took deep breaths to calm himself. When he locked the car and wandered towards the city centre, he was not musing on the ways old loves had shaped him. He was focused on his reaction to his homeland.

Making his way along Dover's pedestrian precinct, Julian reckoned that, for some minutes, he had fallen victim to the illusions that had done for many expatriates he had known. Shadowy expectations had crept into his consciousness, had warped his memory. He was anticipating dark suits, bowler hats, and men marching to work with rolled umbrellas or newspapers tucked under the arm. These men would politely greet one

8

another while red buses emerged from a swirling mist and passed the telephone boxes, which stood on every corner.

He turned to his right, intending to comment on his native land. He opened his mouth to speak, but said nothing. He wanted to put his reactions into words, to articulate and clarify them so that they would have some meaning for him. He was about to express his surprise that after twenty-seven years, the Italian view of English life had become his. He wanted to comment on English people, clothes and buildings and compare them with their Italian equivalents. Italians were smarter, tidier, cleaner and better looking, but these words stuck in his throat. He had forgotten that since his wife had left there was nobody beside him. That space was now filled by an aching void, an emptiness that said without a partner with whom he could share feelings and thoughts, his experiences and his life were abstract and barren.

So, he said nothing; but he knew that his feelings and thoughts could not attach themselves to any word or expression that he could identify. He meandered from one shop window to another, pretending to be interested in the merchandise. He was hoping to see old friends reflected in the glass so that he could turn and say: *Hi, I'm back*. Seeing nobody he recognised, Julian decided to retreat from the town centre, to walk on the cliffs and collect his thoughts.

Stirrings of fear were replacing his loneliness. The fear was born of displacement, and of having lost whatever he had been hoping to find in England. The gun emplacements from World War Two and the Napoleonic fort went almost unnoticed. He knew they had registered on his consciousness because they prompted a vague feeling of contentment that here at last was the England of his memory. A crooked smile followed when he saw that rediscovery of his national identity lay in relics from past conflicts. He had little to time to consider this oddity because while he was walking back to the town, he saw Kathy.

He had stopped to wonder at the ships that steamed in and out of the harbour when he saw her at his feet. He could not mistake a face that had dominated his teenage years, and nor could he forget a face that had filled the front pages of the local press thirty years previously. The page of this paper, discarded somewhere on the cliffs, had arrived in a downward blast of air and blown against his leg. He shuffled backwards and looked down. He caught sight of Kathy's face before it tumbled away. It rolled slowly at first, and then faster and faster down the hillside.

Eventually, he decided to chase after her, but the paper got caught in another current of air and it rose towards the sky and beyond his reach. As he watched her sail away, his guilt and shame were overlaid in rapid succession by feelings that stunned him with their freshness. These feelings were connected to love and hate, to betrayal and jealousy, and they belonged to Kathy, to Hampton Court and to 1968.

Thirty years had passed since then. Julian stared at the paper pensively for some time. Thirty years, he thought, or were those years a dream? But dream or no dream, there she was, disappearing again. He gaped when he realised that once more and as always, Kathy was flying beyond his reach.

He convinced himself that it was gusts of wind from the sea that were making him shiver, that it was not shades of feeling from 1968 sending cold waves of foreboding through him. Nonetheless, needing to break away from himself, to allow his thoughts to find shelter from the past, he raced down the cliff. The dim and distorted shapes from the town beckoned him with promises of warmth, but memories were coming so fast it was impossible to escape from them.

In his mind, Kathy and her world still glistened spring-green. Those days were a time of promise, full of the dreams of Martin Luther King, of Woodstock, and of eternal youth. He looked around for someone to talk to, someone who might offer moral support. Finding nobody, he consoled himself with the notion that although he and his generation had sung the songs of hope, those times were definitely gone. He and his friends had aged, passed along and vanished.

But Kathy had not passed along. She had remained in the sixties. She had been beautiful to him, and her beauty had not worn as he had worn. For a brief moment, nostalgia and illusions got the better of him again, and he lowered his head. Images, masks of the people he had known at the Tiltyard Cafeteria solemnly returned to crowd his thoughts. He could only watch as these people from that summer of love filed past, unreachable and untouchable, under the scrutiny of his inner eye.

Julian muttered a string of curses and looked up. He was shocked and disgusted with himself, with this rush of feeling that had broken through his defences. He stared at the approaching town and decided to get a grip, to prevent these memories from taking hold and absorbing his emotional energy. He shook his head to clear it of an unwanted residue of images. He questioned the accuracy of any recollections from Hampton Court. For a moment, he believed he could see himself as he had been in 1968. Unmolested by thirty years, he was eighteen, absorbed in himself, and at the centre of the universe. But so distant was that place where memory beckoned, he had doubts. It was difficult to identify with that young man, his fine and high forehead, his shoulder-length hair, and the red, silk neckerchief. It was hard to recognise the person who used to quote William Morris and Davy Cohen in the same breath, and who carved hearts and intertwined the initials of K and J in the kiosk beside the Tiltyard Cafeteria.

The most difficult thing of all was to understand who it was that memory brought to mind. Was it giving him an image of the boy he had been then or a picture of the man he saw in the mirror every day when he shaved? Julian could not really say. The face in the shaving mirror was middle-aged and heavily lined around the mouth and forehead. The once curling and blond hair was stubbly and greying. He told himself that the Bohemian and romantic youth was detached from him now. At that time, his life had lain in front of him, but in 1998, half of it lay behind him. He was unable and unwilling to sing the songs that had once given him hope. The words of those songs now belonged to another and lost time.

Setting off down the cliff, he reckoned that even the erratic flight of the sea gulls in the wind was ordered and logical compared to his thoughts. He longed for somebody to turn to, someone whose words would fill the intolerable silence, still his inner voices and remove the unwelcome need to find out why Kathy was in the news again. He wanted to hear that the past was a dead place, that there was no longer any relationship between Kathy and him, and all that remained was the memory of her face - nothing more.

Julian glanced idly around him as though looking for something or someone he had lost. He considered the possibility that he should get into his car and drive away, that it was the future that should have been occupying his thoughts. He had come back to England to find peace amidst the turmoil of a destroyed relationship. He had come to find a lost feeling, a sense of security he thought he had once known.

Halfway down the cliff he stopped under a tree, scanned the town and listened to the faraway sounds of life that reached out to him. Shapes emerged from the distance, and occasional lights flickered in the centre of town. The lights brought with them the promise of new times, new places, new situations, and new faces. He watched all the miniature people going about their business. He imagined them leaving their pasts behind them like invisible vapour trails. Julian smiled at this image. It told him that 1968 was indeed a dead place, and that people's lives had not been standing still, frozen in time and waiting for him to come home.

He congratulated himself on having recognised this illusion before it had a chance to grow beyond his control. Earlier that day he had been hoping to see people he had once known, but untouched by the years. He received a powerful but absurd image of his old friends moving like ageless but animated photographs along these pedestrian precincts. He even managed another crooked smile when he imagined himself recognising faces, Paul's perhaps, amongst those of the faintly threatening youths grouped on street corners.

The cool air shifted and touched his hair, his face and his smile. He bathed in the conviction that there was no need to revisit the past. It was all abstract. Life had moved on. Then a starker truth revealed itself. A second passed before the importance of this revelation reached home, and he smothered the smile in his hands. The fact of Kathy's face in a recent paper was sending contradictory messages. She was telling him that life had not moved on, nothing had changed, that time may have passed and consumed identities, but everything else was the same.

He continued to argue with himself for a considerable time. In the end, and in spite of his best efforts, it was curiosity that got the better of him. A little excursion into the past, he thought, would do no harm. He turned to his right and said in an authoritative tone, "We'd better find that newspaper." He nodded as if he had heard some confirmation from a voice at his side. "Yes, that's right," he said, "just for the sake of understanding and knowing why Kathy's face is on the front page again after thirty years."

3

Strolling down Dover's main street, Julian spotted the newsagent's and the travel agency at the same time. They stood on opposite sides of the road and confronted each other, titanic challengers for his attention. He rubbed at his temple and frowned into a shop window. Reflected in its glass were the images of shoppers. They were shadows passing through the doors of the travel agency behind him. He shook his head. Kathy was no mirage. He had managed to keep her imprisoned in his diaries, but that day she had escaped and now sang to him like a siren. He took deep breaths of the sea air and stepped into the newsagents.

It was late afternoon, and the newspapers had boiled down to the fatally soiled or the unwanted. He grabbed at the first paper and scanned the front page. The faces of Bill Clinton and Tony Blair smiled at him. The headline stated they were to visit the site of the Omagh bombing that day. He flung the paper down and paced up and down the magazine rack like a caged animal. The paper he wanted could have been an edition from the previous week. It might even have been from the previous month. He almost ground his teeth when he saw the local papers, the nationals, the dailies and the weeklies. He marched up to the cashier and, indicating the papers with an outstretched arm, he confronted her with:

"Yesterday's papers. Where are they?"

His voice sounded like that of an overindulged child, and he winced as though he had let slip a surprise confession. Glancing towards the entrance he saw his way blocked by men and women looking in his direction. He tried a conciliatory smile.

"I'm really looking for yesterday's papers. Do you happen to keep them?"

The cashier eyed him suspiciously while disapproval rippled from the top of her nose to the corners of her mouth.

"We don't do yesterday's papers."

She was looking past him and at the next customer, but Julian shifted himself into her line of vision.

"Don't you know," he said, "where I can get hold of past copies?"

The ripples of disapproval turned to waves.

"Nobody reads yesterday's news," she said. "All the remaining papers go back to the printer."

Julian had a clear picture in his head of the type of person the cashier thought she was dealing with. This person was a synthesis of hundreds of similarly tired and grumpy middle-aged men with bags under their eyes, men who had left their wives to spend money in Marks and Spencer. The cashier put out her hand towards the next customer.

"Yes, please?"

Cashier and customer exchanged a glance which effectively bound them, made Julian feel excluded, an alien from another planet.

Believing further communication to be now

impossible, he spun round, snatched "The Sun" from the racks, and paid for it at another cashier. He hurried out of the shop, and strode towards the churchyard. He saw himself, left in peace, happily working his way through the paper and finding some news about Kathy.

With only memorial stones to the dead for company, Julian regained the composure he was hoping for. A bench in a hidden corner of the cemetery gave him the physical and mental space he needed. He straightened out the paper and settled it on his knees. Sitting amongst moss-covered and lonely gravestones, he clawed at the front page. He vaguely registered another image of Clinton and Blair and cracked open the paper at page two. This contained photographs of ferries and angry dockers under the caption, "French scuttle talks." There was a warning to continental travellers to check with operators before leaving home, but there was no sign of Kathy.

He was about to turn the page when he was distracted by a grave immediately beside him. The cross had broken off at the base and lay at an impossible angle. He fingered the paper, but the impossible cross demanded an explanation. It seemed to be held up to the sky by an invisible thread, and the thick layer of moss that covered it gave the impression that it had once grown like a plant from the earth itself.

He leaned over and peered at the inscription. It read:

In memory of my dear son Thomas Norman Cairns Captain second battalion Kent Regiment killed in action in France during the battle of the Somme in or near Delville Wood 30.07.1916.

The sorry and forlorn state of this memorial suggested that the captain's relatives were all dead. And if they were no longer alive, then the captain's memory had died with them, and with nobody to remember him, this man had simply never been. So it was with Kathy.

With nobody around who remembered her, Kathy had never existed either. Julian could not ask a stranger about her and yet he was surrounded by strangers. The reason for her presence in the news would be forever unknown to him.

He flicked through the advertisements and reached the sports pages. His hopes at finding Kathy had faded to nothing, but he was painfully aware of an inner voice. It was whispering to him, telling him he was happy she was not there, that he could now avoid the issue and run away from responsibility and the truth.

He tossed the paper into a bin and made a decision. It was hardly a decision at all; certainly not a conscious decision, but he had simply discovered what he had always intended to do. Instinctively, he turned to one side, his mouth already open, feeling the need to explain, the need to receive Paola's approval.

"There's no point staying here," he said. "I'm going back to Italy, to my marriage, to pick up my life."

And as he said these words, Julian convinced himself that if it was security for which he hankered, he had come to the wrong place. England was now a country of strangers. What he needed was the security of the familiar, something that belonged to him. It was only as an afterthought that an unwelcome voice in his inner ear said: *Running away again? If you do that, you'll never know why Kathy is in the news again.*

He hurried out of the churchyard, towards the place where he had parked. Fumbling in his pocket for the keys, he was struck by a wave of disharmony, the recognition of wrongness all around him. Instinctively feeling for his wallet and passport, he saw that the top of the driver's door was bent outwards at an angle of about twenty degrees, enough to get a hand inside. He allowed his gaze to travel over the back seat.

Carelessly registering the absence of his suitcase, his

eyes urgently probed for his box of diaries. With his mind racing he grabbed at the broken door. He tugged it open and plunged inside.

The box of diaries had been tipped up, and the volumes, these records of his life, lay discarded on the floor of the car. But the 1968 diary had been opened. An unexpected and unseen hand had touched the pages of the most secret year of his life. He snapped the diary shut in a way that suggested he would crush some horror which was emerging from between the pages.

"This your car, sir?"

Julian started and for the second time that day, he banged his temple against the door. He opened his mouth and silently groaned in pain. He saw the policeman through a veil of tears.

"The station's just around the corner," he said. "You're going to report this, aren't you, sir? If you'd like to follow me..."

And Julian followed meekly, rubbing his temple, wondering how this situation had come about. Why, he wondered, would any sane person willingly seek out their worst nightmare? He wiped away his tears. Then he cursed the day he had decided to come back to England, into the arms of the Police and a crime that had been waiting for him all these years.

4

In the consulting room at the local station of the Kent Constabulary, Julian blocked out the panic that stirred within him by concentrating on his surroundings. His eyes focused on the old and battered table in front of him while his fingers explored every scratch and chip of the chair beneath his backside.

His discomfort was eased by the fact that the consulting room disappointed him. He had been anticipating something more substantial, something that might match the enormity of his fears and expectations, but nothing in the room suggested power or punishment. Feeling more balanced, he got to his feet, but a distant voice forced him back into his chair. He shuffled and fidgeted, breathed deeply, and told himself it would all be over soon. This silent monologue was not helped by the drab, institutional aspect of the place. Its eternal greyness influenced his thoughts. His life had stopped, and he was waiting for the police sergeant, waiting to be pronounced guilty for a crime he had forgotten.

There was a shuffling from the corridor. Someone was about to come into the room. Julian told himself to calm down. He had come only to report a theft, but an urge to run out of the building had settled on him and would not go away. He took another breath and reminded himself that tiredness often brought out these weaknesses in him. He consoled himself with the thought that he had never yet embarrassed himself by giving way to them. The possibility of bolting reassured him, but when the policeman bustled into the room, he effectively blocked all escape routes. What was worse, there was nothing about him that promised human warmth or sympathy.

The sergeant was sharp creases, sparkling buttons and boots. He snapped to a halt behind his chair and took methodical pains to ensure that it was correctly angled. Grunting in satisfaction, he lifted the pleats of his jacket, swept them under his buttocks and sat down. Julian blinked. This surprisingly feminine motion had reminded him of graceful swans tucking away their wings as they settled on the water. The movement was completely at odds with the man's face, which was so crumpled it resembled a road map. A delicately tended moustache lined his upper lip and apparently irritated the policeman's nostrils. They constantly quivered as if the sergeant were about to sneeze.

"Sorry to keep you waiting, sir," he said.

Julian gritted his teeth, focused on the table and managed a smile while his fingers urgently probed the underside of his chair. The sergeant took a mechanical pencil from his top pocket and a sheaf of papers from a tattered document-wallet.

"What was the nature of the complaint?" he asked, flicking through the papers.

Julian coughed, cleared his throat and belched. The police sergeant looked up and raised his eyebrows.

"Everything all right, sir?"

Julian grinned.

"Stomach's a bit upset."

"Toilet?" said the sergeant. "Just down the corridor."

"I don't need a toilet."

The sergeant tilted his head, let his eyes rest on Julian's face, and appeared to assess him, and then, to recognise something. His lips parted in a smile, and he said:

"Overdid it a bit last night, did we?"

"Actually, I don't drink."

The policeman seemed profoundly hurt - the look on his face suggesting that he was about to be shot by humanity.

"Don't drink? What sort of man are you, sir?"

"A teetotaller," Julian said. "In Italy..."

His words faltered and died on his lips. What was the point, he wondered, telling the sergeant that in Italy a man's masculinity was not measured by the amount of alcohol he consumed?

"I see, sir," the policeman said.

For several seconds, not a word or a glance passed between the two men. But Julian was aware of a connection between them, a heaviness in the air of a feeling or opinion not expressed. He guessed that the policeman did not trust teetotallers.

"So, what was the nature of the complaint?"

"My car's been broken into."

"So, car crime," the sergeant said, selecting a fresh document from the sheaf in front of him. The document was marked with faded lines and boxes. Julian supposed that it was the last in a long line of photocopies. The sergeant raised the pencil to his ear and clicked its top several times.

"Name?"

"What?"

"Your name, sir. I need the facts, you understand? I need the simple facts."

Julian imagined all the other interviews that must have taken place in this room and wondered what unhappiness, deceit and sadness lay hidden behind the facade of simple facts. His thoughts were interrupted by the sergeant's voice, its tone exaggerated, weary.

"So, your name is?"

"Julian Everet."

"Date of birth?"

"21.01.50."

The sergeant looked up quickly, brushed Julian's face with his eyes and then looked down at the form he was completing.

"Age?"

"Forty-eight."

"Distinguishing marks?"

"What?"

"Distinguishing marks, sir. You know, what makes you different from other people?"

A good question, Julian thought. Until he had gone to live in Italy, he had always considered himself an average person. Italians were quick to show their appreciation of elegance and distinction and admired his hawkish nose, his fine northern European bone structure. Compared to most Italians he was tall, his clothes hanging neatly on his upright frame. But distinction, he knew, was comparative, dependant on where you were living. His hair, cut and brushed with Italian precision, was queer in England, and so were his clothes. These were elegant, neat and fashionable in Italy. Now they were simple expressions of vanity.

Neither Italians nor English mentioned his lop-sided, supercilious smile, the result of botched dental work from early adolescence. The smile still disturbed him when he saw it in the mirror. He did not consider himself to be supercilious. But he sometimes noticed other people pulling away from him, their eyes turning inward for a second as if to consult some inner jury before looking outward again, the pretence of friendliness gone, and Julian convicted of an arrogance he did not feel. Apart from the lop-sided smile, there was nothing much to distinguish him from others, and there was certainly nothing distinguished about being forty-eight and ageing, wherever he was.

"No," he said. "No distinguishing marks."

"Occupation?"

"University lecturer."

The sergeant looked up and held his eyes tightly to Julian's. The policeman's nostrils were twitching alarmingly.

"You're a teacher then," he said, spittle almost exploding from between his teeth.

"Not quite," Julian said, feeling the need for a shower. "A university lecturer. History."

"Teacher," muttered the policeman, scribbling something down on his paper.

The sergeant clearly had no time for anything that did not fit comfortably with his preconceptions. He concentrated on words and never saw the important things beneath the facade of simple facts. In short, Julian decided that the policeman had no peripheral vision in life, that he was just a stupid copper.

"And you're married, Mr Everet."

Julian looked at him in genuine surprise. Did it show? Was there some special badge or mark of distinction that marked him out from non-marrieds? Another emotion rippled across the policeman's face. He indicated Julian's hand with his pencil.

"Your ring, Mr Everet."

"Separated," said Julian, rolling his wedding ring between thumb and finger. The sergeant made a movement of the mouth that could have been anything from a smile to a scowl.

"All the best people are," he said, curling his wrist and marking a box. Then he surprised Julian still further with:

"Any form of attachment sooner or later brings pain, you know?"

"Really?"

"Address?"

"It's Italian, actually."

The sergeant looked at him with pencil poised between arched eyebrows.

"Via Veneto 20, Verona," Julian said.

The policeman's arched eyebrows dropped.

"Italy," the sergeant said. "Sunshine, sports cars and beautiful girls, Mr Everet, sir."

"Absolutely."

"Make of car?"

"Fiat Ritmo."

"Number plate?"

"VR 6234."

The sergeant raised his head and looked down his nose. He shuffled on his chair and sniffed. Julian expected the man to sneeze violently at any moment.

"That's a foreign number, isn't it?" the sergeant said.

"Yes," Julian said feeling dirtier.

"Purpose of visit to the UK?"

That was not an easy question. Initially, he had come to find peace and security, to reassess his life. Less than twenty-four hours later, he had decided to go back to Italy. But it was not as simple as that. He had come home also because he was tired of being a foreigner. Being a foreigner carried both privileges and responsibilities. The privileges concerned a certain freedom from constraint. No longer bound by English moral values, you were not expected to conform to Italian ones. The responsibility was to yourself. With neither English nor Italian moral values to guide you, foreigners lived life in a sort of limbo, and amorality could become a real problem. Julian knew this. He had fallen into the trap.

"I'm on holiday," he lied. "And I'm looking at the job opportunities."

A frown gathered on the sergeant's brow, the crease marks spreading rapidly down his nose and into the road map.

"You're forty-nine," he said, as if he had a direct line to some eternal truth. "If I were you, I'd go back where you've come from."

"Forty-eight, actually."

The two men looked at each other, hostility gathering. The sergeant took a deep breath and centred his eyes somewhere around Julian's left ear.

"So, Mr Everet, sir," he said, with an ominous calm. "Something's been taken from your car."

"Yes."

"That'll teach you to leave the doors open, won't it?"

"They weren't open. I locked them."

"Then how did he get in?"

"He must've got his fingers in the top of the door and forced it. It's been bent back at an angle of..."

"Always fall apart those Italian cars. You'll need a new door, won't you, sir?"

"Yes, I suppose I will."

"Buy British next time, sir."

Another of Julian's illusions shattered before his eyes. In Italy he had convinced himself that the English were tolerant and fair. But foreign things, beautiful things and intellectual things were greeted with suspicion, and a good fart was valued more highly than a discussion about the meaning of life.

"There are strict safety laws in this country, you know," the sergeant added.

"Yes, I do know actually."

The policeman waved his pencil.

"You can't drive around with doors that fall off. Not in England, sir."

"Quite."

"So, what exactly was taken?"

"A suitcase and my belongings."

"Just one suitcase sir?"

Julian nodded.

"And what," the sergeant said, nervously smoothing his moustache between his words, "did it contain, this one suitcase?"

Julian caught the official tone of the policeman's voice.

"Personal effects," he said, "clothes mainly."

"What else was there?"

Julian turned his head as if to catch a thought or a memory that might be hovering at his ear. From the corner of his eye he glimpsed blotches on the wall by the door. The sergeant noticed his victim's attention had wandered and took the opportunity to make his version of a joke.

"You didn't have one of those in your suitcase, did you, Mr Everet?"

With his eyes, Julian followed the nod of the sergeant's head and then turned further round. The blotches were two posters. One was new and white, and the word "Crimestoppers" was written across the top. The other reminded him of a thin potato-crisp. He recognised Kathy's face immediately. It was the same photo he had seen in the discarded paper on the cliffs, but this photo was sandwiched between two lines of writing. "Missing person," was written above the hairline and, "Have you seen this woman?" was written under the chin.

"They do turn up from time to time," the police sergeant said, "in all shapes and forms."

Julian pressed his palms into the chair and leaned forward, hoping for the crack of the starter's gun that would send him sprinting out of the room. He concentrated on the table but memories flooded in from the wings and stunned him. There was the rustle of her dress, and the petticoat peeping out from beneath the hemline. The faint whiff of her perfume made his nostrils quiver, and then she was in front of him, feet together, leaning forward, shoulders back almost like a diver about to spring off into the air. But the magic of her was the way she turned her head sideways and slightly upward, a look of expectation in her brown eyes, her lips open and rounded, the musical Irish lilt which blended so perfectly with the sound of his name and which made his heart flutter.

One memory sparked off another so that he recalled a number of gestures, of snatches of conversation and other moments he was unwilling to deal with. He decided to fill the intolerable silence, but his voice had become very faint and thin.

"So, what's Crimestoppers?"

"What?"

Julian cleared his throat and pointed to the wall.

"What's Crimestoppers?"

The sergeant stiffened, rose to his feet and, walking over to the posters, he crossed his hands behind his back and braced his shoulders.

"Crimestoppers is a police initiative," he said. "It's a nationwide crime-intelligence and investigation network."

"So, what's new?"

The sergeant's eyes widened in injured disbelief. He appeared to meditate for a while before continuing with:

"Crimestoppers enables members of the public to contact us, sir. Callers are not required to give their names. Anonymity and trust, sir; that's the name of the game, trust."

The sergeant's sparkling shoes squeaked on the institutional linoleum. Then, Julian heard the man's voice in his ear.

"You don't have any information to give us, do you, sir?"

He swept past Julian's elbow and took his seat again.

"How long have they been missing?" Julian said.

"Depends," said the sergeant. "The one on the left? Two months. That other one - McCullagh? She's been gone for about thirty years?"

"Thirty years? Don't you ever give up?"

Medleys of sound were competing with each other for his attention while he watched the sergeant gesticulating and mouthing hugely.

"Give up?" he said. "We never give up. In fact, sir, we're still anxious to interview people who may or may not be connected with Miss McCullagh's disappearance. No, sir, we never give up. We have records dating back to 1946."

Somehow Julian managed to stop himself from jumping the starting gun and running out of the room. He removed himself from his body, watched himself sitting quietly, numbed and deadened by the policeman's words.

"Fifty years is a long time."

He could hear his voice quivering, and there was a film of dampness under his hairline.

"Fifty-two actually, sir," the sergeant said with practised calm. "And yes, fifty-two years is a long time, especially for their families."

There was another long pause. Julian's mind was blank. This time, it was the sergeant who filled the silence.

"And how long have you been abroad, sir?"

"Twenty-seven years," Julian said swallowing his

spittle.

"Twenty-seven years? But you didn't disappear, did you, sir? I mean, somebody knew where you were, knew you were alive, didn't they? Are you all right, sir?"

It was at that moment that Julian turned a mental corner, and waiting for him there was a memory from 1968. It seemed that someone was sketching a familiar shape inside his skull. The shape was the suppressed memory of a person who had once humiliated him, and it was clawing its way out of the subconscious. A mental glimpse of the managerial suit and white shirt-cuffs came and went in an instant, but the image came relentlessly forward and soon it had a name, John McKnight.

McKnight was half-in and half-out of memory, and Julian was flustered, unsure how he was going to deal with this bully. Should he face him as the older man from 1998 or as the young boy from 1968? The dregs of the boy were still there and trembling while John McKnight came forward. But the memory was changing while it approached. There was now a younger man present, and both he and John were moving in Julian's direction, two figures, side by side. There was a sense that they were floating just above the grass of the beautifully tended Tiltyard lawns, and a suggestion that one of the two had said something amusing for both men seemed to be smiling.

The image of McKnight evaporated, but the younger man returned. He seemed to shed light as he came forward, and in the light, Julian saw his thinning hair and his glasses, balanced on the end of his nose. With this image came a name - Dick Duncan-Smith, and a string of words associated with him. Suddenly, like McKnight himself, the man disappeared, a stray thought in the black hole of lost time. Only the echo of his words remained, "If you're not with us, you're against us."

The memory passed Julian by, and he was left with a feeling of amazement that such people could have been forgotten for so long. Why, he wondered, had these men decided to crawl into the present at that particular time? He supposed they had been brought back to life during the earlier incident in his car, and its associations with violence, fear, lawlessness and the mention of the emerging person's name, John. But above all, it would have been the sight of Kathy's face that revitalised the two men.

Julian made a quick decision, a statement of intent to himself. He was not yet ready to free and attend to these unwelcome ghosts, and he forced the men back into the darkness in which he had imprisoned them thirty years earlier. The eighteen-year-old Julian might be dead, but he was unsure whether he would be able to face McKnight as the forty-eight-year-old person he actually was.

"Sir? Are you sure you're all right, sir?"

He looked the policeman right in the eye and smiled his lop-sided smile. In a distracted tone, he said:

"Am I all right? Yes, I'm absolutely fine."

He was listening to a new, strong and determined voice sounding loudly in his inner ear, and it was a voice that prompted another lop-sided smile to appear on his face.

Pity you have decided to go back to Italy, the voice said. *If you stayed a while longer you could find out whether you are man enough to face McKnight. Now could be the time for Kathy's retribution.*

5

The turrets and gables of the Albert Guesthouse loomed darkly through the evening. Their familiarity challenged Julian to place them in the perspective of time, and he scanned his memory, searching for an experience he had forgotten. He soon realised it was not this particular example of Victorian architecture that was prodding at his memory, but the house was prompting a powerful emotional response to an incident in his past he was reluctant to visit. He stood still, on the watch for some sight or sound that might jog his memory and bring the occasion back to life. Both place and event refused to reveal themselves but he sensed they were somehow associated with Victorian houses, with fear, with Kathy and McKnight.

He paced up and down the pavement rubbing at his eyes with his knuckles. Occasionally he stopped and stared at the ivy-clad walls or the huge sash windows before shaking his head and shrugging his shoulders.

He had been feeling emotionally strained before he found the guesthouse the sergeant had recommended. Now he was exhausted. Setting off back to town to pick up his car, he dragged his feet over the uneven paving while his thoughts hovered on the edge of absurdity. Dover's streets held suggestions of a place populated by the sick or terminally ill, a people who marked their brief presence by leaving vomit pools and the acrid smell of their urine hanging in the air.

He even felt a surge of compassion when he saw his damaged car. It was as if it represented part of him. But the compassion carried another emotion with it; the emotion magically conjured up by the sight of all that Victoriana. He caught and nearly lost the word in the same moment - loss. No sooner had it come than the feelings associated with it, newly released by gathering exhaustion, rushed at him.

Driving back to the guesthouse, he mourned inwardly. He mourned the recent loss of his wife, the loss of his clothes, and even the fact that somewhere, he reckoned, he had lost his national identity. When he pulled up outside his accommodation, he was mourning all three of these, bundled and distilled into one. His remaining emotional strength was taken away when two memories from 1968 snapped into his consciousness. He blinked and ducked away from the emotional blows that assailed him, but he stared helplessly at his humiliation from long ago.

Julian is eighteen and looking upwards into John McKnight's face. Rays of the sun are pouring through a skylight and make McKnight's pale face paler. His blue eyes appear distant and cold like frosty moons. John McKnight gets to his feet and leans over a desk. He lowers his voice to a whisper.

"Just fucking tell me," he is saying, "why I shouldn't ring the police now? If you're so fucking intelligent, give me one good reason."

The second memory was blurred at the edges, but Kathy and McKnight are both sharp and distinct. They are sitting in John's Austin Healey, and his fingers are fumbling at the gear lever, too close to Kathy's slightly open and inviting thighs. She is staring mockingly through the windscreen, across a thirty-year divide, and right into Julian's eyes. He flinched at a memory that brought with it a suggestion of the torture he had once endured. The pain was still there, thirty years later, vibrating deep inside him.

He doubted the accuracy of his memories, but he was so disturbed to discover the existence of these old wounds that he threw the car door open, grabbed the box of diaries, and hurried away from the pain and disgrace.

A few moments later, he was waiting inside the Albert Guesthouse. The lobby was laden with Empire, kings, queens and ghosts. Prints and pictures of Victoria and Albert adorned the walls, and interspersed with these were Union flags and pennants. Above the pay-phone there was a poster of a London bus, and another showing a man with a bowler. Tiredness forced Julian's mind another step closer to abstraction. He experienced a staggering sense of the absurd, a flash of a notion that imagination had created a past, and this creation had become real history for the tourists of 1998. Logic suggested that the tourists could no more walk away from this invented reality than he could walk away from the inviting thighs, the fumbling fingers or the humiliations of his own creative imagination.

He shook his head in an attempt to shake it free of Kathy. He tried to mentally engage with the photographs of ships and sailors he found in a dark corner. Perhaps, he mused, these photos reminded one sailor that at least once in his life, he had been loved enough to merit a permanent record. *Ah yes,* said an intrusive voice. *Your permanent record of Kathy lives in the pages of your 1968 diary, doesn't it? Remember? It was the one you secretly snapped on one of those many days when you*

34

followed her across the bridge.

That image was stamped upon his memory. Fixed and frozen in time, the face was as familiar to Julian as his own. The photo showed Kathy under the large clock on the concourse of Waterloo Station. Her head was raised, and she was leaning aggressively forward. As the shutter had clicked, her mouth had opened wide and round. Thirty years later, she was still calling out to him from the past. Standing in the lobby, Julian once again wondered what it was she had said. There was the sound of a nearby voice.

"Can we help you?"

He blinked, readjusted to his surroundings and looked around. It was a woman's voice, a mildly suspicious voice carrying a mid-Atlantic accent.

"Are you looking for something?"

He wondered how long she had been standing there. She had, perhaps, been watching and evaluating him from behind her desk. When he turned to face her, she had stepped away from the desk and stood in the middle of the hallway on strong and purposeful calves. Her face was heavily painted with rouge; and her eyes, black with mascara, produced a repulsive effect as though she were cross-eyed. She waved Julian to the desk and suggested that if he was looking for a room, he might like to fill out the register. Her tone implied that if he was not looking for a room, he should leave immediately.

And so, Julian was confronted with more fact and fiction. Name, address, passport number, contact telephone number and other information which says nothing and which guarantees anonymity. While the ink flowed from the nib and formed letters on the paper in front of him, it finally sunk in that he was homeless. Via Vittorio Veneto, Verona, Italy, was disassociated from him. He no longer lived there. It was one thing to know this. It was another to give the place as a false address and say the street name as he had said it out loud to the police sergeant. But for Julian, the last straw was putting his lies down on a piece of paper as a permanent, written record.

The landlady glanced at what he had written, and when she opened her mouth to smile, he was struck by her eyes. Seeing everything or nothing, they stared at him as if from some deep and dreamless sleep. He felt naked before her. She had seen through his permanent written lies, had probably seen that he was of no fixed abode and feeling vaguely criminal. But all she said was, "Do follow me up the stairs," and he walked after her in the sweet perfume-cloud she left in her wake.

All the rooms in the guesthouse had pink doors, and they had names like Balmoral and John Brown. She ushered him into the Empress of India suite. It smelled of roses and was, she assured him, the only room they had left. She glanced at his box of diaries and, treating him to another smile, she said:

"I expect you'll want to fetch your suitcases."

"I don't have any suitcases," he said. "My car's been broken into."

Before his words were out, he wanted to kick himself. He was sure that in her eyes, any brush with the underworld would have left its stain on him. He was right. The corners of her mouth drooped, and she eyed the diaries with increasing suspicion.

"A flying visit then," she said. Her front teeth were covered in a film of saliva-diluted lipstick. This imperfection made her somehow more human. Julian smiled sweetly.

"Been abroad?" she asked.

He glanced at the floor in a way that suggested he might have lost something.

"Actually, we live in Italy."

Earlier that day, he had used the word "separated" for

the first time. He was still coming to terms with the sense of dirtiness and failure that accompanied the word. He longed to be associated with something acceptable and respectable.

"My wife and me I mean."

"And you're on your way to visit friends?"

"That's right."

Feeling slightly sick, Julian saw how easy it was to allow one lie to lead to another. In what way, he wondered, could the word "friend" be applied to people he had not contacted for twenty-seven years? Essentially, he had disappeared as completely as Kathy had done, and his life had no relevance for those he had left behind. And yet, he had been expecting England and its people to be unchanged and waiting for him. He had only to pick them up again, like photographs, and animate them. The truth was out. There were no more relationships, no more friendships. All that remained were shared memories of the same photograph.

"How long do you intend to stay?" she asked.

"Five days."

"Five days?" she said, the corners of her mouth drooping still further. "In Dover? Most of our clients are only passing through."

The word "clients" touched a nerve. Julian replied quickly:

"Isn't that the essence of life? Only passing through? The ghosts that crowd upon life's empty day."

He felt sicker as he rolled out this quotation. The words had appeared involuntarily on his lips. He was now getting flustered.

"I mean, aren't we all here one day and gone the next?"

And perhaps here again, he thought, like Kathy. He had been hoping that if he forgot about her then so would everyone else. Close your eyes, go to Italy, and she would vanish. He shuffled uncomfortably. With tiredness weighing heavily on his eyelids, he was unable to prevent the idea of a young man from appearing. It was the young man the police were still looking for, and he walked into Julian's head and stood there daring anyone to challenge his presence. He knew this young man had every right to visit. He was, after all, a reflection of himself at eighteen, the photograph he had left behind.

"We only have vacancies for one night," the lady said firmly.

The corners of her mouth collapsed completely, and her lips fused together. She looked at Julian from head to toe, and leaned her head at an angle as if to assess him. He could only guess at what she saw. A strange and wretched man with criminal associations, his youth passed away, his mind addled with tiredness, creeping through the streets of Dover to look for a bed for the night. He hated the woman, but was consoled by the idea that had he told her the truth, that the middle-aged man in front of her was homeless and still wanted by police, she would never have allowed him to stay in the Empress of India suite.

"I'm leaving in the morning," he said.

"And you have to vacate the room by ten o'clock."

"I'll be away after breakfast."

He discovered that he was still unsure as to his next move. His older self advocated going back to the police station and telling them his version of events. But if he did that, he thought, he would never find McKnight, never put Kathy's soul to rest. What was more, Julian's younger self, so recently revived, recoiled at the idea of a confession to the authorities. He was ignorant of the law, but it was not unreasonable to suppose that they could put a person in prison for withholding vital information. He did not even know how vital that information was, and he never would know unless he found out why Kathy was in the news again. He stilled his mind with the notion that these problems were hypothetical anyway, that he had made his decision.

"Actually, I shall be going back to Italy in a few days," he said.

"Breakfast is at seven thirty, and don't forget to read the fire-notice on the back of the door."

She swivelled on her high heels and clattered down the stairs. As she dived into the hallway, Julian heard a man's voice.

"Full English or Continental?"

The voice was youthful; its power suggesting a man in his prime, but it did not correspond to the sad and old appearance of the man himself. Julian thought he recognised the face that looked at him expectantly from the downstairs hallway, but recollection came with a touch of sadness. He had seen this man's younger self in Royal Navy uniform. The vitality that he had noticed in the photo above the phone had been snatched away, bore witness to the failure of the attempt to master time with the push of a button. This man now had the shadow of death on his face. Julian nodded towards the photo on the dark, corner wall and said:

"Did you serve on that ship?"

The naval man immediately threw back his shoulders and clicked his heels.

"Twenty years in the service," he said.

Julian thought the man wanted to say more, but the woman put a hand on his shoulder.

"Don't forget," she said, "to tell the gentleman about the window in his room."

The ex-sailor looked at Julian helplessly like a man drowning. The woman continued, her voice singing, the vowels drawling.

"And don't forget to tell him this is a non-smoking

house."

"I don't smoke actually," Julian said from the top of the stairs.

"And don't forget to tell him we don't allow guests."

She brushed past, swept into another room and closed the door a little more forcefully than was necessary. The word "management" was clearly visible on the woodwork. The seaman looked up and, raising his eyebrows, he shrugged and said:

"You heard the captain."

Julian disappeared into the Empress of India Suite and showered in a dribble of lukewarm water. Emerging from the tiny cubicle, he felt something was not as it should be. Initially he thought it was the unaccustomed softness of carpet underfoot that was wrong, but it was the absence of a clothes basket that troubled him. He found himself stranded in the middle of the room and wondering what to do with his soiled clothes. He was used to putting them in their basket at home. But the word "their" was no longer appropriate. Their car, their house, their balcony and their life had ceased to be. It was only a week ago, but that life had ceased to exist as irrevocably and as completely as Kathy.

He recalled his last day at the house he used to call home. Only two weeks previously, it was the day he told his wife Paola about his behaviour. He recalled telling her one sunny Sunday just before lunch. There had been nothing special about that day, nothing special about the Sunday-people pampering and polishing cars in a Verona suburb. There had been nothing extraordinary about the car radios playing or the strains of music drifting through the window in the breeze. Nor had he chosen that particular Sunday to tell Paola, but as he watched the net curtains gently playing around the window frames, he knew he was going to tell her. It was like a spasm; he could not prevent himself, and out it all came, on impulse, the bitter cud of a festering soul.

Paola had been mixing spaghetti with their favourite sauce, and the kitchen breathed the freshness of olives, the aroma suggesting blueness and the deep-green of Italian hills basking in sunshine. Paola dropped everything on the floor, and she stood in the centre of the kitchen, the slippery spaghetti writhing like snakes at her feet. With widening and moistening eyes, she asked:

"Why?"

The question echoed and rang in his ears. He recalled an anguished pause, the sound of curtains playing on the woodwork and Nat King Cole singing to the breeze, "When I fall in Love, it will be forever."

Then, there was another sound, soft and trembling; it was his name she was whispering. Julian felt detached, not quite there, as if she were appealing to his shadow while the real he stood exposed in another place. His detached shadow frowned. He was as vulnerable as Humpty-Dumpty with the inside scooped out. And what if the shell cracked? Perhaps there was nothing inside except a poisonous and pustulating imagination, the dark-yellow foulness of rotting things. He recalled feeling sick, but he could not answer her question.

"Why?" she had asked.

Perhaps the answer lay in some distant and faraway place.

Before getting into bed, he extracted the journal for 1998 and filled in the page for 3 September. It had indeed been a day of expectations and surprises, but as it all came to a close, the biggest surprise was still to come. As though it were the most natural thing in the world, he picked out the 1968 journal. He had never before read his entries for November of that year, but he turned the pages until he came to that forbidden month, that forbidden day - 28 November. He read the first sentences.

Midnight. God help me to sleep. Keep these diaries safe after what I've just seen and done.

He gazed thoughtfully at the words and then read on. After several minutes, he closed the journal, lay down on the bed and closed his eyes to sleep. Once that night, he woke up from a dream, and it was then that he heard his wife Paola again. Maybe it was the sound of the gulls, or perhaps it was the shout of a reveller, but he was sure he heard her question, her strength, her pain, her confusion and her despair. He heard it all in one long and distant, "Why?"

6

By first light Julian had recaptured some peace and composure, although Paola's question still troubled him. He guessed that the answer was in his secret journal, and he eyed the volume lying open beside his bed. The diary contained details of his obsession with Kathy and her responses to him. He was sure that these had predicted his behaviour towards his wife, had been ticking away for years like a bomb. Two weeks previously the bomb had finally exploded, and now he was alone. He turned his back on the diary, switched on the television and threw himself into a chair.

The faces of Clinton and Blair materialised on the screen. They were standing at the spot where the device had exploded in Omagh. Julian grimaced, hit by a wave of incomprehension. What heights of feeling, he wondered, caused such acts? Incomprehension became laced with guilt when he stared at the sanitised news, the shots of distant smoke filling the air like an ink stain, the burst water main and streams of water running down the street. These made it easy to ignore the unacceptable reality; the real bits of body washed up against the kerbside, the real roars of pain, real confusion and wailing sirens.

The next item dealt with the ferries and confirmed fears of a forty-eight-hour strike, which had already begun from midnight. Julian leaned forward, pressed the off-button, and the white cliffs of Dover disappeared into a pinprick of light on the screen. While the television went through its death throes and crackled its way to silence, he considered his options. He fully grasped the fact that even though the answers to his marital problems might be found in his journals, his historical roots were not going to help him. It was the direction he took next which mattered. He jumped up and made his way down the stairs to the pay phone. He dialled the number of the ferry agent and while waiting for a response, he re-examined his surroundings.

Neither Victoria nor her consort were as forbidding as they had been the night before, and by the time he had rebooked his sailing for the 6 September, Julian was sensing echoes of the contentment he had experienced on seeing the gun emplacements and the fort on the cliff the previous day. The smell of frying eggs, and the sound of crackling bacon reinforced this comfortable reconnection with the past. The history suggested by the flags and pennants on the walls took possession of him. It was saying: *You may have been out of my sight for twenty-seven years, but you can never leave me, you can never go away.*

He replaced the receiver and made for the breakfast room. On the threshold, he took in the scene with a sweeping glance. There were about ten tables, all of which had been laid and prepared with a care and precision that he thought odd. He had not seen other people or heard other sounds from the building. He supposed the ferry strike had kept people away.

He chose a seat at a window table. While waiting, he decided that, with forty-eight hours to kill before his boat sailed, he might as well look up a few people he had once known. His thoughts shifted to Paul, to friendships and whether they too, like history, could take possession of him again. Of all his friends and acquaintances from pre-Italy days, Paul's face stood out from the others and shone like a beacon.

Images of Julian's primary school, images that for years had been packed away, rose up again. He saw the stained, russet brickwork which cloistered the playground. He saw the cricket stumps painted on the walls, and the nooks which offered protection from bands of Apache Indians. He recalled the asphalt, frozen in the winter of 1961, slippery and fun but sometimes the cause of scraped knees and shins.

Paul is eleven years old, has slipped on the ice, cracked his head on the painted cricket stumps, and tears are rolling down his cheeks. Julian stares at him. Until that moment, Paul has been just another boy, a sketch with a lock of hair hanging over his forehead and enjoying the winter slide like everyone else. Then, Paul starts to cry and Julian sees his humanity.

At the day's end, the two boys walk away from the school, trudge homeward while undecided flakes of snow nestle on their duffel coats. The two ramble through the streets in silence. Paul screws up his face and says:

"There must be more than this."

"More than what?"

"All this," Paul replies with a sweep of the arm. "More than all this."

Julian ponders for a while. For some seconds, there is just the sound of their footsteps crunching through the snow.

"Who knows?" Julian says.

"And who cares?" Paul replies.

The boys smile at each other as they hatch the banter that becomes one of the trademarks of their friendship.

On impulse, the two boys clamber up to the Bowstones on the hill that overlooks the houses. Visible from the village streets, the stones are the shafts of Saxon crosses. The crosses mark the boundary of some ancient kingdom, and from this vantage point, the village stretches below them. When the wind comes from the south, the smell of resin will waft up from the timber yard, blow over the roofs, and reach the boys on the hill. When the wind is from the east, a syrupy-sweet odour will blow over them from the soft drinks' maker that flanks the river.

Julian was distracted, his memories truncated by the smell of frying eggs and bacon, the clinking of cups against saucers, coffee percolating and a song from Bob Dylan. He looked up and vaguely noticed that the music came from behind a door on which the word "Galley" had been painted in large letters. The power of the music arrested all other thoughts and transported him back to 1969. He and Paul have come to enjoy Hendrix, Dylan and Davy Cohen. Paul has put both hands on the Bowstones and he is contemplating the view.

"I feel here," he says. "I feel in contact with lost and dead souls."

"With what?" Julian asks.

Paul is silent for a while and then he shakes his head.

"Do you think people leave something behind when they go?" he asks.

"Go where?"

"You know. Go. Away. Forever. Do they leave something behind them?"

Julian thinks about this question, but all he can do is shake his head. For a moment, there is nothing between the two save the smell of resin. Paul turns to look at Julian.

"Do they leave feelings? Is there a spirit of themselves remaining?"

"God knows," Julian says.

"Yes, maybe God knows," Paul says, and he is not smiling as he says it.

Wondering why he had let Paul get away with such a statement, Julian did not hear the ex-sailor enter the room. One moment he was alone with his thoughts. The next moment, he was aware of a presence. It might have been an air of sadness that suddenly filled the room. He may have glimpsed the white of the seaman's hair or the spotless striped apron, or he may have caught the squeak of his polished shoes as they stroked the carpet. The seaman greeted him with a bow and an unobtrusive, "Good morning, sir." Padding around the tables, he paused occasionally to correct the angle of a knife or a fork. He then sailed away and, with a distant smile, he took his air of sadness and futility back with him into the galley.

Julian was about to reach out, to try and engage the man in conversation, when he was assailed by the power of a memory and its intense sadness. He was amazed at how easy it had been to let Paul go, at how he had never known that it would be the last time.

The last time is an afternoon in the summer of 1971. All day long, he and Paul have been waiting for the rain. It has been so hot and sultry that when at last the rain comes, it is a blessed relief.

"I'm going abroad," Julian says, "to Italy."

Paul nods and lays his hands on the stones.

"So," he says, "when will we meet again?"

"Who knows," Julian says. Looking down because tears prick his eyes, he asks, "Who cares?"

"I do," Paul says, and then he looks Julian right in the

eye. "I care."

His voice echoed down the years to reach Julian in the guesthouse breakfast room, and the voice carried with it his feelings for Paul, and they were powerful, flowing and warm.

The seaman chose this time of reflection to give him a punctuated account of his life in the navy. Julian fixed an interested expression on his face and went on automatic pilot. The ex-sailor told him about the conflict in the Falklands but Julian was reliving that moment on the hill when the smell of resin blew over him. He did not retain very much of the sailor's story. He was concentrated on Paul and wondering whether he still cared, whether a shared childhood and common memories could bind two people after a gap of twenty-seven years. With the toast and marmalade, the seaman described the polar expeditions he had been on, but Julian heard only the rhythm of the man's voice, and nodded in time to it while considering his imminent drive to Thames Ditton. He reckoned it would take about three hours to get to Paul's house; three hours in which to reflect and consider what he might have left behind when he had gone abroad so many years previously.

*

The carriageway rushed under the wheels of his car, and the wind, allowed free passage by the damaged door, blew in his face and through his hair. He sang and hummed at the lightness that had taken him. It was, he supposed, a lightness that came from a decision made and a direction taken. Above all, it was the absolute delight he often found in solitude and freedom. He did not know whether he would find Paul again or a shadow of someone he had known. Paul's airiness of character made him unpredictable. The ex-sailor would have

48

found an expression for it.

He always had a line, no longer than a caption under a photograph, to describe each of the variety of characters he presented to Julian during breakfast. "Nice man, but liked his drink," or, "Always away with the fairies that one." Julian guessed that the sailor had invented these lines to help him unlock a door to a mental room, in which he had placed those who had impressed or influenced him. Julian imagined this ex-sailor, tray in hand, knocking on these doors every morning to wake the occupants for an early morning tea and a chat. He also guessed at the caption he would have created for Paul. "Too sensitive for his own good that one, never satisfied and wanting more."

A light mist was falling when he turned into the road that led to Thames Ditton village. Nothing had changed, but nothing was the same. It took him some time to realise that he was looking at everything from a different perspective. As a child, he had known this road, its houses and its gardens as a walker. He had developed an intimate relationship with every tree and every tree trunk. He had tripped over every loose paving stone, he had peered through every piece of fencing that needed repair, and he had known every monster that lurked in the darkness where street lamps had ceased to function. As a child he had experienced this road and its houses and gardens in their totality. He had given little thought to where he stood in place or time, had cared nothing about where he was going. But now, he was an adult, was already letting his mind race ahead to the bay tree and the bench beneath it. The paving stones, the street lamps and the monsters went past in a flash, unnoticed. He simply felt the road surface passing under his wheels while he leaned forward.

At any moment he was going to see the bench and the tree in the centre of the small roundabout. Left of the roundabout he was going to see the shops in the high street, and he knew he would see the house where Paul had lived. Julian was expecting to see a white gate with the inscription "Dove Cottage," and he would see again, as he had seen it in the total world of childhood, the high and steep-sloping roof with its single chimney stack.

At the end of the road, he had to stop at traffic lights. He tried to blink away this contradiction of his childhood memories and he blinked again when he saw that the bench and the roundabout had disappeared. What was more, the village centre was a pedestrian precinct, and he had no choice but to turn right and park in the village car park.

With eyes now wide open, Julian emerged from his car. He leaned the door shut and spread both arms over the roof. He let his gaze wander slowly over the village. For years he had wanted to revisit Thames Ditton. He had enjoyed his memories of the village in the same way that he enjoyed replaying favourite songs. He laid his chin on the roof of his car and wondered whether he should have left the past in peace.

As if in reply, a faint murmur, a mournful expiring sound as of something dying reached his ears. He raised his head to listen, and then the sun appeared and spread its glow over the sky. The mist lifted and broke into patches, flew away in little white balls. It was at this point that he saw them again. Rising majestically out of the thinning mist, and still marking the boundary of the ancient kingdom, the Bowstones stood triumphant.

He stared at them for a few moments, remembering. He had been away for twenty-seven years, but his memories lived in this village and it still belonged to him. He had grown up here, had gone to its school, and yet, as he skipped across the road, he found himself just a couple of strides ahead of an uncomfortable and nagging voice. It followed him up the high street, snapped at his ears and forced him to stop in his tracks. *Your memories may live here,* the voice said, *but you are a stranger in them.*

Glancing back up the high street towards Dove Cottage, he tried to understand what he was hearing. Paul had once suggested that people left their spirits behind them when they went away. Julian knew that it was not his spirit he had left behind. It was guilt that haunted these familiar streets, guilt and images of Kathy. He shuffled his feet until he was stilled by another starker truth. He had not come to find his old friend. It was Kathy he would ask about and why she was on the front page of a newspaper again.

7

Julian pushed at the gate but his hand initially recoiled as though it had come close to something too hot or cold. It was vibrations from the past he had connected with, a sense of himself as a little boy with the words ready on his lips, "Can Paul come out to play?" Julian strengthened the grip of his hand to prevent the gate from closing. He stood for several seconds, listening to the vague murmur that travelled the streets of the village. It was a sound like that of blood rushing through his head, there but not there, like an echo of history. He told himself that perhaps it would be better not to disturb the past. Nobody had seen him arrive. Perhaps he should drive back to Dover immediately, wait for his boat and return to the life he was familiar with.

He calmly closed the gate and made towards the back door, muffling the click of his heels, afraid of upsetting those vibrations and echoes from another time. He rapped on the door with his knuckles. He was poised, but his emotions were numb, and his thought processes had apparently ceased to function. There was a prolonged creak and a muted thump from inside the house. Then, through the frosted glass, a shape appeared. He heard a woman's voice, its pitch and tone familiar, another vibration from days gone by.

"Yes, who is there? Who are you?"

Julian was fumbling for words. Finally, and with the impatience that is born of frustration, he blurted out:

"Julian. It's Julian Everet, a friend of Paul's."

A bolt slid back with a clunk, and the door knob squeaked. He managed a smile, but it seemed inappropriate. He tried a look of compassion, but when the door was pulled open, he was gaping like a fool, and Paul's mother was gazing at him with questioning eyes. Julian recognised the curls that fell over the forehead, and at first sight they banished all sense of time. But what once had been thick and black was now fine and white. She was shorter than he recalled. Her legs and back were bent and twisted as if under some terrible burden. A shawl was pulled tightly across her shoulders, and she gripped it together at the throat with one fist. Julian had once heard it said that if people looked long enough in a mirror, they could see themselves slowly growing old. He had not seen this face for twenty-seven years. She watched him with raised eyebrows, aware that he had to receive the whole and slow process in one shocking second.

She nodded, and without a word, she pulled at the door. It brushed on the doormat and reluctantly opened in a wide arc. He stepped into the living room. The tray, the cups, and the teapot on a table by an open fire suggested that the old lady was expecting someone. It crossed his mind that Paul might be coming for tea. The fire crackled and hissed, and its flames threw dancing shadows on the walls. Paul's mother released her grip on the shawl and settled herself on the sofa.

"You'll have some tea?"

"Yes, thank you."

He half-closed his eyes, and his nostrils twitched, picked up the odour of tea and currant cakes that breathed in this house, lived in the wallpaper, the furniture and the carpet. Each intake of air tugged out a memory. A child's birthday party, Grandstand on winter afternoons, an adolescent conversation, bottles of light ale, the sounds of Bob Dylan, Davy Cohen, or Jimi Hendrix.

"I suppose you want to see Paul," she said.

Julian laughed and coloured his tone with a familiarity he did not feel.

"I just dropped in to see if he's still in the area."

Before the words were out, he was wondering why he was not able to say that he had come specially to see his old friend, that he had come because he loved him. A smile passed like a shadow over the old lady's face.

"Well, you won't find him here. He went away a long time ago."

He tried to interpret her tone and that fleeting smile, to understand the inner thoughts or feelings that had produced them. He said:

"Do you know where I can find him?"

She eased herself forward and poured the tea. She said nothing and Julian wondered whether twenty-seven years had stolen her hearing. He said:

"Is he still around?"

She placed the teapot on the table. He noticed that her hand was shaking. A penetrating silence filled the room, and shadows of a distant time crowded into the empty spaces. Paul's mother lifted her shoulders.

"He fell in with a bad crowd."

Julian took a seat on the sofa beside her. He tried to look concerned and surprised. She slid a cup and saucer across the table.

"Didn't you know?"

He shook his head, and dropped a lump of sugar in

54

his tea.

"I've been away."

"And he was such a lovely little boy," she said.

He got the impression that she was conversing with some inner voice, but he smiled and nodded.

"So, where's he living now?"

He watched her for several seconds. The murmur of life in the streets had been shut out when he closed the front door, and it occurred to him that they both resembled two figures in a photograph. She leaned towards the fire and folded her hands in her lap. Her breathing was soft and low, and the flames from the fire threw a glow upon her cheeks, but her eyes were in darkness.

"Such a lovely baby," she said.

A number of questions were taking shape in Julian's mind. He leaned towards her and tried to cross a twenty-seven-year divide.

"What happened?"

There was a loud crack from the fire. Julian flinched. Paul's mother did not move.

"Happened? He wanted to change the world. He said he wanted more. I asked him what he meant. He said there must be more."

She shifted on her backside, and he heard her whisper as if to herself.

"But what more is there? Can you tell me?"

He was not prepared for this from Paul's mother. He had approached this very same question himself, but had got no further than the eternity of darkness that follows death and which renders it all meaningless.

"Well, I…"

"Too many questions, aren't there?" she said.

"I suppose so, but…"

"And all for nothing."

"Yes," Julian said.

"The silly boy had it all. He couldn't see it. He just kept on asking questions."

Julian wanted to ask questions of his own, but thought it best to keep them to himself.

"We did our best for him, but it was too late. If we weren't with him, we were against him. He said it all the time."

Her voice was distant. She was lost in some private world, and he remained silent, unwilling to intrude upon it. For a long while, there was the crackling of the fire between the two of them. He sipped at his tea and tried to make as little movement as possible.

"So, does he still live in this area?"

A lift of her shoulders suggested a shrug. He heard a sigh, hardly more than a breath, the faint stirring in the air of a memory passing slowly through the room. Paul's mother replaced her cup on its saucer with a sudden and shocking clatter that seemed to say: *Drink and leave.*

"As if I, his mother, would ever be against him," she said. "But he just fell in with the wrong people and when he tried to break away from them, it was too late."

Julian stared at her, his mind at last emerging from slumber. It was the second time in twenty-four hours that he had renewed acquaintance with this uncompromising tenet of Marxist ideology. He sensed a personal tragedy. In many ways, Paul had been one of the simplest people he had ever known. In restaurants, Paul would eat the same food. When he went to the gym, he would repeat the same exercises with the same weights. He had simple hobbies too - a walk, in sensible and simple clothes. What went on inside his head was another matter. His mind held no boundaries. Feelings, senses and intellect seemed to merge and produced a world of black and white, of good and evil, but it was impossible to know on which side Paul would fall. It was this that made him unpredictable and, essentially, one of the most complex people Julian had ever known. But he doubted the accuracy of an assessment made twenty-seven years earlier. Perhaps it was time to unlock the door to the room in which he had placed Paul's memory and re-examine it.

"When did you last see Paul?"

The old lady's eyelids flickered but she said nothing.

"Can you tell me where he is?"

He waited a long time for the answer. He was expecting her to tell him that Paul was with friends or relatives, or perhaps living in a bedsit. She said:

"He lives in your memory."

The air seemed cold to Julian's face, and from afar the sound of a siren pierced the daylight. He leaned forward and turned an ear towards her.

"Sorry?"

"You might find him on Waterloo Station," she said.

He feared for his old friend. Perhaps, he thought, the things he worried most about in life had already happened. Maybe he should have helped Paul twenty-seven years earlier. In 1998 it was probably too late.

"Tell me," she continued, "what would you both do together now? What would you do if you saw him? Have you come back to relive the past?"

He saw her shoulders move as if she had taken a deep breath. He shook his head.

"No, not that."

"Then what?" she asked.

"I'd just like to find him."

There was another long pause. Then, she said:

"But why, Julian? Why?"

He recognised irritation developing inside. He did not know whether this was due to her persistent questioning or to his inability to answer. His inner voices were babbling again, telling him that he had come to get information about Kathy, that there was nothing more.

"He's my oldest friend," he said.

She pulled the shawl round her.

"You may see him. We see him. He wanders the streets. He sleeps rough. You will find him on Waterloo Station with the others."

More questions came to Julian's mind. The questions concerned Paul's exact whereabouts, and what he might know about Kathy. There were also questions about his own motives and integrity. He was trying to untangle them when the old woman spoke again.

"So now you know. We did our best for him, but it was too late. In the end he believed everyone was against him."

She stared into the fire, her hands now folded on her lap. This woman had always been Paul's mother. She had been someone they never questioned, an authority figure and part of the natural order of childhood. Julian realised with a jolt that he was looking at a sad and old woman whose only child had gone bad, a child who now, like Kathy, was just a blurred face in his memory. Then, she spoke to Julian in a way that suggested she had become aware of his presence for the first time.

"And you, Julian? Did you ever marry?"

"Yes."

"Are you happy?"

He hesitated. He thought it might be easier the second time. He had used the word the previous day, but he could taste its bitterness even before it had left his lips.

"Separated."

He saw her eyelids flicker again, and she rocked forward in her seat. The fire crackled and hissed its warmth upon his face. He should have been expecting her next question but when it came, it packed the power of all the other questions that had come before it. It almost knocked him backwards in his chair.

"Why?" she asked.

Why? He heard Paola's voice again. The sound was strong and powerful but muted like distant city traffic. It could have been his own voice he was hearing. Why? Because the poison took hold on an Italian train before he and Paola had ever spoken? He saw himself as he had been then; he was twenty-three, holding a book, but staring through a window at the fog that covered the north Italian plain. He recalled the train, or was it the idea of a train, bumping along the track to Venice? The compartment had been warm, but it seemed dingy and damp, in sympathy with the world outside. The light was deep-yellow and sombre. Only when the train lurched violently sideways did he look up in alarm. He was searching for reassurance in the faces of fellow travellers, and the girl opposite just stared at him with big, brown eyes. Julian held the gaze for no more than a second, but there was something in her eyes that questioned, and it made him uneasy and insecure. At the time, he told himself that she was flirting with him and teasing, that he should avoid her.

Is that how it had been, he thought, or was he playing selected parts in his memory? And what of those parts that had been forgotten? He did not recall leaving his seat, but he remembered the train, stationary at Verona, and he recalled returning to an empty compartment. Picking up his book, he saw that a piece of paper had been inserted between the pages. At first, he thought the conductor must have put it there. But his heartbeat quickened when he saw the telephone number and the note inviting him to use it. At the bottom was a name, the uneven letters betraying the capricious movement of the train. The name signalled the end of a note from the girl with big, brown eyes.

The living room fire crackled and hissed. Paul's mother was motionless.

"Why?" she repeated.

"Trust," he said.

"Trust?"

"Yes, trust."

The word that had troubled him - trust - the word that explained everything was now out. But once it had been articulated, it sounded isolated and ineffectual. He looked at the old woman, expecting a reaction, a show of horror or understanding. She barely moved.

"What was her name, Julian?"

"Paola," he said.

Yes, her name was Paola. She was more than a flirt and a tease. She had written that daring note. And Julian, condemned to decipher it, never tried to understand the person who had written it. She was forward, flirtatious, and she was daring, and, as such, by these fragments of memory, she lived out her sentence. It had never once occurred to him that perhaps Paola too had been looking for reassurance in the eyes of a stranger.

Paul's mother poured herself another tea.

"Why didn't you trust Paola?"

He shook his head. His mouth was dry, and his tongue was glued to the roof of his mouth. Why? Because of those big, brown eyes and a look of fear misinterpreted as flirtation?

Paul's mother was insistent.

"Why, Julian? Why?"

He felt his back pressing hard against the sofa. He certainly had not wondered why when he used the telephone number Paola had left. He recalled telling himself that he was only doing it for the experience, a dummy-run to practise for the real thing. At twenty-three, he still told himself that he would fall in love only once in his life. Nat King Cole had it right; when Julian fell in love, it would be forever.

He and Paola met for the second time in a bar near Verona city centre. She marched through the entrance.

Her head was tilted back, and there was a look of defiance in the brown eyes. The moment she walked into the bar, she appeared to dare and to tease him, and it reinforced the impression he had received on the train. He took her proffered hand as they introduced themselves. In later years, he liked to think there had been warmth in her hand, a surge of electricity. He liked to think it, perhaps to create the myth that once he had been happy. Probably there had been no electricity, no warmth. Almost certainly, he had been wrapped up in himself, and they had been just another couple in a crowded bar. Where now was that fabricated charge of electricity, that pain of fleeting joy?

Why? Paola had asked.

"Why?" Paul's mother was asking.

Her question was a punch to the solar plexus. Julian did not know why he had not trusted her. Maybe it was because of that look on a train. Perhaps trust had been absent from the beginning because she had written him that note. Or maybe it was because she had held her head so high, and seemed to challenge him to touch her. Or was it because he was sure such a girl had been with so many other men as Kathy had been?

He started violently. His tea spilled out of the cup and onto his trousers. He stared in front of him and muttered the first thing that came into his head.

"Because of her eyes. She had such beautiful, brown eyes."

But he was not thinking of brown eyes. He was thinking of Kathy, and silenced by a shocking moment of clarity. It was as though a theatre curtain had moved and allowed a vision of what lay on the stage behind. The scenery and the actors were suddenly there. Then the curtain was snatched shut. The scene was half-forgotten immediately, but the moment terrified him. He decided to change the flow of conversation.

"Did Paul ever talk about Hampton Court?"

There was a long silence.

"Those were the days," she said.

"Where we used to work back in '68," Julian insisted. "The Tiltyard Cafeteria."

"Were they ever as good as we recall?"

"Did he ever talk about a girl called Kathy?"

The sound of that name as it emerged from his lips unsettled him. His face glowed with embarrassment. He wondered whether Paul's mother had heard the question. Then, in a disinterested tone, she said:

"She was the girl who disappeared?"

He nodded and then tried to sound as though he were inquiring about the weather.

"I thought she was in the news again."

His heart pounded against his ribs. There was another pause before the old lady said quietly:

"We don't get much news here."

"I saw her face in a newspaper and I just wondered why."

"Who knows?" she said.

An instinctive response came to his lips but he suppressed it. He longed to be away. This house, which had once seemed so large, was now suffocating. The familiar odour of tea and currant cakes had become stale and sickening.

"Thank you for the tea."

"You're welcome."

He picked up his car keys.

"Well, I'd best be going."

"Yes."

"If you see Paul, would you tell him I called?"

Then he made a decision.

"And would you tell him that I'm staying at the George and Dragon?"

She turned her eyes from the fire and looked at him

for the last time. They stared at each other. Paul had been the bridge that joined him to this woman. Now that Paul was gone, there was just an emptiness that no words could fill.

Closing the front door behind him, he allowed the sweet smile to drop from his face. He was angry because his memories had been corrupted, and nobody had asked his permission. Memories were bitter-sweet, memories were personal and could give pleasure and pain. They were for the bad times in life when he could look back and remind himself that those had indeed been the days. But Paul's mother had laced his assessment of those days with the poison of doubt.

He wandered towards the car park in a huff. The murmurs that lived in the streets seemed unnaturally loud and matched his mood. He roundly cursed Paul's fate and Kathy's demise. Her reappearance in the news had already thrown his safe interpretation of the past into turmoil. He looked for comfort in clinging to the known facts. In the afternoon of 28 November 1968 Kathy had left work and, according to the papers at the time, she had not been seen again. But he was uncomfortably aware that the known facts were not true, that John McKnight had seen her in the evening. For a moment, Julian's thoughts were stilled by the realisation of this deadly secret. He stared and listened to the sounds of life that surrounded him until a wave of new ideas rushed at him.

He supposed it had been the old lady's use of the tenet of Marxist ideology that had raised Dick Duncan-Smith to Julian's consciousness, but the notion that he might find Dick, question him to get the information he needed, caught Julian as he entered the car park. While he was driving towards the George and Dragon the notion was transformed into a good idea that would put his last day in England to good use. By the time he reached the pub, the idea had become an urgent decision, one that might give him the opportunity to find out about McKnight. It would be interesting, he thought, to find out whether he was alive or dead, whether or not he was still in the area.

Julian emerged from his car, tense and concentrated. When he reached the pub entrance, he was tripping over his feet. He burst through the door like an enraged bull. He strode to the reception desk and, without asking permission, he snatched at the phone directory. Flicking through its pages, Julian recalled Dick's passion for Royal Enfield motorbikes, and a minor panic enveloped him. Dick used to ride his bike like a madman and he was probably dead. If he was alive, he might have moved out of the area. His heart leaped when he saw Dick's name and number. He looked around for the phone booth. He did not give any thought to what he would say to Dick after nearly thirty years. He rushed towards the booth, pushed through the heavy curtain and grabbed at the phone.

8

He scanned the phone booth while the calling tone buzzed in his ear. Retaining nothing of his immediate environment, his eyes flickered, and their gaze turned inwards, to Kathy's face on the front page of a newspaper. He rapped his knuckles with increasing force on the booth window He was struggling with ripples of irritation, trying to prevent them from becoming a wave which would break beyond his control and flatten everything before it.

He pinched the bridge of his nose between thumb and forefinger, and rubbed at his eyes. The world was restored to normality, and a string of large and bold letters jumped at him: C-R-I-M-E-S-T-O-P-P-E-R-S. While the calling tone continued to buzz, the letters slowly developed a meaning. Julian blinked. The word touched off a network of increasingly complex messages. He heard again the words spoken by the police sergeant: *Anonymity and trust, sir. That's the name of the game. Trust.* Kathy's face swam in front of his eyes, frowned and disappeared again. With frustration creeping into his tone, he said:

"Come on, come on."

When the ringing droned on, a string of words emerged like a muffled explosion from between his clenched teeth:

"Answer the fucking phone, damn you."

He tapped his finger on his temple. Despite his anger, his thoughts had taken on a life of their own. Trust was not a word that he had ever linked with the face that had intruded on his thoughts. Betrayal would have been more accurate. *Could have any man she wants,* Paul had once said of Kathy.

He was about to slam the phone down when there was a click. A voice crackled down the line.

"Richard Duncan-Smith?"

Julian was breathless and flushed. His heart was pounding so hard, he almost bellowed into the phone.

"Dick? It's Julian. Julian Everet from Hampton Court. 1968. Remember me?"

The pause that followed was long enough for him to recall why he had never much liked Dick Duncan-Smith. His motorbike leathers had always looked like a second skin, one that Dick was able to shed at will, like a snake. Sincerity and integrity were not words he had ever associated with this ex-acquaintance from 1968. He despised Dick's uncompromising politics, politics that suggested the end would justify the means. He guessed that these means included the friendship of John McKnight although it had always been a mystery to Julian what these two men had found in common.

He and Dick exchanged pleasantries for a while. Then Dick asked what he was doing in the neighbourhood. Julian hesitated, trying to gather his wits, but he was still thinking about Kathy. *More men than hot dinners*, Paul had said of her. Julian was unable to recall and live again the pain this comment had caused. It had detached itself, had flown away, leaving him nervous and suspicious in case it returned and gripped him once more.

"I'm over from Italy for a few days," he said. "I'm looking up old friends."

"Well, we're having a barbecue tomorrow afternoon," Dick said. "Why don't you come and make up the numbers?"

He did not like the idea of helping Dick by making up the numbers, but he did want to talk to him. He lifted his cheeks in an imitation smile.

"I'd be delighted."

Dick gave him directions to his house in Tolworth. When Dick had finished, Julian decided to make some initial inquiries.

"Do you remember a girl called Kathy and a man called John...?" The pips started. He thrashed around and dug in his pocket for some change. He pulled out a one hundred lira coin.

"Shit."

The line went dead.

"Damn and bloody shit."

He held the phone at his ear as if it were a spear. He was wondering at how easy it had become to be dishonest; or was it called pragmatism? Delighted to make up the numbers was a lie, and withholding vital information from Paul's mother amounted to another. She had asked him why he was separated. Trust, he had said. But he had not told her about his own infidelity. Paola had loved him and he had betrayed her. Since Kathy, he had sworn that he would keep pain and anguish at arm's length, would never allow anyone to take advantage and betray him again. *Kathleen goes out with any man who asks her. Kathleen's had more men than hot dinners.* No, Julian thought, never again.

He replaced the receiver and lowered his eyelids as if in prayer or meditation. His first affair, he recalled, had started shortly after his marriage to Paola in '75. Somehow, it had not been he who was betraying. It was another person, a person he would eventually leave behind. He had never considered the possibility that all his lovers would leave their shadow on him. At the time, it all seemed so harmless. His lovers came with the present, but the future would take them away from him.

While he and Paola lived in Italy, the future was some faraway place. Every weekend was an adventure. There was always something new, a new town, a new beach, a new skiing resort and new people to meet. There was no time for reflection, no time for remorse. He knew that one day he would change. He even dreamed of it. But his dreams were made of things that had happened to him in the real world, and in the real world they would come to rest.

Picking up the phone directory, Julian backed out of the booth and made his way down a long and narrow corridor. At the reception desk, he expressed his apologies at his hurried earlier entrance. He and the pub landlord then went through the formalities. Handing Julian his room key, the landlord looked at him with an expression of mild concern.

"Rooms are not equipped with telephones, Mr Everet," he said, tapping a finger on the phone directory. "Both the booth here and the directory are for public use. We trust you understand and we hope you have a pleasant stay."

Julian smiled his thanks and wandered towards the saloon bar. He ordered dinner and sat for some time over a bottle of wine. Someone put a coin into the jukebox. A few seconds later, he heard a familiar song, a familiar voice. It was Nat King Cole. There was a lull in the conversation as he sang out: *"When I fall in love..."*

He allowed his thoughts to drift along with the song until they found their natural resting place in a Verona suburb, with car radios playing and strains of music drifting through the window in the breeze. He recalled telling himself that he would stop his affairs and his deceptions in the future. Why, he wondered, had he never changed? Why had he continued to have these affairs when what he really wanted was Nat King Cole's love forever?

He supposed it was because his twenty-seven years in Verona had been years of constant newness. There was no time or room for change when everything was new. It was a changeless and unchanging world, a world of neither shape nor shadow, a world where the paint had not yet dried. This was not a place where time stood still; time had simply never begun. There was no future in a changeless and unchanging world; tomorrows were always out of reach, and he lived in a never-never land of self-deception. But he had not reckoned on the guilt, and this was his fundamental error.

He recalled an evening earlier in the year. He had been walking home past the prostitutes who stood in line outside Verona station. One of them had been apart from the others. She was on the threshold of the bar and sitting astride a table that gave on to the street. The light over the doorway framed her in its glow like a deformed halo.

"Want a good time?" she said.

She spoke indiscriminately to the passers-by. Depressed men, feigning shock and horror, shaded sad eyes and stole one last glance before turning away. It was their own lives from which they turned, but they were forced by some baser desire to look with longing eyes and look in vain for their discarded days. These melancholic men turned homewards, dreaming again the dreams of things that could never return. Julian remained motionless, incapable of turning from the shadow of guilt. He saw this prostitute through a golden glow. She was the embodiment of his infidelity, his conscience personified. He could hardly believe what he had done. He had held love in loving arms and he had let it pass away. He would change in the future, he had always said, but it was too late to see that in his life, the future would never come.

So, he had told Paola just a few weeks previously on that sunny and hot, summer morning, that nondescript Sunday with Sunday-people cleaning their cars while net curtains billowed outwards in the breeze and brushed the window frame when they drifted in the calm. But as the memory recurred, he realised that some things were already different. This time, the memory was accompanied by the sound of his own voice, echoing painfully in his ears.

"I've been unfaithful."

"Why?" Paola asked.

He stared at her, memories flitting through his head. He studied her big, brown eyes for a second. There was something there that stirred some long-lost fragment of time past.

"Why?" she asked again.

She isolated the final vowel. The sound was long-drawn and despairing like a distant train whistling in the night. Tears of anguish streamed down her cheeks. She was talking to him. She was asking him. Memories of his infidelity, shards of glass, pierced every strand of his body.

"Paola."

Julian's voice shook.

"Paola. I'm here now."

But it was too late. There was nobody to hear him. There was just a stirring in the air of someone who had come for an instant, passed by and gone.

"I'm sorry," he had whimpered.

There was the soft rustling of a curtain drawing back,

and he heard the words of Nat King Cole drifting through time.

"When I give my heart, it will be completely..."

He shook his head and looked around the saloon bar of the George and Dragon. Then, he started slipping. He tried to get a grip. He got to his feet and, feeling faint, he almost fell through the door and stumbled into the street. He was gulping for breath.

"Sorry," he said, "yes, I'm sorry..."

The words were hollow to his ears, sounds uttered into a vacuum. Being sorry would not bring Paola back to him. He took in air like a man drowning. He rested his head against a shop window and, looking up, he studied his reflection. What he saw made him cringe. It was an image of a middle-aged man, isolated from his culture, haunted by his past, and completely alone. He started slipping again. He clawed at the windowpane but the slide downward continued. He was on a slippery pole with no handles.

Then it hit him. The stirring curtain moved again, and suddenly the truth was there. It was a sort of Punch and Judy show, a tit for tat. Julian was the pathetic Punch punishing his Judy for crimes that she had never committed. And how each blow, each word, must have cut into her.

"I - have - been - unfaithful."

He hung his head. With each calming breath, he wondered how he had never seen the truth before. Were all personal revelations so obvious but so difficult to swallow? How misguided to think that he had been unfaithful because of Paola's brown eyes or because she had held her head so high or that she had challenged him to touch her. The truth was much simpler.

He was almost soothed by his revelation. His safe and regular reactions and responses, those patterns and hooks on which he had hung his marital identity were being removed one by one. The truth, now seen and accepted, was that he had been conditioned and corrupted by Kathy's bad behaviour. The most obvious symptom of that corruption was that he had punished someone else - Paola. He had somehow managed to convince himself that she had indulged, and would indulge again, in a variety of sexual encounters with a variety of men. There never had been evidence to support this conviction, but it was resentment at what Paola might have done, and at what she might do again, that prompted his behaviour. He had expected Paola to behave like Kathy, to go with other men as Kathy had gone with McKnight and God knew who else. But with Paola, Julian had got his hand in first - just in case. It was a sort of pre-emptive strike. Punch punished his Judy for someone else's crimes. It was obscene.

Therefore, life with Paola, he thought, had been nothing but a lie from start to finish. Their twenty-three-year-old marriage was damned because of Kathy and McKnight.

Julian wanted to stamp his foot on the ground. He had an overpowering urge to take his troubles to some higher being, to confess, to hear his words saying that he had punished Paola for Kathy's infidelity. He needed a reply, reassurance from the mouth of this higher being, that twenty-three years had not been wasted on McKnight's lies and Kathy's deception.

Setting off towards the pub, Julian was strangely calm and at peace. Now and then, he brushed shoulders with another walker, and in the sky the full moon shone, was bathed in a soft, reddish glow. Deep in thought, he turned to cross the road, hesitated and continued on his route towards the pub. He smiled broadly while he focused on the pleasures of a plan to flush out John McKnight. The plan was an outline, an interesting idea that he might seriously consider if he was going to stay in England. The more he considered, the more the plan became part of something bigger. He tugged at his shirt collars, pulled an imaginary jacket closer around him and smiled at the road ahead while imagining sweet revenge.

Arriving at the pub car park, he made straight for his car. He opened the boot and took out his briefcase and the box of diaries. Cradling his life in his arms, he went directly to his room. He washed his face and combed his hair and, for several minutes, occupied himself with a series of other calming and mindless activities. He extracted the 1968 diary from its box and conversed with himself, tested his thoughts. He found that the more he questioned, the more possible were his ideas of revenge. His knees vibrated while ideas flowed and passed the scrutiny of his inner eye.

He threw himself onto the bed and pulled open the covers of the diary. He raised his head, gazed at the ceiling and, putting out his hand, he searched for the photo. He let his fingertips linger for a while over its fractured surface and the worn edges. Then, he snapped the diary shut. With his mind's eye he saw the image the old photo showed. Kathy was standing under the large clock on Waterloo Station concourse. She was leaning forward, her mouth open. Julian shook his head and muttered.

"What on earth did she say?"

But before he could even begin to search for an answer, his mind had skipped a beat, jumped to another time, an evening in 1968, and he found he was watching himself as if he were acting in a silent film. He is following her across Waterloo Bridge. He has decided. He cannot live without a vision of her. He needs her face every day. She turns and looks back along the pavement. She seems to look straight at him, but she just hurries on. He knows that to her, he is just another blur in the darkness over the river - just a walking shadow.

He tells himself he will speak to her tomorrow, tomorrow, and always tomorrow. That is the way to dusty death. And he manages to console his aching heart by telling himself that at least the thought is there. But thoughts without words are mere shadows, he is thinking, and he is the poor player who sits and dreams in his empty room.

While she is waiting under the clock on the station concourse, he pulls the camera from his bag. It is no longer enough to see her in his mind's eye. He will look at her whenever he wants to. He knows now that with the photos she will be safe, forever young, and his until the end of time.

"Whatever did she want?" he muttered again. "Whatever did she say?"

In theory, one man could answer that. His back had been to the camera, but the head was turned as if he had been slapped in the face. John McKnight had heard her words, had felt her anger. Julian knew that expression on her face, knew that stance, could almost feel her fiery temper.

He wondered what McKnight could have done to make her so angry. No sooner had these words appeared than he started banging his fists on the bed. He lifted his legs and brought them down as hard as he could on the mattress. He lay still, while the strong desire to kill McKnight passed quickly through his mind.

He rubbed at his forehead, reached out for the 1968 diary and flicked through its pages. He came to the month of July. Then, with a mental reminder to himself to put the diary safely back in the boot of his car in the morning, he started to read.

9

Journal of Julian Everet. 10 July 1968

I have been waiting for her so, so long. I've been waiting for her since the spring when fresh green burgeoned in the trees. I was waiting when April arrived, and we started again at the Tiltyard. I was waiting when July came, and the days began to shorten. Sometimes, I think I'll still be waiting when September comes, and they tie up the rowing boats on the Thames for the winter. I'll probably be waiting when the season ends, and I go to university, and she returns to her job in London. "Hast thou longed through weary day, For the sight of one loved face?"

11 July
The morning trip to the bottle store is the highlight of my day. If I time it right, I can see her as she walks up from the Lion Gate. Today, the sunlight was filtering through the trees on a group of tourists who gathered around the maze. I saw only the couples. Some were talking secretively, others were touching a lot. Whatever

they were doing, they all looked happy. So why am I so miserable? Perhaps I should ask her out. What am I afraid of? Why don't I do it? Am I afraid of rejection?

I know I'm not good enough for her. Nobody's good enough for her. Nobody's good enough for an angel. Perhaps it's best to keep her at a distance, to put her on a pedestal. The worst thing is that even if I ask her out, I don't think I can kiss. And she'd expect me to kiss her. Do you suck or blow?

Today, I took an extra crate of Pepsi from the store. Thirty shillings! Maybe I can take her to London with it.

10 August 1968
This was the most terrible day of the year. The worst day of my life.

"Here we were for the last time face to face, thou and I... And I love thee, whatso time or men may say, of the poor singer of an empty day."

Is it the last time? Is there any hope for me? There was that look in her eye.

I took her out. We went to London. We saw "Gone with the Wind." I'll never forget the smell of her perfume - it filled the evening, and will be forever associated with her and nervous excitement. Cinemas and Clark Gable will always be associated with her. Never realised before, but she looks like Vivien Leigh.

I told her after the film. We were walking over Waterloo Bridge on the way to the station. She had her arm in mine. The touch of her was intoxicating. Was it the first time? Was it the last time? Was it?

I started by telling her I had strong feelings for someone at the Tiltyard. I was hoping for a sign, some indication that she knew I was talking about her. She gave me none. It was horrible. So, I just blurted it out. "It's you," I said. And she physically recoiled as if I'd hit her over the head with a cricket bat.

The journey back home was a nightmare. She seemed unconcerned. She talked and talked the whole time. She told me about a new flat she's going to move to - somewhere in Kingston, down by the river. She said this was just the beginning and that she wanted to change her job and her life. She didn't invite me to see the new flat or suggest I'd be part of her new life.

I walked her home over Kingston Bridge. At her front door we stood looking at each other. Then, I took a step forward, grabbed her by the shoulders, and kissed her. I should've waited. I should've played it cool as Paul would've done. I've closed the door forever on a relationship with the girl I adore. She simply stood and stared at me in surprise. I was breathless and tongue-tied.

There was a strange expression on her face. What did that look mean? I thought for a brief moment I saw some deep emotion reflected in her eyes. Then, she and the emotion were gone. Vanished! I didn't hear the slamming of her door. There was just an empty space where she'd been. I was alone in the street. Then, it began to rain.

"Look long, O longing eyes, and look in vain! Strain idly, aching heart, and yet be wise, and hope no more for things to come again that thou beheldest once with careless eyes! Like a new-awakened man thou art, who tries to dream again the dream that made him glad when in his arms his loving love he had."

16 August

"Probably had more men than hot dinners," Paul said. How does he know? How can he understand? She is not like the tarts he picks up, those bits of stuff that hang around on the Tiltyard lawn. They are the worthless products of warm, sunny days, and he's always on the lookout for any talent that might be daring enough to show its knickers. She's not like them. How could he think that of Kathy? How does he know she probably has several boyfriends already? Is he jealous?

No. Kathy doesn't belong to Paul's world. She's an angel. She's perfect. She'll remain virginal and untouched. My own feelings are pure and beautiful. I expect the same from her. How can Paul, with his earthy and lustful passions, be expected to understand?

Kathy doesn't go with men for money or material things. Yes, John McKnight has wheels, but she'd never be attracted by that, would she? Paul said he saw her with JD in the pub. JD has experience. He'd know how to kiss. This worries me.

We made ten pounds each today. One penny on all the ice creams and drinks, and a packet of Embassy that Paul got from the store. Good day's work!

17 August
I wish Blodwin would leave me alone. She hangs around the kiosk all the time and sits next to me in the pub. She seems to think that because I put my arm around her once, that we've developed some kind of relationship. If only she knew I did it because I was aware that Kathy was looking. It was only a game! But I won't be unfaithful to Kathy. She's waiting for me. She likes me too. I know this. The look on her face and the expression in her eyes said she likes me. For some reason, she's holding back. One day, I'll know why. One day, she'll give me a message. Please, let me help!

I saw her today. She always comes at ten o'clock and I made sure I was at the bottle store as usual. The trees that lined the avenue were flat and boring without her presence beneath them. When I saw her, I panicked and ran back to the kiosk.

I finished off the heart. Our initials are inside it. I don't care who sees it. I've carved it deep enough so it'll last forever and ever and ever. One day I'll come back here and say:

"It was me who did that, a long time ago." My love and the hearts will last forever like the Bowstones!

I was disturbed by a girl's voice from behind me. It was Blodwin, and she asked if I was going to the pub tonight. What a slag she is. Why can't she leave me in peace with my dreams?

Three hours I worked like a slave. Every ice cream I sold meant a penny in my pocket. The heart reminded me constantly of her. But I can't erase the image of JD and Kathy that Paul put in my mind. JD has experience. He's been married. He can kiss. The doubts tortured me, and the image of her in his embrace took root. I decided to speak to him but I have to wait until tomorrow.

Relieved in the kiosk by Dick. He's a peculiar bloke. He claws his way through the air as if he's impersonating James Cagney. People often distance themselves from Dick. They do it by instinct as though they feel uncomfortable in his presence. Is it because he's older than us? Perhaps it's because he's a chameleon. He behaves in a way he thinks others want him to behave. He must think I'm a crook. He stands like a gangster when he's with me. I always expect him to straighten his jacket with a shrug, and produce a revolver from his pocket.

I wonder why.

18 August.

Only two short weeks before the season ends. And then?

"What vision wilt thou give me, autumn morn, to make thy pensive sweetness more complete?"

When will I see Kathy again? I can't imagine a life without her. Her presence gives me hope. There's nothing without hope. But there's no chance if she's seeing someone else. Of course, she isn't seeing someone else. But I had to see JD in order to banish the idea once and for all.

I went to the restaurant via the Wilderness Gate. Walking across the restaurant lawn, I tried to look as though I had some important business to attend to. I tried to stop myself looking in the high glass of the restaurant window. I couldn't. There was no sign of her; I just saw my own reflection. Why do I feel so guilty? Is it because going to the restaurant is the place where she walks and breathes? Perhaps it's a forbidden planet for me – or is it just the planet of my dreams?

Mrs Croucher grabbed me outside the back door to the restaurant kitchens. She told me she had done her best for me. I suppose she means for me and Kathy. Good sort Mrs Croucher! When she left me, I stood for a while to listen. Apart from the bees buzzing round the bins, there were simply the usual kitchen noises. I managed to get a good view of JD. He had his back to me. He was smoking a joint as usual and dropping the ash on the chopping board.

Why does it give me such a thrill to stand on the fringes of another person's world? He never let me in to his world. He's given me more questions than answers. When I left, I saw John and Kathy standing close together, their faces almost touching. She was angry. Or was she afraid? But why were they standing so close? Closeness doesn't mean anything, does it?

24 August
One week to go before the end of the season. And then - darkness. Must I forever shade my eyes from the rising sun, "and weep because the day is done?"

I'm sure she wants me. There's something stopping her. But what? Somehow, I must keep in contact with her when the season is over. There's still hope for me.

Strange things happening here! Paul and I were in the

bottle store. Good old Mrs Croucher is in some sort of trouble. We heard her talking to the colonel. How exciting it was to be, just for a minute, unobserved and part of her world. Funny chap the colonel. He is Mrs C's escort but nobody is sure why he's called "colonel" or whether he's ever been near an army base. But he looks and sounds ex-army. He barks orders at everyone and matches Mrs C gin for gin. She was like a little girl. She promised she would never do it again. I was astonished. Mrs C is usually so authoritative and self-assured. Whatever it is she has done, she has apparently done it before. The colonel said so. Mrs C said she couldn't take any more risks. Not here. She said she couldn't get involved in "McKnight's little game with the boys." What boys was she talking about and what on earth is McKnight's little game?

I've never heard her sound afraid like that. Whatever Mrs C has done, it concerns Beattie's the clothes shop in Kingston. The colonel said he thought the doctor had cured her, but Mrs C said she couldn't stop herself. Poor Mrs C. I saw her shoulders tremble. She's really afraid of something.

Paul was more concerned by her next comment. Apparently, she did a stock take yesterday morning. Apparently, things are missing. Things don't add up. Well, if you steal things, I'm not surprised. Paul brought me two hundred extra cigarettes yesterday. Nice one!

I don't know what Mrs C and the colonel decided to do. She muttered something about going to the police, something about an obligation to stop McKnight in his tracks. Then they were both swamped by a crowd of tourists. Paul is shitting himself about the stock take. I am untouchable. Nothing more can happen to me. I'm hurt enough. Next week is followed by a black hole. The cafe closes. No more trips to the bottle store. No more walks in front of the restaurant. No more living in the hope that I'll see Kathy. She fills my thoughts. She controls my life. She's pure and untouched. She would never go with JD. She would not be seen dead with John McKnight. No - she would not be seen dead with anyone else but me. She is pure. She is perfect. She is mine. She belongs to me.

30 August.

Disaster has struck. I'm desperate. I've been found out, and on the last weekend of the year. Kathy will never look at me again. What'll she think when she knows I took her to London with someone else's money? What'll she think of me when she finds out I'm a thief? Where there was hope there is now despair. Will McKnight tell the police? If he does, I'll be in real trouble. It could ruin my life. I feel like screaming.

Mrs C tried to warn me, and I should've known. McKnight gives his time as if it were money. He pays you what he thinks you are worth. He's never given me more than a few seconds of his time. Today, he gave me ten minutes. I remember every one of those terrible minutes. Every detail's now etched into my memory. Every word's still ringing in my ears.

I went to his office but I had no idea what was coming. He didn't accuse me immediately. Sadistic bastard. He really made me sweat and began by telling me that this was my final day at the Tiltyard cafeteria. He was smiling too! I didn't understand at first. What did he mean by final day?

He made me sit on a low stool so that I was almost cringing before this monster. He probably did it on purpose and it must've given him pleasure to watch me in agony. He asked me about my future plans, and I told him that my plan was to go to university next month.

He started on about bloody students and he asked me if I thought he was stupid. He said that just because he never had the chance to have a university education, it didn't mean that he was a fool. Then he told me that he knew what I was up to. It was then that the truth slowly sank in. I knew I was in deep trouble. When he started talking about the stock and he asked me if I really thought I'd get away with it, I knew what "it" was. I'd been exposed. By whom? Who has told him?

He asked me how much I'd made. That shook me and it shakes me now. What if he asks me to pay it all back? How will I be able to do it? I won't - not on a student grant. How does he know I've been overcharging on the drinks and the ice creams?

Then he started with the morality bit. I've never felt so miserable. Suppose Kathy finds out what sort of person I am? I felt that all eyes were upon me as I walked out into the height of a busy Sunday at Hampton Court. I went to the bottle store and slammed the door behind me. I didn't and don't care about McKnight. I just didn't want to be seen. I wanted to hide from the person I love, but the one I love is the only person I want now. And she'll never look at me again.

Was Paul right all along? Is John McKnight seeing Kathy? Is he getting rid of me because I'm standing between them?

31 August

I've lost everything. Even my future looks shaky with what McKnight knows about me. Branded a thief, I stayed inside the bottle store this morning so Kathy wouldn't be able to see me. But I watched for her through the gaps in the fencing. It's the end of the world for me.

Mrs C grabbed me outside the bottle store this morning. Only ten o'clock but I could already smell the gin. It seemed to come out of her skin. She told me everything I needed to know, and things I didn't want to hear. She told me that I wasn't the only person who'd ever been on the fiddle. She seemed to think I'd be happy to hear this! Some consolation! I told Mrs Croucher I did it for Kathy, that I needed money to take her out. Even as I said this, I had doubts. I think I would've done it anyway. Still, the explanation sounded plausible. Mrs C believed me. But she was pretty angry. She told me not to blame it all on someone else.

She said I wasn't the only one with problems, that there were bigger, much bigger things going on. She told me Kathy and JD had their worries too. And it was then I understood. Kathy and JD. The coupling of names is always associated with established relationships. Laurel and Hardy, Anthony and Cleopatra and now Kathy and JD. So, at last I know. Kathy's going out with the chef - he who's been married. He who has so much experience in bed - oh the thought of it makes me want to throw up.

Mrs Croucher told me McKnight was trying to involve them too. She said they needed our help. McKnight'll find your weak point and exploit it, she said. She told me I've been walking around with my eyes shut. She said I've trod on his toes and I can't see it. Can't see what? Does this point to Kathy and McKnight? Is this the reason why she won't go out with me? Is this why he was so angry with me? I can't bear it, but it makes sense. Suppose she's going with both of them? Paul said she'd probably go out with any man who asks her. More men than hot dinners, he said. No, she's not that type of girl. Anyway, just because she goes out with them doesn't mean she has to sleep with them. Of course, it doesn't. And she isn't that type. I am sure she isn't. Please, please, she isn't that type of girl. Please God, don't let her be that type of girl.

I wasn't allowed to go near the kiosk. Still, I've left our hearts there. It's the end of the Tiltyard for me. No more glimpses of my dream. Without a dream, what is there to life? One day I'll look back and say, "Those were the days." I wonder what I'll be doing in twenty-five years' time. Will I visit the places I once knew? Will I laugh or will I cry when at some future date I look back on my life now - this life without dreams. Surely, unrequited love, and a girl who goes out with other men are not things I'll be able to laugh about. Will I ever forget what I feel now? I don't think so. I'm doomed to unhappiness. JD and McKnight've denied me the future pleasure of nostalgia. I shall never forgive them for that.

One day, I shall get my revenge. One day, one day, one day, I will get my revenge. Somebody is going to pay for this. Someone will pay for taking Kathy away.

"Nay never will I love again, for loving is but joyful pain if all be at its very best; a rose-hung bower of all unrest; But when at last things go awry, What tongue can tell its misery? And soon or late shall this befall – The Gods send death upon us all."

1 September
Last evening in the King's Arms. It's strange. JD's probably the man who's walked off with my dream, and I know nothing about him. Our world is the weekend-world of Hampton Court, the Tiltyard cafeteria, and the restaurant. JD's never given me much information about himself. He's a good listener, but he talks in riddles. When he walks out of the pub and crosses the road to the bus stop, he takes your secrets with him into some unknown territory. But he leaves me scratching my head and wondering what it was he's been trying to tell me.

When I walked into the pub, JD was already there. He greeted me as usual and I told him I'd been sent home. I said it with a smile, but I was expecting him to walk away in disgust. He didn't. He seemed interested in a strange way and told me I was in good company. Riddles again! What did he mean by good company?

When I told him, I'd been selling a few things from the stock room, he nearly choked. At first, all he said was that he was surprised that such "a scholar and gent" would do such a thing. He warned me not to mess around with people like John McKnight. I wonder if I have been walking around with my eyes shut. For me, McKnight is a rival - someone who might be going out with Kathy.

JD must know! Why doesn't he tell me? Withholding information is as good as telling lies. So, who is Kathy seeing? The uncertainty's unbearable. I suppose not knowing means there's always hope for me.

Don't remember much of the rest of the evening. Too many *Bacardis*. I was sick. The last thing I recall is McKnight standing by his car, and JD and Kathy walking to the bus stop.

I have a terrible headache. I feel so miserable. Next month, I'm off to university - as long as McKnight doesn't tell them I was caught fiddling. University never seemed such a faraway place until yesterday. Until yesterday, I knew I had the future to look forward to. There was always next year and a new season at Hampton Court. It's horrendous. The one place in the world I wanted to be and this place is now barred to me. It's so unfair!! I can hardly believe what has happened. I am SO angry - so bloody angry...

10

Julian drove carefully over the sleeping policemen and nosed the car up to the bush at the end of Inkerman Avenue. He had no trouble spotting Dick's house. The front door had just been painted and it was, as Dick had said, a glossy pink. The BMW in the driveway caused Julian to raise his eyebrows. He associated Dick with motorbikes. He used to boast that on leaving the Lion Gate of Hampton Court Palace, he could make sixty miles an hour by the time he reached the pond in Home Park. Nobody had ever doubted that his Royal Enfield was powerful enough, and nobody had doubted Dick's daring. But with death lurking in every corner, nobody had ever doubted that one day Dick would kill himself.

Not only had he survived, he had clearly prospered. For the most part, Inkerman Avenue consisted of restored Victorian mansions, which reflected the arrogance of their age and the material success of their current owners. Strolling up the curving driveway, Julian assumed the pink, stone pigs on the front lawn were a fashionable version of garden gnomes, but when he rang the doorbell, he saw a painted pig on the letter box; and looking down, he saw a smiling pig on the doormat. From inside the house, he heard Jimi Hendrix singing: *Hey Joe.*

The door opened, and a middle-aged woman in a caftan and beads stood before him. He supposed it was Dick's mother. He had never met Dick's mother, but this woman knew him. Her face was open, and held an expression that seemed to signify recognition and welcome. Her shoulder bag swung under their noses and brought the word "trough" to his mind.

"Julian," she said, exaggerating the first vowel, "how nice to see you again."

She was giving him conspiratorial looks that implied they had something in common, some experience that the two of them had once shared. As far as he knew, Julian had never seen the woman in his life. Her clothes and the music of Jimi Hendrix suggested she had remained at the dawn of the Age of Aquarius. Surely, he thought, the era of peace and love would never have approved of the powdered and white face, or the painted lips. And the permed blond hair seemed so uncomfortable on the head of one of nature's children.

Probing his memory, he planted a smile on his face and stood at the door beaming. She moved the bag in his direction as if she wanted him to look at it. She then snatched it away and groped inside. With a disconnected movement of both hands, she pulled out one cigarette and let another fall to the floor. She almost lost her balance leaning forward to pick it up. Ushering him into the house, she fixed a smile on her face.

He put his hands in his pockets, took them out again and wiped his palms on his trousers. It was clear that the woman was under the influence of some drug, and he had no idea if he had known her well enough to kiss her cheeks. He wondered whether he should put his arms around her and give a hug. He proffered his hand as a compromise. When she took it, her smile widened and her nostrils flared. The connections to the past cleared like an unblocking pipe.

"Blodwin," he said.

She waved her hands and lost her balance.

"Forgotten, hadn't you, naughty boy."

"Of course not," he said.

Until this moment, the woman had been a name in his diary, an individual whose personality had been erased from his consciousness. They used to call her Blodwin Pig. In part, this was because she looked like a pig, but she also liked the rock group of that name. Above all, she believed in free love and practised it. Blodwin Pig had been what Julian and his friends at the Tiltyard called, "A bit of a slag."

"We're out the back," she said, "come on through."

She spun round, lifted the unlit cigarette to one ear, and holding the bag outwards as though it were ballast, she swung down the corridor. He set off after her, breathing in the stale cigarette smoke and alcohol fumes that she left behind her.

"Yes, I know," she said, "the place is in a bit of a state."

Her beads rattled, and she waved a hand around the house.

"Bloody decorators..."

He made appropriate appreciative noises. A smell of paint mingled with the incense and alcohol. The woodwork was the same colour as the front door.

"Really wanted to do it ourselves," she said. "But Richard is so busy with his new job. Touche Ross, you know."

"Touche Ross?"

"The accountants," she said, her tone suggesting

disappointment. "Richard is senior economist, you know." She raised her eyebrows and gave him another conspiratorial grin.

He nodded and congratulated himself for not trying to kiss her cheek. He had once asked Blodwin out. His intention had been to use her and her reputation in an attempt to get back at Kathleen. It had not worked out in the way he had hoped, but as they walked through the house, he decided that if she did not mention it, neither would he.

Another thing he recalled was Blodwin's inclination to contact your inner being and express it. This child of her time had become adult, but she had held on to this belief in self-expression and developed it. The pigs on the lawn were matched by pig candlesticks in the hall, pig clocks on the walls, and in the kitchen, Julian saw pigs everywhere. On the kitchen table stood a pig teapot. Beside it, were pig cups and pig mugs. On the pine dresser were pig egg cups, pig place mats and more pig clocks. Everything was painted pink, and Blodwin was dead drunk.

With a flourish, she threw open the back door. Julian was almost overcome by the marijuana smoke. The first thing he noticed about Dick was his flower-patterned apron. He was standing at a sizzling and smoking grill and absorbed with a piece of meat that refused to be turned. He raised his head.

"Glad you could make it."

"How are you doing," Julian said.

Dick nodded his head and pouted his lips. He had always been slim, but now he was shrivelled at the edges like the meat he was wrestling with. He still wore his hair long and swept backwards, but it was now grey and receding. His long face was cast downwards in a concentrated and careful way, and his eyes looked out through the glasses, which balanced on the tip of his nose and reminded Julian of telescopic sights. What saddened him was not that Dick had aged, but that there was something about him that suggested he would change no more. In 1968, Julian had known a person in one stage of development. The middle-aged shell by the grill was the end-of-the-line product.

There were two men and two women sitting round a table. Blodwin introduced him.

"A friend from Richard's schooldays."

One of the men was asleep. There were grunts and nods from the others, but nobody looked in Julian's direction. The couples were Vince and Sandy, Frank and Christine, and their names seemed glued together in the manner of Pinkie and Perky or Tom and Jerry. The couples apparently thought they were as ageless as the cartoons. Christine was reclining on a sun-bed and smoking dope through a hubble-bubble. The only connection to her youth was the hair. Reaching her stomach, it brought to Julian's mind an image of Beatniks and Peter, Paul, and Mary.

Sandy was smoking a joint and drinking a gin and tonic. The corners of her mouth were turning downwards, but her lips had yet to set into permanent middle-aged bitterness. She was swaying from side to side and appeared to be listening to Jimi Hendrix and: *The wind cried Mary.*

Without warning, she leaned backwards in her chair and crossed her legs. Her eyes became hard and suspicious. Julian sat down opposite her. She said:

"Richard tells us you've been abroad. So, what brings you back?"

The voice was slurred, and her words were uncertain so that Julian wondered if she was wearing loose dentures. He thought she might have been addressing someone else, but through the cigarette smoke he saw her eyes fixed on his. Blodwin then arrived and put a glass of beer in front of him. She swivelled away giggling and brushing his shoulder with her thigh. He smiled his thanks for the beer.

"I'm on holiday, actually..."

Sandy shot forward and rested her elbows on her knees. Staring through the smoke, she sipped at the G and T. While Julian waited for her next comment, Frank put aside the book he was reading. The cover illustration showed a motorbike, and the title concerned Zen and mechanics.

"You know," he said, "I don't remember you from our school days."

"Didn't go to school together," Julian said. "Dick and I knew each other at the Tiltyard cafeteria in Hampton Court in '68."

"Dick? Richard? Well, those were the days, eh?" he said, and picked up the book again.

Julian watched Sandy's eyes narrow as she continued to stare at him. She leaned further forward and poured gin into her glass. Some missed the glass, fell to the ground and splashed her brown, cloth shoes.

"So," she said, "what were you running away from?"

The tone of the question held a very poor opinion of him. Julian guessed that her hostility also held clues to her own disappointments: things never done, people never met, and dreams never realised. He reckoned he was in for a row. He removed himself from his body and watched his performance from one side.

"What?"

"Running away from," she repeated.

"Sorry, I don't understand."

"Running away," she said with force, "easy to understand, no?"

He peered at her, feelings of contempt playing with his top lip. She had pulled her head back between her shoulders as though she were avoiding a blow to the face. She said:

"I mean, people don't usually leave the country...twenty-seven years for nothing, do they? Are you Lord Lucan?"

"I wanted to travel, you understand, no?"

She looked at him sullenly before shaking her head in slow and wide arcs. The silence between the two grew oppressive. Julian decided to break it, but Sandy surprised him by covering her face with her hands and shouting into her palms:

"No...no. Why did you...?"

Dick came to the rescue. He dropped a piece of meat on Julian's plate.

"Sunshine, sports cars and beautiful girls," Dick said.

Julian turned his head sharply but held his lips tightly together. For the second time in three days, most of his life had been judged to be banal.

"There's more than that…," he began, but he could not finish the sentence. Sandy's alcoholic moods were changing rapidly. She was now so composed Julian could hardly detect her breathing. The two stared at each other, but he saw only barrenness between them. He heard her voice, indistinct through the fingers.

"Who are you? What makes you think you can just go and then just come back?"

Julian was attempting to decipher the meaning of this question when he heard a clatter of beads and earrings, and he felt the pressure of a hand on his shoulder. It was Blodwin.

"What do you teach, Julian?"

"History."

Nobody was listening. Frank was deep in his book, Sandy appeared to be nodding off, and Christine was busy with the hubble-bubble. Dick sat down opposite him. Blodwin leaned over the table and, pushing her breasts into Julian's face, she poured her husband a glass of wine. Julian shuffled and looked sideways at Dick.

"Why have you come back?" Dick asked.

Julian muttered something about jobs and holidays. Then he said:

"By the way, I went to see Paul but spoke to his mother instead."

Dick nodded. "Did she tell you anything?"

"Not much."

Blodwin settled herself on the arm of Julian's chair.

"He's rotten," she said in a burst of alcoholic anger. "No grit, no integrity, no good..."

"What do you mean?"

"No persistence, you see? Walked away from his ideals, his friends.... We were trying to help but he was drinking himself to death. He's probably dead now." Blodwin had pursed her lips and held her nose in the air. "Used to see him sometimes wandering about and muttering."

"What happened?"

Blodwin took a huge gulp of wine. It was hardly down her throat when she said:

"Started drinking."

Julian noticed a red smear on the rim of her glass. Dick stared at the floor as though waiting for the Blodwin-effect to pass. He looked up.

"Lost his grip on life," Dick said. "Started drinking. Whole life collapsed. Was it the drinking that caused the collapse or the collapse that caused the drinking? He lost everything; thought the world was against him."

Dick glanced in Blodwin's direction in order to keep her in the conversational process. Then Julian said:

"Is nobody trying to help? I mean..."

"Why should they?" Blodwin interrupted.

Dick got up and pretended to busy himself with the fire. He prodded at it for some seconds and then sat down again. He turned his head and aimed his glasses at

Julian. His question was equally direct.

"Did you ever get married, Julian?"

"Yes, I did."

Frank turned the page of his book. Sandy had begun to snore, and Vince was still asleep. There was a bitter taste in Julian's mouth as he formulated the next sentence. He decided to affect an air of worldly wisdom.

"Separated now, actually."

Everything around him went still. It seemed he had entered a prohibited area where ideas and possibilities were never spoken, a place where cowards feared to tread. Still sitting at his shoulder, Blodwin tensed but, with admirable calm, Dick asked:

"What happened?"

This time, Julian was prepared for the question. He had a ready-made answer.

"We fell out of love."

Blodwin and Dick looked at each other as if both were waiting for a sign from the other, a signal to begin some action, dispute or negotiation. With what appeared to be genuine interest, Dick asked:

"Why?"

Before Julian could reply, there was a hiss and a flash of fire from the grill. Dick jumped up to attend to it. For a moment Julian was left to himself, remembering. Dick came back to his seat. In a casual tone, Julian said:

"By the way, I thought I saw Kathy's face in the newspaper."

Blodwin moved one of her hands as if she would throw Julian's words to the floor. Dick flicked his head sideways as if to avoid a flying and menacing insect. Then, he turned his glasses straight at Julian, but his eyes seemed to be staring into emptiness.

"Who?"

Julian was stunned by a crushing sadness. What he remembered as important in his life was forgotten, and the examinations and explanations of twenty-seven years were not even given a second's thought by others. The whole notion was preposterous.

"Kathleen - Kathy. You know, the waitress from the Tiltyard restaurant. The one who…"

He watched Dick search his memory. Dick's eyelids dropped, and he said:

"You mean the one who disappeared?"

Blodwin stood up, fetched a fishing stool from the floor, unfolded it and sat down at her husband's side. Now, it was Dick's turn to affect an air of worldly wisdom. He glanced in Julian's direction but avoided his eyes and spoke as though he was talking to a distant memory.

"You probably weren't here but…"

"Of course, he wasn't here," said Blodwin.

Dick did not move a muscle. He said:

"They…. A body was dredged…a body from the river a few days ago or the remains of a body. But they don't know who the remains belong to; in a manner…"

Julian suddenly felt that all the people around him had woken up and were staring at him. He gripped his chair while his lips groped for a response.

"But why did they…, why the photo?"

Dick shrugged. He slipped the glasses up his nose with a push of his forefinger.

"The remains are thirty years old…at least," he said. "Quite well preserved in the silt or something. Could be Kathleen…the police are not sure…. Could be anyone…. There's nothing sensible to write about, so the papers decided to run the story again."

Dick punctuated his story with slight laughs and spasmodic shrugs of the shoulders, and his glasses seemed permanently aimed at his knees. Julian was unable to stop a succession of pictures and sounds that appeared in his mind with each thump of the blood in his ears. He wanted to take his head in his hands, wrench the pictures from inside it and bury them again. But one memory refused to budge.

It is Waterloo station. The young Julian is buying a paper so that he can cover his face. He gets in Kathleen's compartment and watches her reflection in the glass. He loves watching her every move, her hand brushing her hair away from her eyes, the way she is sitting with her hands folded in her lap. Just for half an hour, she is all his.

She gets off the train at Kingston, and he keeps a good distance as she turns left outside the station and makes towards the Hawker works on the Richmond Road. He loves watching the grace of her movements, and when she stops to buy some apples from a roadside vendor, she bends from the waist and her hair falls away from the collar of her leather coat. How he wants to touch that delicate and slender neck, to run his fingers through her hair. He is so absorbed with this idea that he hardly notices her turn up a side street. He hurries after her. Riverside Road. This is the street where she lives. There is a song by that name, so he knows he cannot be all bad. If there is a song, then he knows he is not the first person who follows his beloved home. It is common practice, and he is in good company.

She disappears between two gate posts. He keeps his distance and looks through the hedge that flanks the gateway. He sees a fine Victorian mansion, and behind it, the river flows. "Old Father Thames - flow softly till I end my song," he thinks.

Then he hears footsteps. He has to pretend he is looking for something in the hedge, but a woman with a dog gives him a suspicious look.

"Ever heard of DNA testing?" Dick asked.

Shaken from his dream, Julian looked up and answered with a nod. He was soothed by this display of

English arrogance. Why should he not have heard of DNA? He put it down to the attitudes and beliefs that saw only ignorance beyond one's own national borders. Dick said:

"They're doing tests now. If it is Kathy, we'll hear about it."

Julian nodded again. The tumult of dissociated images and sounds had passed like a tidal wave. He now seemed wrapped in silence. The terror was out and nothing had changed. The world had not ended. He was still there. He said:

"But they don't know yet?"

"Not yet," said Dick.

Blodwin leaned over and put her hand on Julian's arm.

"They're interviewing JD," she said.

Dick got to his feet and disappeared into the house. Julian's head was spinning. He wondered whether he was passively stoned. He had not expected to hear about the chef from the Tiltyard restaurant. Over the years, Julian had only occasionally let his thoughts lightly touch on his one-time rival for the affections of Kathleen. Julian's last sight of him was a grinning figure walking across the road to the bus-stop, and running away with his dreams.

Dick came back waving a newspaper in his hand. He tossed it on the table. With a plop, Kathleen's face appeared again.

"Only a few days old," said Dick. "Tuesday's in fact."

Julian glanced at the date, 1 September.

"Has there been any more news since then?"

From the other side of the table there was a snort. Sandy was asleep. Dick took the joint from her fingers and stubbed it out in an ashtray.

Julian hesitated before picking up the paper, but once

it was in his hands, he became surrounded by a perfect stillness in which he was the powerless spectator. The tormenting images appeared again and with them came the sound of her laughter, and thirty years melting away without a trace.

He scanned the article feeling a need to visit the toilet. The first part of the article told him no more than what Dick had already explained. Bodily remains had indeed been dredged up from the bottom of the river near Kingston Bridge. The remains were as yet unidentified but police suspected they might be those of Kathleen McCullagh, who had disappeared without trace in 1968. They were waiting for the medical examiner's report.

There was a shuffling sound from the other side of the table. Sandy was staring at him with unseeing, bloodshot eyes. It seemed to Julian that her face was streaming with water, that locks of her hair were clinging to her forehead. Christine released him from this nightmare by jumping up to put another cassette into the player.

"A bag of bones," she said. "How can they identify a bag...?"

Dick shrugged.

"Dental records, face reconstruction and DNA," he said, "genetic finger printing."

Christine seemed unconvinced.

"Is this evidence? I mean..."

"Depends," said Dick.

Julian read the rest of the article to the sound of *Waterloo Sunset*, Sandy snoring and Dick and Christine arguing about the latest methods of identifying a corpse. Reading the story was like reliving a terrible dream. He knew what was coming, but such is the power of hope he could not stop himself from reading every detail. He guessed he was searching for some evidence that his memory was faulty or that something had changed. But every detail was a hammer blow; and each one forced him to realise that this was one dream he would never wake up from. The article described how Kathleen McCullagh went missing on 28 November 1968.

She was last seen leaving her office in the Strand at 5.00 p.m. The Police were aware that some months prior to her disappearance Kathleen had been receiving threatening calls from person or persons unknown.

At this point, a wave of panic spread through him. His head sang, and his knees were quivering. Sandy chose this moment to wake up. He heard her laugh, and then she said:

"What *were* you running from?"

Unable to say a word, he stared at Sandy and watched her head, apparently drained of life, fall backwards over the chair. He read on.

Police are interviewing Justin David King, butcher from Stockwell, London. Mr King is thought to have been the missing girl's boyfriend. Police are also still anxious to interview a young man who was seen near her house on the evening of the disappearance. A bouquet of red roses was found inside Kathleen's flat and Police believe they were put there on the evening of her disappearance. Kathleen was employed as an accounts clerk in a London office, and in the summer months, she worked part-time as a waitress in the Tiltyard Restaurant at Hampton Court Palace. She was reported missing by family and friends, and her disappearance was described as totally out of character. Did you see anyone acting suspiciously on that evening, 28 November? Do you remember seeing anyone with a bouquet of red roses? Police are appealing for anyone who may have information which could help detectives with this investigation, to contact the Incident Room at Kingston police station or (if you wish to remain anonymous) Crimestoppers on 0800 555 111.

"You all right?" said Dick. He had come over and put his hand on Julian's shoulder. "You look like you saw a ghost."

Julian patted his stomach and made to stand up.

"Inside. Second door on the left," Dick said.

As Julian rushed through the door, he heard the Kinks singing and Christine saying, "He all right?"

But Julian is in a place of memories and dreams and he is listening to another question from thirty years previously.

"What can we do for a scholar and a gent like you?" JD is asking.

The shuttered half-light of the restaurant kitchen suggests coolness, but Julian is wrapped in a thick and warm dampness that catches at his throat and makes him cough. Exact and ordered on a series of iron stoves, pots are lined up like soldiers on parade. Clouds of steam spiral to the ceiling.

"I need to speak to you," he says, "about Kathy."

Bustling and busy, JD appears to be engaged in a losing battle to force the billowing steam back into the pots. Every clatter and ring of lid on pot makes Julian jump. JD's silence makes him suspicious, but when he eventually speaks, his voice reaches Julian as a disembodied mumble. There is something about JD that suggests embarrassment, and his shoulders are hunched as if in protection from an unseen but striking hand.

"I'm doing my best for you," JD is saying. "What more can I do for a scholar and gent?"

He scoops salt from a container and tosses it into the boiling water. The salt hits the water with a prolonged hiss. JD says:

"Kathy won't be around for you much longer."

He reminds Julian of a cruel and calculating magician bent over his recipes. More salt hits the water but Julian shivers as if chilled.

"Things are happening here," JD says.

"What things."

"Bad things between Kath and McKnight. And I'm involved too."

"What do you mean?"

"Don't ask."

Julian is shivering, and there is a coldness round his heart. Why, he thinks, does JD contract Kathleen's name? The contraction suggests a familiarity which sickens him. He asks himself if JD is involved with Kathleen, whether this is the reason why she refuses to be his girlfriend.

"She isn't the innocent thing she looks," JD says. "She's made of tougher stuff..."

And in that sunless room where clouds of steam soak the walls and coat his skin, JD's words touch Julian like ice. She is not a tart, he thinks, she is not like that. Oh God, please don't let her be like that. Please, please...

JD continues tossing salt into the pots. He tells him that Kathleen has quite a mind of her own, but Julian's mind is in turmoil Why, he thinks, does JD go on telling him that Kathleen stops at nothing to get what she wants, to get what she thinks is right? Why is he telling Julian that he will be better out of it? Out of what?

Just before he leaves, Julian catches a glimpse of her through the door that connects to the dining room. She is standing close to McKnight. They are face to face, eye to eye. They must be whispering some secret, Julian tells himself, or they must be sharing a joke. They could be doing any number of things. Closeness doesn't mean anything, does it?

Julian stayed long enough in the toilet to empty his bladder, to allow his thoughts the time they needed to run their natural course, and to regain his self-control. When he went back to the party, the dregs of pain were still tugging at him. He tried smiling, but Dick said:

"You look none too well."

"Bad stomach," Julian said.

"Spanish tummy," said Blodwin.

"Doesn't live in Spain," said Dick.

"Same difference," said Blodwin.

"The point is," said Christine, "they can't arrest without a body, right?"

"Sort of," said Dick. "They won't arrest unless there's overwhelming evidence against the suspect."

Julian sat glued to his chair. He was remembering the expressions on JD's face. He was remembering the glitter in Kathy's eyes, snatches of conversations now emerging and echoing down the years. Interspersed with these, Dick's voice came and went like a poorly tuned radio.

"In this case there...no overwhelming evidence, no suspect. If the body...be Kathleen's...have enough evidence to arrest JD. The body isn't...they will have to leave him alone."

"And the mysterious prowler," said Christine, "and those roses. It's bizarre. What kind of man would do that?"

Dick shrugged. Julian said:

"Someone who loved her?"

At the last moment, he managed to put a questioning intonation to his voice. He was staring, terrified at how easy it was to become involved again after so many years. With a laugh, Dick said:

"Maybe the prowler was JD, but it's useless speculating until we know whether the bones are Kathleen's."

Julian listened with increasing irritation. He had accepted the fact that England had not been waiting for him. He saw that, in his absence, life had moved on, people had got older and lived in another world. His observations were right and wrong. Dick and his friends had got older, but they had chosen to hold on to the past. Julian had decided to move on, but the past was pulling him back, and it was a place he no longer wanted to visit. For him, time had been standing still for thirty years. In 1968 a woman had disappeared. In 1998, bodily remains were pulled from the river.

"Maybe," said Dick, "JD is at last going to get the punishment he deserves."

For some time, Julian sat at the table nodding along with the others. But, before long, his inner eye saw an increasingly familiar face taking shape and watching him again. For a second, the suit, the curly blonde hair and the thick lips were immersed in shadow. Now was the time to attend to John McKnight, to put a name to this ghost, time to try out his ideas. Julian had carefully rehearsed his words but saying a name in the presence of others and attaching it to this shadowy figure was more difficult than he had imagined. He coughed and cleared his throat.

"You were friendly with John McKnight," he said. "Do you know what happened to him?"

Dick did not remove his eyes from the fire. Julian wondered if he had heard the question. His eyes were stony and vacant. Too much grass Julian told himself. He heard Dick take a deep breath, but before he could utter a word, Julian added:

"I have some things he may be interested in, things that suggest he was closer to Kathleen than anyone knew and things that may implicate him..."

He interrupted himself as though startled at the drift of his words, but in reality, it was the realisation that Dick had not been smoking grass that forced his voice to trail off. Dick was now alert, his eyes pin-pricks of light. He said:

"Implicate him in what?"

Julian grimaced, wrestling with ideas that he was unwilling to release. Absently as though talking to himself, he said:

"In Kathleen's disappearance. I have photos and diaries to prove it."

Dick flicked his head sideways again. Julian wondered whether it was another sign of middle age, a spasmodic movement beyond his control.

"You've got these things with you?"

"Here?"

"Umm."

"In the George and Dragon."

"Thames Ditton?"

Julian nodded. Inside he was sparkling. The cat was out of the bag and John McKnight was out of his cage. Dick was still staring at the grill.

"What are you going to do with this evidence?"

"Don't know," Julian said. "Expose him?"

He gasped in silent surprise at his use of these daring words. He had not planned to utter them but now they were out they charged him with the excitement of the unknown. But his mental hold on the possibilities was so weak that he judged it necessary to repeat the words to himself so that he could possess them, believe them, act on them.

"Expose him."

"Expose him for what?"

Julian looked up and surveyed the other guests sitting around the patio. They seemed distant, irrelevant and unimportant. He shrugged away Dick's question, and everything changed in an instant.

"Why don't you stay for dinner?" Dick said.

"Like to," Julian lied, "but I must be getting back. I've a booking for tomorrow's sailing."

He rose, said his farewells and, with unfelt exhortations of good luck and insincere expressions of hope that they would all meet again, he left. Dick muttered something to Blodwin, and Julian felt her presence behind him as he made his way through the house. She followed him through the front door and onto the lawn. She seemed nervous and anxious. As he was about to turn and say a final goodbye, he felt the pressure of her hand on his shoulder and he heard her voice in his ear.

"Julian, I must talk to you."

11

Julian shrugged off Blodwin's hand and twisted away from the cloud of stale alcohol and cigarette smoke that seemed to hang permanently over her. He turned slowly and stared at her as though she had intruded on a private moment and refused to go away. His gaze drifted to her caftan and then sideways to the trees where he could remain with his thoughts and loiter in his imagination with its fanciful plans to expose his one-time adversary.

He was so far away with intricate details and delicious possibilities that he forgot Blodwin's presence. From somewhere near at hand, a church clock struck. The vibration filled the garden, distracted him and diverted his attention from idle thoughts. He lingered for a while in some intermediate mental place between present and future, and then he heard her again. She was speaking with an urgency that forced him to tune in to her.

"Should've stayed," she was saying.

She was fingering at her caftan and looking at him for a response, but he had no idea what she was talking about. She lifted her fist to her mouth and, holding her knuckles lightly between her teeth, she sobbed out:

"Should've stayed where you were."

Her face was white and drawn. Whether this was due to the light of early evening or an excess of alcohol, Julian could not say. While he watched her struggle to get a grip on herself, he tried to think of some words that would continue logically from what she had said.

"It's getting late," he said.

He frowned at the sound of his voice. It was not the tone he had intended to use. He had wanted to sound apologetic, but instead he had sounded abrupt, had adopted the tone of one who has no time for another. Part of him cursed himself for saying the wrong thing, but part of him still rebelled at having had his privacy invaded. Thoughts of revenge were wonderfully entertaining, and he was impatient to get back to them. He was also aware of his impending trip back to Italy, the drive to Dover and decisions about where to spend his last night in England. He also had bags that needed packing. In a more conciliatory tone, and one that was intended to communicate finality, he added:

"It was time to be leaving."

Before he could turn away, Blodwin placed her hand on his arm.

"No," she said. "You must listen..."

Julian became aware of the trees that separated the garden from the road, heard the wind blowing through the branches. He thought it was the rustling of leaves but it was Blodwin continuing in a whisper:

"You don't understand what you've been saying. How could you?"

A leaf settled precariously on Blodwin's hair. Other leaves were swaying through the air and settling on the lawn around them. Blodwin lifted her hand from his arm and leaning forward, she gazed into his eyes.

"Julian," she said, "you really don't know what you've started."

The words, which had danced lightly and quickly from her mouth, were followed by a bottomless pit of silence that beckoned him, dared him to speak, to ask the question that her statement appeared to require. He let his head fall forward and, avoiding her eyes, he muttered:

"Started what?"

She laughed and shuffled sideways. Lowering her head, she looked up at him, and her beads set up a rattling overture to what was coming next.

"Tell me first," she said. "The pub, tell me about the pub."

"What about it?"

He was only mildly interested in hearing her answer. His eyes kept wandering to the leaf that was slowly rolling off her hair. He wondered whether he should tell her about it. Somehow, the leaf made her look ridiculous.

"Only you can tell me," she said. "I've been wanting to know for thirty years."

The breeze swept down from the trees and brushed Julian's cheeks. He shook his head and planted an encouraging smile on his face. Blodwin's frown had set up deep creases and shadows on her forehead. There was very little trace of the girl he had once known at the Tiltyard. Perhaps in the nose and mouth there was a resemblance to someone he had briefly known. Even there, time had destroyed youth, obliterated the person he and his colleagues had once referred to as: *A bit of a slag.*

"You remember," she said, "the last night in the King's Arms? The summer of 1968?"

He turned his eyes inwards. Fragments from time, pieces of a missing dream, fell in place.

The public bar is full of faces: Paul, Dick, JD, Mrs Croucher and the colonel. And in the lounge bar, there is a World War Two reunion; Americans who served in England, and the women who remember them. A group of middle-aged men are hesitantly mingling with a group of similarly-aged women. The two groups look as though they are playing blind man's bluff, but without the blind.

From the lounge bar, music curls and whirls, and candles are burning softly, their flickering flames revolving with Julian's spinning head. One tune but many dances, and all the people are dancing to the music of time, but all of them are doing it in a different way. Then, there is the accordionist and people singing out: *"Those were the days, oh yes, those were the days."*

And there is Julian, lurching towards the door. His hands are on his knees. He is vomiting on the pavement.

He heard Blodwin's beads rattle, and felt the pressure of her hand on his arm.

"Why did you say that to me," she asked.

He tried to recall Blodwin or the idea of Blodwin. He dug down deep, but all that emerged was the music, the dancers, the shadow of a feeling for Kathy, and an image of her and JD walking over the road to the bus stop. He slowly shook his head.

"Say what?"

"You recall, don't you, Julian?"

He shook his head with more vigour and screwed up his cheeks to signal an apology.

"Sorry."

He tried to focus on her face as he said it. He wanted to show her that he was sincere, but in the dying light, he found she was difficult to focus on. He did see her eyes close, and she swayed backwards as though he had slapped her. Her mascara had run and a black tear was rolling down her cheek.

He watched her dig into a pocket and fumble for a packet of cigarettes and a box of matches. She extracted a cigarette and slipped it into her mouth. Then, she struck a match and held it in front of her. Her hand was shaking so violently, it was all he could do to stop himself from grabbing the match and lighting the cigarette for her. She cupped her elbow in her hand and held the cigarette under her chin. She spoke through the curling smoke.

"You were sitting by the bar. You were alone and surveying the place and people as if the rest of the world didn't exist, had vanished without a whisper."

It was getting darker, and Blodwin was herself vanishing, her beads rattling and echoing as though from some distant and forgotten place.

"Was it someone else you were waiting for, was it?

He suddenly took a step towards her, found that he had lifted both arms as if to grab her. Certainly, he knew that the need for caution, the need to protect her fragile dream had vanished. With no attempt to conceal his growing frustration, he said:

"That's enough."

He saw no resentment in the way she glanced at him. Perhaps she was aware that it was not her he was annoyed with. Perhaps she knew that he did not want to hear his name mentioned in the same breath as Kathy's. He had got used to his own thoughts and secrets, was frightened of hearing his name and Kathy's in the mouth of someone else. Blodwin grabbed at his arm. He wanted to pull his hand away but forced himself to let it stay still. She smiled suddenly but the brightness in her eyes had an odd quality - something unstable, almost deranged. She said:

"You don't remember what you said to me?"

Julian recalled the street. He remembered watching Kathleen enter another world with JD. He hardly recalled Blodwin at all. Her beads rattled again.

"It was Mary Hopkin," she said.

"Those were the days?"

She nodded.

"Don't you recall what you said at the end of the evening?"

He had to shake his head. Blodwin took a drag from the cigarette and blew out a long stream of smoke from her nostrils.

"You said that whenever we heard it, the song would remind us of the King's Arms, would remind us of the year, the people, and the dream we lived. Once upon a time there was a tavern; but of course, you don't remember, do you, Julian?"

Blodwin was looking at him through narrowed lids.

"But then you never meant it in the first place. It was just a sham, wasn't it?"

Her mouth snapped shut, her beads stopped rattling, and she looked at him in such a way that suggested she had received a revelation, had seen through his skin.

"Well fuck you," she said, and threw the cigarette on the ground and stamped on it. "Yes, fuck you, but I want that time back..."

He watched for some moments, untouched by the anger that gripped her.

"It's a long time ago," he said.

"You didn't know what I felt about you?"

A cold wind touched him as the sun went down over the house. Blodwin said:

"You never got my signals?"

She was frowning again, and her eyes were pools of disbelief.

"You never got my messages?"

"It is thirty years and..."

"Just fuck thirty years."

The pools of disbelief threatened to turn to rage, but

Blodwin blinked it away. She held out one arm, the palm of her hand facing outwards as if she would push his words away.

"And it was stronger because you were so inaccessible, so distant..."

He looked at her blankly, paused for a moment and simply repeated:

"Thirty years is a long time."

"Thirty years is nothing," she said. "The dream of '68 is a dream in '98. No longer real, perhaps, but still a dream."

Her face, now with no tears, and the voice with no emotion caused him to open his eyes wide in something approaching fear.

"But it's not a dream I've been living, it's a nightmare with monsters. I can tell you…"

She suddenly lunged forward and grasped at his shoulders.

"I've seen such terrible, terrible things..."

Julian tore himself away and staggered sideways, but her voice followed him, its tone now betraying desperation.

"Please help me, Julian, please..."

He was silent, aware that he wanted to get away, to get back to his room and close the door on the rest of the world. Blodwin glanced nervously over her shoulder as if she was expecting to see someone standing there. In a whisper, she said:

"Help me to find my way back to the life of those days."

She stepped back into the semi-darkness from which she had emerged earlier in the day and, making a dismissive gesture with her hands, she muttered:

"Too late now. You've changed and you should've stayed where you were."

He thought that it might have been easier for him had

her words been infused with hate, had she closed her fists and struck him. He could then have echoed her feelings and thrown them back at her. He could have shouted out his words and given them the power he wanted to give them. Instead he said rather weakly:

"In Italy?"

She ground the dead cigarette further into the turf with her heel.

"No," she said, "in my memory. You should've stayed there. You know, Pictures of Lilly and all that. But you came and destroyed my dream..."

Then, suddenly, Blodwin's eyes were pressed close to his. In reaction to some imagined crisis, her eyes were threatening as if someone or something had become a danger to her.

"Don't recall what happened outside either, do you?"

Her eyes narrowed further. He was trying to remember what he was doing. Vomiting? Yes, and he did remember a girl's features floating in his tears.

"I'll never forget the look on your fucking stupid face," she said.

He was mentally breaking away from her. It was the decision of one who fears being contaminated by another's instability. Blodwin was full of malice and bitterness.

"And do you know what that look was?"

He shook his head. He did not need to be reminded. He had been in love, and there was nothing wrong with that. She answered her own question. And when the words came, she hissed them out.

"Hate," she said. "Sheer fucking hate."

He took two steps backwards and turned his face away. There was no guilt when he spun round, no pity when he walked towards his car, no pity that he left her standing all alone in the garden. No guilt, no pity; nothing. Blodwin shouted after him:

"You're a marked fucking man. Watch your back. And fuck you."

Blodwin was still screaming at him when he got into the car and reversed down the street. Rows of Victorian buildings passed him by. Waterloo House and Balaclava Villas suddenly appeared to him as diseased versions of what once had been, their grand facades echoing long-gone and certain days. Was this, he wondered, what the past had all come to? He continued on his way through the early autumn evening seeing nothing else but the pointlessness of it all, the wretched decay and crumbling grandeur that was the end result of all that energy and all that hope.

*

It was around seven thirty when Julian started up the stairs that led to his room in the pub. As soon as he placed his foot on the bottom step, he knew there was something wrong. He could not put his finger on it, but it was in the air. He was being played with. There was something wrong all around him.

His heart thumped. His legs took the stairs almost by themselves as if powered by a morbid curiosity. On the landing outside his room, he hesitated. He stared at the door, wondering what he would find behind it. Tentatively, he reached out and wrapped his hand around the cold, brass knob. Then, as though some demon was following him up the stairs, he threw the door open. He let it bang against the inside wall. He stood there waiting for something to emerge.

There had been very few times in his life when he could truthfully say that a drink was something he needed in the way people needed a tranquilliser after an emergency, something indispensable during a crisis. He needed a drink when Paola told him she was leaving. He needed one when he saw Kathy's face in the police station. That night, he needed another.

When he entered his room, only the traces of person or persons remained. His box of diaries had been tipped up for the second time in three days. The volumes were scattered over the bed and the floor. Their pages, now upturned, were turning slowly in the slight breeze that had come with him through the door. His life was once again exposed for the entire world to see. He hurriedly checked through the volumes. They were all there, apart from the one he supposed the intruders had come to find. He had remembered, that morning, to tuck "The Kathy Years" safely away in the boot of his car.

If he had expected this intrusion, he had not expected it to happen so quickly and nor had he anticipated the fear that accompanied it. He took a sharp intake of breath, and his legs crumpled. He sat down heavily on the edge of the bed and cradled his head in his arms while the tension ran out of him. Consciously he tried to breathe, to fill his lungs. He raised his head, inhaled deeply and stood up. A horror had emerged from the shadows, had declared himself and his involvement in Kathy's disappearance. But what frightened him, made him sway as if someone had struck him, was the certainty that sooner or later, the horror would come again, would come looking for the damned evidence.

Later, while he was opening his door, the thought came to him. He was on his way to the bar for that much needed drink. As the doorknob rattled in his closed palm, he saw that he had no idea from which direction the horror would appear. He was aware of two stark alternatives. Either he could be the helpless victim and react or he could be the perpetrator, take positive steps and deal with the problem proactively. He took a few steps forward and stumbled against a table. With a great effort he pulled himself together and, breathing unsteadily, he set off in search of the bar.

12

Sleep that night was evasive and fitful. Whether awake or half-awake, Julian was continuously in some troubled place where nightmares and thoughts merged together and moved in his mind, uncontrolled and uncontrollable. It was the recurrent image of Paola which at first haunted him. As though from a great height, he watched her beckoning. He was the helpless victim, able only to watch and wring his hands at his inability to reach out and touch her.

Then he was facing Paola across the void. He revealed to her that his infidelity had been determined by unhappy experiences in 1968. He was telling her that he loved her. But it was all a dream; she could not hear him, and he could only whisper.

When fully awake, he reflected that his twenty-three years together with Paola held nothing on which they could draw to help them. Their situation was so unfamiliar that he and Paola resembled newly blind people stumbling about and trying to make sense of the world.

He had come to England on the rebound. It had been an unthinking move, a sort of conditioned reflex that would take him to a haven, a place of rest from life. But now he had regained his balance, he reckoned he had made a mistake. It was the wrong haven. England was no longer the secure home it might once have been.

And when this dream and his reflections had passed, there was the sleeping nightmare in which he was forced to relive a moment in his life from 1968, a moment which had been unconditionally released by his return to England.

In the nightmare, McKnight is leaning forward in his chair, and his hands are clasped in front of him. Mrs Croucher is standing at his shoulder When Julian appears in the doorway, she raises her eyebrows and then her arm. Opening her hand, she beckons. A stool has been placed near the door. John McKnight nods to it with his head.

"Come in," he says, "and sit down."

Julian notices a flatness in McKnight's brogue that suggests calm before a storm. He drags the stool to the desk and sits down. He is looking upwards into McKnight's face. McKnight leans back in his seat and cups his head in his hands. Staring vacantly in front of him, he flicks the tip of his tongue between his front teeth. Then, he smiles and says:

"So, this is your last day at the Tiltyard cafeteria."

Julian's stool is so low to the ground, his chin so close to his knees, that he is curled up and cringing in front of his tormentor.

"Tell us," McKnight says, "about your future plans."

From the corner of his eye Julian watches Mrs Croucher. Her gaze is shifting about the office. She is holding her hands together at stomach height and rubbing her palms as if she wants to keep them warm.

Every now and then, the corners of her mouth turn upwards to smile, but her eyes are sad and haunted. Julian says:

"I'm planning to go to university next month."

John McKnight lets his chair fall forward with a clatter.

"Good at planning, aren't we now?"

He turns to Mrs Croucher.

"Hear that? The boy thinks he's good at planning, by God."

Mrs Croucher nods, and the corners of her mouth turn up still further. John lets his own lip rise to a sneer and says that university is hardly the best place for criminals. Mrs Croucher shuffles uncomfortably. John McKnight gets to his feet and leans over his desk. He lowers his voice to a whisper.

"Can you tell me why I shouldn't ring the police now? If you're so fucking intelligent, give me one good reason why."

His unexpected and sibilant whisper has an almost hypnotic power that makes Julian want to hide his head in his shoulders. John McKnight leans further forward. He lifts one arm and taps his head with a finger.

"Do you think I don't know what you've been about here?"

He lets his words and his hand hover in the air. His face is like the dark side of the moon. He talks about the stock and he asks how Julian thought he could get away with it. John McKnight reaches forward and pulls the telephone violently from the desk.

"And don't tell me, by God, don't tell me you've no idea what I'm talking about."

He holds the receiver under Julian's nose and shakes it.

"Give me one good reason why I shouldn't call the police right now? Come on, Mr bloody student, you who are so fucking intelligent. Give me a good reason why I shouldn't call the police."

Mrs Croucher's cheeks turn crimson. John McKnight's face is taut and quivering.

"Come on, Julian. Come on, boy; one reason. Just one fucking reason."

Julian can think of none. He is sitting with a hanging head. He knows he has been exposed, found out. It is as if his skin has been peeled away to reveal the rottenness beneath. The phone under his nose still shakes menacingly.

"You've been greedy, haven't you?" McKnight says. "And by God, we've just had a complaint."

He looks at Julian with an expression of utter disbelief.

"Did you only think of yourself? Didn't you ever think of the people who saved up just to give their children a treat? And what happens? You rob them of their fucking money. What sort of heartless little shit are you, boy?"

Julian lowers his head still further. John McKnight replaces the phone and sits down. He calmly folds his arms across his chest.

"God knows why, but I'll do you a favour."

He stares wildly around the room as if looking for a reason. Then, he whispers again.

"You'll pack up here this weekend. But if I see your arse around here after that, if I see your arse anywhere, I'll be on the blower straightaway. Understand?"

Julian can only nod.

"And you know what that'll mean, don't you? No more university for you, Mr bloody student. You're a fucking thief man. You know what happens to thieves, don't you?"

Mrs Croucher gets redder and redder. John is holding his head as though there is something poisonous on the desk in front of him.

"Don't you?"

Julian nods again. McKnight leans back and cups the back of his head in his hands.

"Do as I tell you and you'll be all right. Disobey me and I'll see to it that you'll be cleaning fucking tables for the rest of your fucking days. Then you'll find out about the realities of life for those who never had the chance of anything, yet alone a university education. And do you know why...?"

McKnight interrupts himself with a smile.

"So, what do you say, Mr fucking student?"

Julian tries to speak but his mouth is so dry, he coughs. John McKnight turns an ear towards him.

"What was that I heard? I'm doing you a fucking favour. You must thank me for that, boy. Thank me, by God. What did I hear you say?"

"Thank you."

"That's better."

He turns to Mrs Croucher.

"Now, Mrs Croucher will give you other duties today. And I don't have to tell you not to go to the kiosk. You're a thief, a fucking thief. Now, get the fuck out, get the fuck out of here."

Julian came to with a start and let his head mould into the pillow while he chased the tail of his dreams. He reached out, switched on the lamp, and the uninvited guests of his nightmare faded. A light film of sweat quickly developed under his hairline while he reflected. He lightly clenched and unclenched his fists until his breathing eased, and he fell asleep once more.

In the morning, he opened his eyes to a changed world. He lay on his back, staring at the ceiling, trying to identify what had happened during the night. Huge ideas were sounding like foghorns, filled the spaces around him as if they were part of the air itself. They were unmistakable and impossible to ignore.

It was while he was shaving that he realised what had changed. During the night a decision had been taken as though in his absence. His face had a strangely balanced smile when it stared back at him from the shaving mirror. The soap, stubbornly remaining in the lines around his mouth, forced him to see that ageing meant a slow descent into ugliness and mediocrity. If his life was to go comfortably from middle age to old age, he would need to confront his demons and deal with them.

He dressed at a rush, picked up the box of diaries and his briefcase, and carried them down the stairs and into the patron's car park. With an absent mind, he placed them in the boot of his car where "The Kathleen Years" still lay hidden under a blanket. Then he strode into the pub and into the phone booth. A residue of indecision obliged him to stare at the phone for a moment or two while he dried the palms of his hands on his trousers. He snatched at the receiver and dialled. Within a minute, he had cancelled his sailing for that day and replaced it with an open return. It was all so simple.

He breakfasted to the sound of Capital Radio, and he emerged from the George and Dragon at around nine o'clock. It was such a beautiful, early-autumn day that a song came immediately to his lips. He sang it softly to himself as he walked towards his car.

"Do you remember, the kind of September when life was slow and oh so mellow?"

The smell of resin from the timber yard blew through the streets and threatened to take him back into the past as the song promised. Refusing to let it, he hummed a different song, a song he seemingly plucked from the air as though it had been waiting for him to grasp it. The shadows of the words touched some deeply buried emotions, but the words themselves refused to break out of his memory and show themselves. Nor was he able to identify the title of the song, and the name of the singer eluded him. The tune itself refused to go away. It was embedded in the rhythm of his heartbeat, and he was breathing in time to it. He put out his hands as though he wanted to stave off the arrival of a horrible truth. He glanced around him, a man looking for somewhere to hide. Then his mind went numb, and forgetfulness pressed all around him with its closed doors and emptiness.

Driving out of the village, Julian reckoned he had tapped in to an echo of a terrible experience he had once chained down. The tune had loosened those chains and, for a moment, he had brushed lightly against some moment of horror and pain. The same shock seemed to be promoting a surge of intense vulnerability. He could think of no other reason why he should feel he was attracting someone's attention.

The sight of the Bowstones on the ridge calmed him. He told himself that many human tragedies had taken place in their shadow, but the accompanying suffering had simply disappeared in a puff of wind. He consoled himself with the notion that whoever might be looking at him now would disappear in the same way.

One or two early shoppers were making their way along the pavement to the village. Not one of these people was looking in his direction. He shrugged and managed to convince himself that it was his imagination or his disturbed state of mind that was making him feel conspicuous.

The sound of gravel crackling under the tyres brought him back to himself, and he parked in a hollow directly underneath the Hampton Court bypass.

He removed the briefcase from the boot, dropped the keys into it and took stock of his surroundings. Two enormous pillars, which supported the bypass, straddled the entrance to Strudwick's Car and Commercial Vehicle

Dismantlers Yard. For the youth of the area, the pillars offered a splendid opportunity for skateboarding. A group of youngsters had already gathered, happy in their adolescence, to revel in the decaying symbols of a consumer society.

It was a sunny morning, and the carriageway cast a long, black shadow across the yard. Water was dripping and spraying down so that an oily, black slime coiled through the centre of the hollow. The shadows, the rain and the spray were not the only things that had descended from above. Cigarettes, paper wrappings, hankies, and even bottles had come down, discarded from the bright and shiny cars booming overhead.

He made inquiries, and a skateboarder pointed the way to Strudwick's office.

"Behind that lot," he said, "in a corrugated iron hut."

The skateboarder had indicated a rampart of scrap metal. It bristled with distorted axles, fenders and exhaust pipes. These wrecks were now absolutely discarded and unwholesome, rusting hulks from which their once proud owners had disassociated themselves as completely as they might reject the old and insane.

Finding Strudwick's hut was not as easy as the skateboarder had suggested. The dismantler's yard was a maze, and the sight of the cars made Julian uncomfortable. Some of them had been involved in bad accidents, and as he made his way forward, he heard noises. He told himself that it was the sound of the breeze whistling through the distorted metal, but the noises were strangely similar to the murmuring - there but not there - that he had noticed outside Paul's house.

From above came the continuous whoosh of cars, and he found the place gloomy and claustrophobic. Underfoot it was slippery with mud and oil, and the smell was something he could almost taste - rusty and cankerous, bitter like blood in the mouth or the tongue upon steel. The wrecks were piled like corpses. Car doors were swinging open in the wind, and the seats were thrown forwards and outwards like smashed and broken limbs.

He stumbled round one such pile, caught his foot on an exhaust pipe and tripped towards the office. Strudwick was a hunched back, blue dungarees and stabbing elbows. Beneath his rubbing hands was the shiniest car Julian had ever seen. Strudwick must have seen his visitor reflected in the bodywork. He stopped his rhythmic movement, tensed and then turned to face him.

Julian stepped backwards, almost lost his balance when the case got caught between his knees. The man's face was grotesquely misshapen and resembled a squashed frying pan or a blob of sealing wax that had flowed sideways. Julian stammered out the purpose of his visit; a door, to replace the broken one. Strudwick merely nodded his head and told him to leave the car for forty-eight hours. Then he stared at Julian, his good eye drilling a hole through him. Julian gaped stupidly until the expression in Strudwick's eye turned to one of recognition, and a smile flitted across his lips. Julian had no time to wonder what it was that Strudwick had recognised in him. Faced with this blighted man, Julian muttered his thanks and turned to hurry out of the maze. He heard Strudwick's voice at his back.

"The keys - don't forget the car keys."

Julian opened his briefcase, groped inside and dropped the keys into the outstretched hand.

"I've left the car at the entrance," he said.

He took two steps backwards and tripped again, his heel finding a patch of oil or mud so that his leg slid away from under him. He mumbled an apology, regained his balance and headed off in the direction of the exit, the roar of the traffic and Hampton Court

Palace.

He was walking across the bridge and admiring the facade of the Mitre Hotel when the feeling returned that he was on stage and under the intense scrutiny of unseen eyes. He tried telling himself that if he was still feeling disconnected from his homeland, this was no reason to develop paranoia. No sooner had he consoled himself with this explanation of his discomfort, than he found himself confronted with another thought. It occurred to him that he was being watched. Although the idea was absurd, he quickened his pace over the bridge and hurried away down the towpath toward his rendezvous with the past.

13

The palace slowly materialised through a thin fog, which had been hanging over the river as a harbinger of autumn since the early morning. Apparently hidden from intrusive eyes he felt safer down by the waterside, where the fog was thick and low enough to obscure the opposite bank of the Thames.

There was a dredger, a shifting shadow, under Hampton Court Bridge. The full mechanical booms and the rattling of heavy chains seemed oddly disassociated from the machinery on the dredger's deck. Dampened by the mist, these sounds drifted and resonated mournfully over the river towards him. Ripples of water from the boat's hull lapped against the river bank, clouds billowed over the towpath, and wispy arms of white reached out to grip the anglers who sat hunched and concentrated over their rods. Wreathed in this milky veil the men were ghostly and still, their floats bobbing and ducking with the invisible flow of the great river. The crunch of Julian's feet on the path provoked little more than an irritated flick of the fishermen's heads.

Further along the path, he slowed his pace to watch

the arrival of the first passenger boat from Kingston. Tourists, who lined the boat's rail, now made space for the deck hands. Revived by the boat's imminent arrival, these men were spurred into action and heaved coiled and heavy ropes behind them. With a shudder of reversing propellers, the boat thumped against the wooden jetty. The ropes were then thrown and tied, and the deck hands stood to one side to allow the passengers to spill down the gangplank and gather in groups on the towpath. Julian joined the groups as they funnelled through a heavy, wrought-iron gate that led into the palace grounds.

And so, after thirty years, he was again standing opposite the Tudor facade of the West Front. Nothing seemed to have changed. The person who looked out through his eyes was the same person who had looked at everything in the summer of '68. The shell was lined, older and perhaps thicker, but Julian had a strong sense that the palace grounds belonged to him, that the tourists around him were trespassers on his territory. And there was a stronger sense, a deeper feeling, that in these ancient building he might find a part of himself that the years had taken from him.

Detaching himself from the groups of tourists, he took a left-hand path and approached the rose garden. From nearby tennis courts came the familiar and intermittent pock, pock, of racket against ball. The sound echoed in the stillness of the garden. Disembodied shouts encouraged and congratulated, and from a not-too-distant radio, the sound of music drifted across the lawns. Julian was not expecting a fanfare of trumpets to greet him, but as he strolled through the garden, he thought, just for a moment, that he could hear snatches of an old song blowing with the breeze.

"Those were the days, young friend," came the words.

"Good shot," cried an invisible tennis player.

"We thought they'd never end."

Pock, pock sounded the ball.

"We'd sing and dance the whole night through."

He was brought firmly back to the present by a clip-clipping of shears from near at hand. A solitary gardener was tending to the borders and she looked sullenly at him.

"Nice morning."

"Indeed, it is," Julian said, breathing in the smell of cut grass.

On impulse he decided to play a harmless game, to ask her a question to which he thought he knew the answer.

"I wonder if you can help me. Is there a cafe hereabouts, where one can get a cup of tea perhaps?"

The gardener let the shears fall against her waist. Her lips moved slightly, but she stared at him for a long time before saying:

"A cup of tea? Bit early for tea. The restaurant serves teas. But there's no cafe here."

This was not the answer he had been expecting. He and the gardener looked at each other with increasing suspicion, two people divided by conflicting experiences.

"There's always been a cafe here," Julian said indignantly. "I used to work in it."

The gardener examined him as if he were a fool. She mumbled to herself and then she woke up as though from a dream, shook herself and looked round with assurance.

"No cafe here. Never been a cafe here."

He stared dumbly at her while she lined up the shears and worked again at the borders. He reckoned she was about twenty-five. Maybe, in her life, there never had been a cafe there, Julian thought, but one of them had to be wrong. Muttering his words of thanks, he left the rose garden.

Julian took a diagonal course across the first of the Tiltyard lawns. He watched his shadow tapering before him as it moved over the crisscross-patterned grass. The centre of the lawn was dominated by an ancient cedar, but long before his shadow had broken over its trunk, he found himself stealing sidelong glances through the high glass of the restaurant window. He knew, by then, that it was ridiculous, but he discovered he was still expecting to see people he knew. In particular, he was stunned to realise that he was half-expecting to see Kathy. The restaurant was still filled with her. Even after all those years, it was filled with the magic of her absence.

And yet, through all the pain, the guilt and the shame, there was the particular smell that he had always associated with the Tiltyard, the long hot summer days of '68, and the drunken nights at the King's Arms. The smell was a combination of tea, freshly mown grass and oldness, and it conjured up something people can only feel once in life. It was the magical feeling of first love, and it seemed to come out of the air itself like Aladdin from his lamp. First love, he thought, would never rust.

He approached the heart of his memory with a light step. He made his way to the high wall that separated the restaurant lawns from the cafeteria. As the thin end of his shadow further darkened the ivy that gripped the brickwork, he was visited by three confused fragments of memory. No doubt they were coloured by the present, but these fragments from summer '68 were as alive and as bright as hill-top beacons, and like beacons they were surrounded by the darkness of lost time. He could no longer remember from which position he had originally viewed these scenes. Perhaps he had been like a photographer, always and ever present, but never there.

The first fragment is an image of Mrs Croucher.

Through the high, glass window of the cafeteria the under-manageress is an indistinct and shadowy figure, moving towards him through the tables. She is easily identifiable by the shape of her hair. Piled on top of her head, it resembles a warped and shrunken busby. People say that back in the fifties, Mrs Croucher looked forward to a bright future as a film star. Somewhere, her life has taken a wrong turn, and she has ended up here at the Tiltyard. Julian has never once heard her discuss her disappointments, but there is an air of sadness and tragedy about her. It is almost as if she knows that the hand of death is pulling at her shoulder. Julian and his friends all love Mrs C, but they all know that she is killing herself with gin and tonic.

"I've done my best for you," she is saying to him. "But you aren't the only one with problems, and you're not the only one who's on the fiddle here. Trouble is you've been walking around with your eyes shut."

She hesitates, looks furtively around and adds in a secretive whisper:

"You don't get it do you? You've trod on his toes. McKnight's trying to involve everyone here in his own little game. That includes JD and Kath too. They need our help."

Still standing by the wall, Julian was struck by confusion, doubtful whether these snatches of conversation had occurred simultaneously here on the cafeteria terrace. All he knew for sure was that Mrs Croucher had given him these warnings thirty years previously, and that they belonged to the summer of '68. But the precise points in time in which the words were spoken had collapsed into other and similar conversations which had taken place at the same period in his life.

He was vaguely aware that this was also true of the second fragment of memory. This is an image of his colleagues. Grouped around a table on the terrace, they are enjoying their morning tea-break. Dick is lazily stretched out on two chairs. His head is inclined and resting on an open fist, and his eyes are trained down his leather-clad legs and aiming through open feet. Dick is two years into a politics and economics course at Trinity College in Dublin and he is practising his rhetorical skills. He waves a finger at his target audience.

"And why should we strike?"

The tone strongly suggests that Dick is about to provide an answer, and his question is greeted with a hostile silence. Dick's audience is leaning over cups of steaming tea, and cigarette smoke is curling over the table. Dick wags an accusing finger between arched eyebrows.

"I'll tell you why. We must show solidarity with Alexander Dubcek."

A medley of muted cheers, laughter and jeers greets this announcement. Someone looks up. A finger jabs and a point is raised.

"It's all right for you," says Mike the sandwich-maker, who always smells of stale milk, "you students. But some of us work here for a living."

There is a low mumble of agreement, but Dick will not be put off by any challenge to his authority. He wags his finger with increased vigour.

"And you mustn't forget that if you aren't with us, you are against us. Remember Martin Luther King and his dream."

"Good serve," cries a voice from the courts.

"Those were the days," says the old song.

And the memory at first dimmed and then faded away, taking Julian's one-time friends and colleagues with it.

The third fragment begins with a shadow and a voice. The voice is strident, urgent, and the brogue bears witness to the Belfast origins of the speaker.

"Right, boys."

The voice and the shadow are accompanied by a jingling sound. The arrival of the cafeteria manager is usually preceded by the sound of his car keys dangling from one finger. John McKnight flicks his keys upwards so that he can momentarily close them in his palm, and then drop them again.

"Back to work you'll go, by God."

The group around the table appear to have set in stone. Everyone except Dick falters in the face of this barely hidden threat. McKnight takes a step forward.

"Didn't you hear me, boys?"

The manager's suit gives the impression that he has materialised from his own shadow. Against this darkness, the white shirt-cuffs stand out in vivid contrast. The sun glints briefly from the bulbous studs that hold the cuffs together. The jangling suddenly ceases, and McKnight digs into his trouser pocket, pulls out a handkerchief and flicks specks of dust from his jacket.

"I said back to work."

His shadow breaks over the table, and McKnight stands in the full glare of the sunlight. The skin of his face is as white as the shirt-cuffs, is almost transparent in the bright sunlight. He jabs a finger at the ground.

"And I mean, now."

"We're on strike," says Dick.

McKnight's top lip rises in a sneer.

"On your fucking bike," he spits out.

Unwilling to lose face in front of his colleagues, Dick says, rather lamely:

"If you're not with us, you're against us. Solidarity with Gerry Fitt and civil rights in Ireland."

There is a moment of silence, a breathless and expectant hush at Dick's daring defiance. But in a tone which is strangely conciliatory, McKnight says:

"OK, boy, but we're open for business and we've customers to attend to."

From the kitchen, the washing-up machine hisses, puffs and clangs.

"Find Julian," says McKnight, stuffing the handkerchief back into his pocket. There is a pause as he straightens his jacket. He looks around and then lets his gaze and a light smile fall on Dick.

"Tell our university friend I want to see him now."

McKnight stands with legs apart, flicking and dropping his keys, and then lowering his bottom jaw, which he slowly moves from side to side, grinding something real or imaginary between his teeth. Then, he swivels on a heel and struts away towards the kitchen. In the twinkling of an eye, this fragment of memory was gone. Standing by the side of the ivy-clad wall, Julian still heard the sound of McKnight's car keys jangling in his ear.

The first thing he noticed, when he peered round the end of the wall, was a gaping hole, an emptiness where the kiosk used to be. He looked at this hole for a second or two and tried to suppress the confusion, the irritation he felt. He supposed he had been looking forward to buying an ice cream from the kiosk. He supposed he had imagined himself pointing to the hearts carved in the woodwork and saying to the ice cream vendor, "That was me who did that, a long time ago." It was a long time ago - so long that the kiosk, the hearts and the love that had prompted him to carve them, had all vanished.

The next thing he noticed was that there were no tables outside the cafeteria where Dick used to hold court during the tea-breaks. Julian strolled across the terrace. It was sad and empty apart from the fallen leaves brushing lightly over the concrete. Then he saw the sign: *Tiltyard Conference Centre.* The gardener had been partly right. The cafe was there in form but not in spirit.

He pressed his face against the highly polished glass and stared at the interior. His gaze was in the middle of the room before he really saw anything at all, but the glass was so polished, the sun so brilliant, that most of the interior was contaminated by the mirror images of his surroundings. The floor he and his friends had scrubbed daily swam in the reflection of the trees. The walls were festooned with pictures and prints that floated and shimmered in the shadows of the old buildings and bushes behind him.

The place was recognisable but so different as to be no more welcoming than an empty tomb. Unable to focus on the interior, Julian stood back from the glass and, in a sort of dazed silence, he paid his respects to the idea of the past. He gazed sadly at this place where he had known first love, but he was not looking with his eyes. His heart reached out and tried to touch and to feel again those things that once upon a time had made him both happy and sad. He was deeply penetrated by the solemnity of this moment, by the beauty and strength of a feeling that could come upon you like a typhoon, inspire you, hold you mercilessly in its power, and then move on. But his heart recoiled in shame and regret when it saw that when the chance to love and live had come in '68, he had looked upon it all with such careless and thoughtless eyes.

Eventually, he drew himself away and set off back to the restaurant. He guessed it was simple habit that urged him to turn, to look back and stare for one more time at his past. To his surprise, it was not too difficult to keep moving forwards. He now knew that the past was non-existent, as illusory as the end of a rainbow.

There was a freshness in his step when he approached the restaurant and walked through its doors. A woman in blue came towards him, her head tilted to one side and at a questioning angle that seemed to challenge him. When he noticed the colour of her uniform calling out to her eyes, a wave of anger swept through him and left nothing but a strong sense of outrage. It was an obscenity that he found this woman attractive, a horror that this should occur in the shrine of his past, shameful that he could betray his own memories and taint them with something as basic as sexual attraction. Worse still, the lady in blue would have been about twenty years of age, the same age as Kathleen had been when she had disappeared. Julian turned his eyes from the magical blue of hers. The badge on her uniform read: *Day and Knight Catering Services*, and underneath, *Susan. Assistant Manager.*

Susan showed him to a seat by the window. He thanked her and, avoiding her face, he looked through the high, glass window. He mused on the failures of his personal history and on his inability to learn or to protect himself from a past that could not easily be hustled away and removed from sight. And while he mused, he contemplated the view of the Tiltyard lawn, the cedar tree and its uninterrupted connection to memory. Under that tree, he had once had a dream, and the dream had faded to such dimness that what remained was the barest outline of a smile upon his face.

He buried his head in the menu card, but as he did so, he thought he saw a youth in a starched, white jacket clearing the rubbish from around the tree. He fancied he had seen the youth long ago. He was looking surreptitiously towards the restaurant as if he knew who Julian was and what he was doing there. Julian knew this was impossible. The figure by the tree was so young, and he, Julian thought, was so middle-aged. Although he tried to ignore the youth Julian's eyes kept returning to the white jacket. He sensed that the youth objected to his presence in the restaurant, so he shook his head and the young man was gone.

He knew immediately that the young man had been no mirage. He was a struggling memory of himself. Julian was sitting in the place which his younger persona had invested with magical qualities. This was the Forbidden City, the place where Kathy had once walked and breathed. She had stood almost on the very spot at which Julian was sitting now. It was a shock to see how ordinary it was and disappointing to see the paint peeling off the ceiling.

Susan approached with an order pad in hand.

"Yes, please?"

He glanced at her and decided to accept her in her role as waitress and nothing more. He said:

"Tea with lemon, please."

"Do you mean tea with lemon or lemon tea? There is a difference, you know."

He squinted at her. A mistake. Perhaps she mistook his squint for a grin. She smiled at him, and her blue eyes crackled. He said:

"Tea with lemon."

"Anything else?"

"Nothing, thank you." Then he added, "Do you mind if I draw the curtain?"

The mist had now dispersed, and the sun, poised low in the sky, was dazzling.

"Sorry," she said, "we don't draw the curtains during the day."

A few seconds later, he heard her shouting through a hatchway into the kitchen. He was distracted again by movement from outside and he peered into the sunlight. The young man by the cedar tree was nowhere to be seen, but Julian saw him in his mind's eye, making his way along the towpath from Kingston. Before this memory could properly emerge, there was a sound and then a voice at his elbow.

"Tea with lemon, sir."

The tray clattered onto the table. Julian smiled his thanks.

"I wonder if you could help me," he said. "Does John McKnight still work here?"

Susan looked at him, emptiness in her blue eyes.

"Who?"

"John McKnight."

"What does he do?"

"He used to be the under manager here."

"Oh, you mean *the* John McKnight," she said. "He doesn't often come here."

"*The* John McKnight?"

She looked down at her badge and giggled childishly.

"Day and Knight catering Services."

Julian nearly choked on his tea with lemon. "He's the boss?" he spluttered.

She nodded and laughed again - a little nervously.

"He's the boss," she said.

"Is he here today?"

"Only comes at weekends," Susan said. "Usually stays in his office in London."

"Where's the office?"

A shadow of fear passed over her face, and her mouth fell open. Suddenly she was not so attractive. Her slightly flirtatious tone now gave way to quick and nervous words that emerged quickly, before they could be pruned, domesticated.

"You're not from the bloody health authority, are you?"

Julian felt sorry for her.

"No, I'm not from the health authority. I'm an old friend."

"Didn't know he had any friends."

"Only in a manner of speaking," he said, giving her another smile.

Susan looked relieved and lowered her voice to a whisper.

"You must be a very old friend. When did you last see Mr McKnight?"

"About thirty years ago."

"Then you don't know," she said, her blue eyes becoming bluer still and twinkling with excitement.

"Know what?"

Susan raised her head and held her chin at a proud angle.

"They say that our Mr McKnight's going to run for MP."

This time he did choke on the tea. He broke into a fit of coughing. Susan leaned forward.

"Are you all right?"

Through his coughing, Julian assured her he was.

"MP?" he said. "MP for what?"

Susan looked slightly distraught.

"Where've you been? Everyone knows John McKnight. They call him a pillar of society."

"A pillar of society? John McKnight?"

His eyes were now brimming with tears. He was about to describe him, the thick lips that would rise to a sneer, the curly but thinning, blonde hair and the watery, blue eyes. He simply stared at Susan. She would never have recognised this description of a ghost from the past.

"The very same," she said and she walked away without giving him the address he wanted. He sat in a dream. John McKnight was head of the catering services. John McKnight was going to run for MP. Given what Julian knew about him, it was obscene. He looked at his watch and decided to go to London immediately, but he sat immobile with the smell of the tea playing with his memories.

It was the feelings that came first. They marked the door to his other world. He was not sure what might be lurking there for he had kept the door firmly shut for so many years. He rubbed his eyes, but he was unable to prevent fragments of memory from emerging.

It was Mrs Croucher's voice he heard first.

"You heard him," she is saying. "He wants you out and out you'll go. He'll humiliate you first. He wants you to go around the Tiltyard and pick up all the litter."

Julian heard the crunch of gravel underfoot, and he saw again the young man who had been threatening to re-emerge on the towpath from Kingston. Julian shook his head and tried to turn his thoughts away. He concentrated on the sugar wrappings, he stirred his tea, but his younger persona was coming on relentlessly.

The youthful Julian is an indistinct figure with a box in one hand and bending over to pick up the litter from the Tiltyard lawns. He is expecting Kathy to see him and give some kind of signal that she needs him. Before arriving at the cedar tree, the young Julian comes to an abrupt halt. The vague outlines of two people are disturbing the shadows of the cedar. The outlines shift and shuffle in a way that brings the word "furtive" to his mind. He is indignant. The people have no right to be there. They are trespassers who have arrived unannounced and uninvited into his dream.

One of the two people is leaning against the tree. A leg is bent backwards, and the sole of the foot is flat against the trunk. "Commanding" is the word to describe the way the arms play and the finger wags in front of his face. The young Julian does not at first recognise that the person is Dick Duncan-Smith and nor does Julian have the time to wonder what Dick is lecturing about. But he is surprised when the other shape steps out of the shadow and McKnight walks into the sunlight. He looks Julian straight in the eye. There is no more time for thoughts, no more time to wonder why the manager should allow himself to be lectured by Dick.

"Get to my office," McKnight says. "Wait for me there. I'm going to pay you off now."

And the light of memory was extinguished. Julian looked up. Susan was standing at his elbow and looking at him with a suggestion of worry on her face.

14

Do you need anything else, sir?"
Julian shook his head and glanced at his watch.
He had been daydreaming for several minutes. Those
events of long ago, so intense in the living of them, had
been distilled and compressed into minutes. Such a short
time seemed so unfair he felt betrayed by life itself.

Susan was bending forward and trying to catch his
eye.

"Is everything all right, sir?"

He smiled reassuringly.

"Yes, perfectly, thank you. Perhaps I could have the
bill?"

He fumbled for his wallet and took a long, last look at
the cedar tree. In 1968, it had been a point of reference
that indicated the restaurant, and a place from which
Kathy was sometimes visible. The tree dominated the
lawn and blocked the view towards the rose garden. A
stunted shadow lay beneath the cedar's branches, and
Julian responded to it with the odd notion that it could
almost have been the same shadow in which, thirty years
previously, he had seen John McKnight behaving so

strangely and out of character. The memory flashed back.

"Get to my office," John is saying. "Wait for me there. I'm going to pay you off now."

This had happened in 1968, but thirty years later, and over a cup of tea in the Tiltyard restaurant, the event resurfaced. Julian believed he had seen the shadow under the cedar tree, the beautifully tended Tiltyard lawns, the ivy-covered wall, and all of this against the deep-blue, summer sky. Suddenly, he was no longer certain. After thirty years, he could not say with conviction he had seen John McKnight allowing himself to be lectured by Dick. Julian believed it was John, and all he could do was work with the idea of the man and blend him in with the nebulous image his name generated. Susan's shadow spread over his table. Then, Susan herself placed a bill in front of him.

"Thank you," she said and she was gone again.

He hardly saw her. Memories came and went, and it slowly occurred to him that they were all, finally, memories of himself or of his feelings. If there was a problem with remembering, he reckoned, it was because he was unable or unwilling to recall himself. The young Julian was so very far away, and his actions had to be viewed and interpreted from across a great chasm. He had been so very young and foolish perhaps, but he had done nothing more than that which so many others had done before him. He had loved, lost and suffered, and nothing more - until 28 November 1968. Until that date, he could shrug his shoulders and say, "Well, it's all in the past, and I can do nothing to change it."

Susan came and removed the saucer on which he had placed a five-pound note. He heard her whispered thanks, and her footfalls were muffled on the carpet as she disappeared once more into oblivion. He turned his thoughts to memory again, but there was a voice at his elbow.

"Are you sure you don't need anything else, sir? Can I help in any other way?"

Susan had returned and was bending forward in a way that suggested she was a concerned mother tending to her charge.

Julian shook his head and said:

"By the way, where did you say John McKnight's office was?"

"London."

He hesitated before asking tentatively:

"Do you know where in London?"

"The Strand."

He stared in miserable astonishment at the tablecloth. If memories were of himself and his feelings, what next emerged was a thing that made him feel slightly sick. He was shaken by the reappearance of his own appalling behaviour from long ago. His mouth was dry, and his breathing rattled in his throat like the sound of a person struggling with death. He dared not look up in case he should find something evil standing at his shoulder. Eventually, he found a faint but rasping voice.

"Have the offices always been there?"

Julian sensed rather than saw the suspicion in Susan's face. A suggestion of mistrust descended on the two of them like a light shadow. He heard her say:

"Are you sure you're not from the health authority?"

"Absolutely. But I used to work here. Thirty years ago, actually. John McKnight was under manager then. I'd just like to look him up. We've a lot to talk about. I've got things to show him."

"What things?"

"Photos and a diary," he said, fingering his briefcase. "Things from our past, things I'm sure he'll be interested in. Actually, I haven't seen John since 28 November 1968."

"Oh, you've a good memory."

At last, he managed to look up at her and as he did so, he waved a deprecatory hand.

"Only for dates; and I remember this one because it was the day Enid Blyton died."

Susan nodded, but he doubted she cared about Enid Blyton. She passed the tip of her tongue over her top lip and said:

"Mr McKnight was your boss too, then?"

He raised his eyebrows and smiled his reply. She seemed relieved. They were now on the same wavelength.

"Did they do company history back in those days?" she asked.

"Company what?"

She shifted her eyes away from his, and told him about Knight and Day Catering. Her tone was flat and matter-of-fact. Julian had the impression she was reading from a page printed on the inside of her forehead.

"Thirty years ago was in the days of Park Merchant Catering," she said. Then, with twinkling eyes and a little laugh, she added, "Mr Day and Mr McKnight liked the company so much, they bought it."

"When was that?"

"In 1988," said Susan proudly. "I'm a trainee, you know."

"Have the head offices always been in the Strand?"

"Always," she said. "Knight and Day Catering, formerly Park Merchant Catering, of the Strand, London."

Susan took a step forward, and the cup and saucer slid away from under Julian's nose. Her lips were now set, and her head was turned from his in a way that suggested she thought she had said too much. He said:

"When I see John, I'll put in a good word for you."

"You're very kind," she said and she walked away in

the direction of the kitchen.

He left the restaurant and sauntered through the rose garden to the main gate. While he was walking over Hampton Court Bridge, he flicked his head sideways to glance behind him, to identify a presence that seemed to be hovering at his shoulder. Wondering if some unseen person had caught sight of him, might call out his name, he felt increasingly transparent, a moving shadow that would disappear in the autumn wind. His walking pace was considerably faster than usual when he approached the station, but no lengthening of stride would remove him from the attentive eyes of person or persons unknown. He spun round in the hope that he might catch the watching person unawares. He scanned the road along which he had walked but there was nobody in sight. Julian put himself in the ticket queue, turned his back on his paranoia, and focused on the events of 28 November.

He tried to bring the whole day back to life; but as he boarded the train, he realised he was trying to animate things that had a life of their own, that would reappear at a time and place of their own choosing.

These mental efforts were not helped by a jammed door, which connected one train carriage to another. He forced the door open with a shove of his shoulder and closed it with a hefty push of his foot. Several pairs of eyes looked up accusingly from behind their newspapers, and he slid his briefcase smartly onto the rack before sitting down in the manner of a person ducking bullets.

Julian was aware that he had dealt with the evening of 28 November 1968 in much the same way. He had left the country, ducked his head and buried his memories in Italy. These had been dredged up from the riverbed along with a body. Whether or not that body was Kathy's had yet to be proved. But the past had come back as though it had never really been away.

He stared through his reflected image in the windowpane and at the long wall which announced his arrival in Wimbledon. The ban-the-bomb signs sat comfortably with *Moseley out* and other bits and pieces of English graffiti from times past. The only vivid and enduring memory of that night in November 1968 remained etched upon his consciousness in the same way as the graffiti. He had seen Kathy with another man, and that man had struck her. Julian was now unsure as to how far the events of that night had been altered in his long-term memory, whether he was imagining or reformulating the man he believed he had seen. Time had gone by, and memories came in fragments with abrupt transitions that laid themselves open to the caprices of the mind.

As the train pulled out of Clapham Junction, Julian got to his feet, was reacquainted with his fellow passengers and their raised eyes following his every move. He was reaching out for the case, was wrapping his fingers round the handle when there was a crash. Julian recoiled, held his breath for a moment. Then a man appeared. Huge and blue, he stood aggressively at the connecting door. He seemed pleased with himself for having pushed the jammed door open. Julian slipped and threw up his arm in an attempt to get his balance. The briefcase flew from his hand and turned in the air. It span round and out of reach until it landed with a bump on the floor. The lid fell open. In his mind's eye he saw the diary and the photograph spilling out in front of his fellow passengers. The face of the blue man swam in front of his eyes. He heard the man's words, "I'll get that mate." Julian was quicker. He lunged forward and grabbed at the case. He was only half-listening to the man's curses. Julian held the case tightly to his chest with one arm while the other was tense, its fist clenched.

But the man in blue was swaying down the corridor, and Julian saw him disappearing through the connecting door to join the next carriage.

He got to his feet, allowed his gaze to travel downwards and rest at last on the floor. A fraction of a second passed before reality struck and the importance of what his eyes said reached him. There was nothing on the floor. His mind raced and groped for possibilities. The big man had grabbed the diary. Maybe Julian had left it in the Tiltyard restaurant. He opened the case wide and let his fingers pass lightly over its interior. Empty. For a moment he was breathless and tense. Then his mind fell quiet, and tension released itself from his body like air from a balloon. In an almost unearthly silence, he recalled that he had left the diary and the photo in the back of his car in Strudwick's yard.

He spent the rest of the short trip trying to convince himself that his experience with the big man had been a coincidence, his reaction to it but another symptom of an overactive imagination. The last Julian saw of him was a huge back powering towards the ticket barrier on the platform of Vauxhall Station. Nonetheless, Julian kept the empty case on his knees, and stroked it as though it were the head of a child.

15

When the train arrived at Waterloo, Julian snatched the case and sprang to his feet. He paused at the slam-door, surveyed the flows and currents of late-morning commuters and waited for the train to hiss and judder to a stop.

He fell in with a crowd pushing and jostling its way down to the Waterloo and City Line. With much irritation and tripping over feet, he extricated himself, and shot through the ticket barrier. The remains of fear stopped him, forced him to look for the man in blue. Sweeping the concourse with his eyes, he absorbed the changes that were transforming the station. Platform one, he noticed was still reserved for the Kingston train. Too late, he swung away from it. He was already staring at the heart of a memory - the idea of Kathy walking along the Strand.

Young Julian waits a moment and, setting off behind her along Waterloo Bridge, he enjoys the power he has. He can gaze at her, and she will never know. At a distance, he is dominant, and she is pure and unspoiled and she will remain like that eternally. How he wishes the bridge would go on forever and ever and ever.

When Kathy arrives at the station, she scans the departure board before hurrying off to the ticket barrier. Once she is safe in her compartment, Julian watches the train pull away from platform one. The words of the song drift through his head: *If you miss the train I'm on, then you'll know that I am gone, you will hear the whistle blow a hundred miles.* He whispers his own farewell as the train lurches round the bend and out of sight. Then, he puts himself at the spot on which she stopped to look at the departures. He senses her presence, a movement of the air in the space she has occupied. He is still feeling her there when the next train for Kingston departs. He doubts his sanity. He tells himself he has had some fun. He wants to stop before it is too late, before tomorrow comes. But tomorrow is always another day.

These shadows of feeling from '68 were blown away by a voice shouting loudly from the present, "Watch your bloody self, mate." Julian jumped sideways and narrowly avoided a cleaning machine that had apparently singled him out and seemed intent on running him down. The driver glowered at him, and Julian scowled in return, but he knew it was his fault.

He left this encounter, the memory and the bustle on the station concourse, and made his way into the subway. A gust of wind tugged at his trousers, and with the wind came the smell of urine, the sound of a guitar strumming, and a voice singing: *"And I can't help wondering where I'm going, where I'm going, I can't help wondering where I'm going."*

The subway walls were splashed with more graffiti, and there were piles of paper and burned wood at scorched intervals on the floor. He emerged in an open circle. The overhead roar and whoosh brought a strong reminder of Strudwick's yard. Although it was early afternoon, the circle was as gloomy as the car dismantler's place. Dampness stained and darkened the walls, and droplets of water poured down the pillars, slid into the oily slime that coiled through the centre of this concrete world. Underfoot it was slippery, and the smell of excrement was overpowering.

He stood for a while wondering which route would take him to the bridge. Slowly he became aware of eyes that stared at him from the edges of this twilight world. The eyes neither pleaded nor argued. They were lifeless and looked out blankly from black, puffy and bearded faces. They could have been the faces of the sleeping but moving closer he saw eyelids blinking, and he guessed the people were in a state of trance or intoxication. He looked back at them with a swift increase of interest, and not because he was afraid or because they threatened him. He was appalled by their dumb immobility. They could have been born from the concrete itself; and like concrete, they lay inert, heavy and so silent that Julian suspected he might have lost his sense of hearing.

There was a cough at his elbow. A head of plaited hair appeared beside him. A woman's face turned to look into his. There were clots of blood on her scalp and forehead, and there were several bruises on her cheeks.

"Got any spare change, matey?" she asked.

Julian shrank from the stinking breath, the rotting teeth, the emaciated neck and face. Then, he got an idea. He plunged his hand into his pocket, drew out a five-pound note, and held it by his ear.

"I need a..."

His words faltered in a wave of awkwardness while he probed for the appropriate way to address a person who no longer belonged, the tone to use with a person who had no status. Eventually, and in a more authoritarian tone than he would have liked, he said:

"I need a favour from you."

The woman frowned into his eyes.

"Favour?"

"I'm looking for an old friend. His name's Paul, he..."

"You think he's here, matey?"

"His mother told me he lives here - on the station - said he sleeps rough."

"Rough? Do you mind? There but for the grace of God, right? So, what's your friend's name?"

"Paul."

"And you are?"

Julian was off-balance, leaning backwards and holding his head away as if the woman was a freak. He glanced over her shoulder at that grim wall of silence from which she had emerged. He wondered at that wall and at the depths of passion and misery it concealed. He said:

"An old friend - Julian - from nearly thirty years ago."

She held out her hand, and he placed the note in her palm.

"See what I can do," she said.

Julian nodded, watched her disappearing towards the concrete world and he mused on the human calamities that had caused so many lives to end up in such a state. He knew that some people did just disappear. One day they were with their friends and family, and the next, their whereabouts were unknown. Perhaps it was in a sort of purgatory like this where they finished up. Nameless and homeless, they ended their days in squalor. He grimaced, and his facial distortions remained moulded on his face while he reminded himself. For thirty years he had hoped the police would believe this is what had become of Kathy.

He allowed the grimace to remain a few moments longer while looking towards the bearded faces that surrounded him. Nothing had disturbed their dumb immobility. He shrugged and told himself he had lost his five pounds.

He was setting off towards the bridge, losing himself in daydreams when a man's voice called out his name, made him turn and gaze expectantly into the circle.

The voice was followed by the memory of a lock of hair. Then came a broken head, the scratched knees and the hint of a person Julian had known. It was Paul. He was shuffling aimlessly as if he had no place to go. He stumped towards Julian and wagged his head, and his face was wrinkled like a walnut.

"Got some change," he said, "for an old friend?"

Julian was assailed by a rapid succession of emotions: guilt, embarrassment, sadness and anger. He wanted to ask Paul how he was, but such a question seemed inappropriate, and he did not know how to say it. If the words remained stuck in his throat, the thoughts and feelings that produced them exploded inside him like violent, shooting pains.

"Got any change?" Paul repeated. "For old time's sake."

With tears in his eyes, Julian reflected that it was twenty-seven years since he and his old friend had seen each other, but their two worlds had become separated by more than time. As children, they had walked the same road for a while and then, when the road had forked, they had gone different ways. As the years rolled by, he knew they had lost the intimacy that can only come from shared experiences.

"Ten pence for a cuppa," Paul said.

Julian's face became tense and cold while he watched this intimacy dissolve before his eyes. His fists clenched tightly when he saw that the images he had harboured for so long were now unsustainable. He wanted to lunge at the man in front of him and throttle him for daring to snatch his memories, poison them and then give them back as though nothing had happened. All those special times together and they had come to fruition in ten pence for a cup of tea.

Paul said:

"Been a long time, old friend."

He spoke slowly, with difficulty, choosing each word as though with a toothpick.

Julian stood still, unable to think of anything meaningful to say. Eventually, he muttered:

"I went home."

"Home?" Paul said. "Whose home?"

"Home. Thames Ditton."

"Mum's house?"

Julian nodded.

"I asked about you. I wanted to know you how you've been."

"No questions," Paul said, "and no lies..."

His eyelids flickered and drooped. Julian became afraid that Paul would pass out or fall asleep on his feet. He made to support him but Paul flinched and cried out:

"Don't touch me."

A number of heads turned towards them, and a distant voice shouted, "You all right, lovey?"

Glancing over his shoulder, Paul mumbled something, recovered his balance and turned glazed eyes back to Julian. Suddenly lucid, Paul said:

"Why have you come back? What can we do together now you've found me?"

The two men stood for a second or two, staring at each other with the tension of memories standing between them. Paul broke the spell. He said:

"Our time's gone, my old friend."

A smile passed over his face and then he asked point-blank:

"What's your business in London?"

"I've come to see John McKnight," Julian said attempting a smile, "remember him?"

He was amazed that this remark, thrown carelessly to connect him with his broken friend, had apparently touched some crazy imaginings in his head. Paul stared stupidly for a moment, then he took a step backwards as though Julian had slapped his face. He cried out:

"So, he sent you."

He lifted his arm, held it out in front of his chest as though to ward off an approaching danger.

"No, no, I haven't seen him," Julian began, "I..."

Staring at the ground as if some horror was passing by his feet, Paul stammered out:

"Only the messenger boy McKnight is. What do they want with me now?"

Julian shook his head and wiped at his eyes before letting his words go one by one.

"I just want to see him again," he said. "I..."

"What do they want now? My soul?"

Paul was breathing hard and beads of perspiration rolled down his temples. He stumbled and leaned his body so close that Julian had a magnified picture of every line on Paul's damaged face.

"You can't have it, see? It's all I have."

Paul threw himself back violently, but Julian kept outwardly calm. Against his wish, he wanted to throttle him again, to punish him for the confused rambling of a drink-soaked brain. He decided to have one last try.

"Do you think John McKnight could be involved in Kathy's disappearance?"

Paul rubbed at his head.

"Didn't you know?"

"Know what?" Julian muttered between his teeth.

Paul lowered his head and vigorously scratched his neck.

"No, you didn't, did you? And they never found the

body, did they?"

Julian bit his bottom lip but he could not prevent himself from exploding in a savage whisper.

"What was going on between John McKnight and Kathy?"

This question apparently caused Paul some inner turmoil. Julian thought he saw it in the way Paul looked wildly around him. He thought he saw it in the way Paul clasped his hands together and shook his head as if he would throw out some haunting vision. It seemed suddenly too hot and airless in this concrete world. Perspiration trickled down Julian's back.

"Do you think, then," he asked, "that McKnight was capable of killing anyone?"

He watched Paul apparently consider the question. And as he watched, his mood was cooled by the sight of this drunken bum. He thought how odd it was that, once upon a time, he believed he had known this person and known him intimately. He asked himself if he had ever really understood Paul. They had shared their younger years. They had made each other feel alive so that they were wanted and liked. But all the time there had been a monster lurking within. The monster was the tragedy of Paul's life, and Julian had never noticed it.

There was a low mumble from the mouths of those lifeless creatures that haunted the fringes of the subway and, eventually, from this mumble, came Paul's enigmatic reply:

"They never found the body. They never knew what she told the police. Do you think the police know? Do they know? Do they know?"

"Can you think of any reason why John should want Kathy out of the way?"

Paul had lowered his eyes and was examining the floor. Julian knew that now they were both absolutely disconnected. With a sinking heart he repeated:

"Can you think of any reason why he should kill her?"

"Kill who?"

"Kathy."

"Who's Kathy?"

"She was the one who disappeared," Julian said. "It was a long time ago."

Paul looked up. There was the barest suggestion of sadness on his face. Then, he staggered away. A group of youths nodded and winked, and pointed at the pathetic sight. Paul swayed away into obscurity, and as he walked, he swung his head from left to right, and there was his voice, waning as he went:

"Do the police know? Do they know? Oh God He knows and God He knows; only God almighty knows. Do the police know? Do they know? Oh God He knows and God He knows; surely God almighty knows..."

16

Julian watched Paul's back with concentrated eyes. Slowly, while his feelings settled, his face developed an expression of indifference. What he found when he connected with himself was the calm of one who knows he has survived in life while others have not. He knew he had never had it easy but he smiled his lop-sided smile when he felt obliged to acknowledge a self-evident truth. In all adversity, he had refused to be the victim. The remaining link between him and Paul was a common past and the same basic chances in life. But Paul, he thought, had allowed his dreams to end in a damned and Godforsaken subway, and he had not. It was as simple as that.

He strode up the ramp that led to Waterloo Bridge and leaned over the parapet. Letting his thoughts drift with the water flowing beneath him, he reflected that it was the ability to take action, to shape his own world, which marked him out as a survivor. It was Paul's propensity to think rather than act that left him a wreck of human existence, drowning in alcohol and living out his days in the subway. The poor bastard was of no use now, Julian thought, and he closed his eyes, inhaled through his nose, and exhaled slowly from his mouth. He needed to savour the air's freshness, to feel it cleanse his body of memories and negative influence.

A cold draught, mingling with the stench of excrement and urine, swept up from the subway. Other travellers were coming up the ramp towards the bridge, and Julian heard the toneless string of words echoing from below, "Spare some change, mate?"

He caught the eye of a stranger, and they exchanged a knowing look, a look that suggested kinship, that brought them together for a brief moment to share a common feeling of disgust.

Julian pushed himself from the parapet and turned to examine what was ahead. An intimacy of shapes and colours leaped at him from along the north bank of the Thames. This familiarity initially puzzled him, but he soon realised that these shapes and colours had always been a part of his life, would always re-create this feeling of warm relationship. He sensed rather than understood that whenever he returned to look upon them, these shapes would appear recognisable but different. They would be different because his eyes interpreted them in altered ways. He had moved on and developed and, unlike his erstwhile friend, he had not allowed himself to stagnate or his soul to vanish in concrete.

Big Ben was striking the quarter when he set off across the bridge. His decision to face McKnight, he thought, was another example of his ability to be proactive, to refuse to sit down and take what others chose to give him. Halfway over the river, he got the impression that the evening was closing in. The rain, which had been falling lightly, intensified and came at him from all angles. By the time he arrived in the Strand, droplets were rolling off his hair and down his cheeks and neck. He decided to make for the phone box he saw in the Aldwych. While waiting at the traffic lights, he cursed the ever-increasing number of cars that sped past. He threw silent obscenities at the blurred and shadowy shapes behind the windscreens and then swore out loud, anything to smother the inner voice that whispered to him, told him if he had time to think his determination to see things through might falter.

When he called directory enquiries, he was still in control of himself but he was uncomfortably aware that the inner voice had grown louder and was diluting his confidence with words and suggestions which promised a way out, excuses for him so that he could walk away, his self-esteem intact.

It was a recorded message which eventually rattled off the telephone number he required. Each number was accompanied by a shot of nervousness that struck at his bowels and made his body tremor. Accurate dialling was rendered impossible, and he poked at the dialler as though it was something dirty or contaminated. With growing impatience and irritation that only he was to blame for the position in which he found himself, he slammed the phone down.

A chill gust of wind wandered through the phone box, and the nervousness in Julian's bowels developed into a feeling of nausea, as though he had eaten something mildly poisonous. He let his eyes take in the jumble of walls and roofs from the world outside. The glass of the phone box distorted everything, and with the distortions came the faint roar of the city, nearby voices, and the sound of police sirens. The sirens were harsh and penetrating and they brought with them a feeling of undeserved personal abasement. He thumped the palm of his hand against the side of the box and swore loudly. Brushing his forehead with his fingertips he whispered between his teeth, "If you don't want to finish up like that fool in the subway, just get a grip." He stood hunched and still for some seconds before dialling again. Someone picked up the phone on the second ring.

"Yes," Julian said. "I'd like to speak to John McKnight, please."

His outburst had left him flushed, irritated, unprepared for a confrontation, but his mental hold on himself was returning. At the other end of the line, the flat and disinterested tone of the girl's voice was somehow reassuring. Julian spoke his own words slowly and enunciated every syllable.

"No, not a company," he said into the mouthpiece. "It's a private matter, actually."

The inside of the box was cheerless, damp, and smelled of fish. Every available space had been filled with dubious visiting cards. He scanned their contents while he listened to the girl's voice.

"What about?" Julian said. "Yes, would you tell him it's about 28 November, 1968? Yes, I'll wait."

There was a click. The sound of Greensleeves crackled over the line. The pastoral music was at odds with the cards and their promise of sexual fulfilment with "Sexy schoolgirls" or "Madam Whiplash." He had no sooner begun to read the cards than he was confronted by a flash of panic and the emergence of a question he had filed away. How was he going to deal with the break-in at the pub? It could not have been anyone but McKnight or one of his men. How would McKnight deal with it? Before he could even think about any answers, there was a click in the ear-piece.

"Eh? Hello?" Julian said.

There was another click, a voice crackled to life and jumped at him.

"John McKnight."

The tone was so familiar that thirty years melted away in a second, but the quality of the voice was lightly touched by something that confused Julian and deflected him from his purpose. He had intended to say something dramatic, something like, "So we speak again at last. I've been looking forward to it." What he actually said, and almost apologetically, was:

"It's Julian. From the Tiltyard cafeteria in 1968. I'm in London and I want to see you."

There was a pause and a shuffle of papers at the other end of the line. He stared at the receiver. His surroundings had now disintegrated, and his eyes focused on the black hole of the mouthpiece and the telephone wire, coiled like a snake and disappearing into nothingness. And from this nothingness came a vision of his tormentor. McKnight was sitting at his desk, with shelved box-files behind his head. He was in his dark suit, settled comfortably in a swivel chair, and annotating papers from a stack on the desktop. The pause developed into uncomfortable silence. Julian stared into the black hole of the receiver. Rather angrily, he said:

"Hello? Are you there?"

There was another shuffling of papers, but the continuing silence did not have a smile in it, a bubbly feeling that suggested welcome or pleasure. This silence had a different quality, one of closing up, a preparation for confrontation or something unpleasant, and it threatened to crush his newly found confidence. He was lost in this no-man's-land for some time until McKnight said:

"Who did you say you were?"

Julian suppressed an exclamation of indignation that this man, who had exerted such a bad influence on his life, could have forgotten his existence. A second or two elapsed before his composure was tilted still further by the realisation that this was how McKnight was going to deal with the break-in - denial. And he prepared himself to play McKnight's game of hide-and-seek, of catch-me-if-you-can, but he knew that by doing so he was playing by his adversary's rules, and playing by his rules meant losing control. He said:

"Julian Everet. 1968. I'm in the Aldwych and I'd like to see you."

There was no immediate reply. He simply heard McKnight's breathing coming at him through the black hole. The sound came and went in short bursts and eluded interpretation. The papers shuffled again. Julian tried to build a clear picture of his adversary and his character; but the man had been out of sight for so long that he was unable to imagine anything more than a vague outline of McKnight's face. Julian was the blind man, trying to replace the lost visionary world with one of sound. But he was still struggling with the man's voice, unable to identify what had changed. In a flash, he saw the obvious. The voice had aged along with the man, and Julian was speaking to a stranger.

"Are you the one who worked in the kiosk, by God? The one I kicked out?"

The word "kiosk" set off a riot of feelings that rattled through Julian like an ague. He said quickly:

"A long time ago."

He had been hoping to infuse his tone with the impression that such a long time had somehow released him from his crimes, but McKnight was unimpressed.

"What do you want now, boy? Your job back?"

The use of the word, "boy" obliterated the passing of time and nearly finished Julian altogether. For a moment, he was unable to speak, but he imagined the supercilious grin playing lightly around the man's mouth. He saw again the watery, blue eyes and the monstrous and fleshy lips. Into this silent daydream, McKnight said:

"It's been a long time, hasn't it? 1968, you say?"

"That's right," Julian said with a snappy edge to his voice, "thirty years, actually."

"Thirty years? Well, well. Time does fly, by God."

"It does, doesn't it?"

"So," McKnight said. "When did we last meet? Can you tell me?"

Julian took a deep and slow breath, and allowed a rush of mixed emotions to pass through him. He focused his eyes on a sexy schoolgirl, forced his cheeks to take on the appearance of a smile and said:

"28 November 1968."

At the sound of these words, Julian's heart at first leaped and then balanced precariously on a knife edge while it waited for McKnight's reply. He said:

"You have a good memory."

Julian's heart thumped into life, was beating hard at his ribs, rising to his throat. Then, he was aware of a nearby presence, a dark cloud falling over the phone box. Simultaneously, he heard the rattling of the phone box door, glimpsed a shadow outside, and from the shadow came a face, hurtling towards him from the real world. The face was pressed hard, flat and distorted against the glass. It seemed that the eyes were rolling, and the teeth discoloured and broken so that this intruder looked like the devil himself. For one crazy moment Julian thought it was the blighted man from Strudwick's yard. The car dismantler had followed and found him, and was now about to open the door and place the 1968 diary in his hands. He blinked and the face was gone, its owner disappearing with a drunken lurch into the crowds. McKnight's voice came back, coiling its way like a snake into his ear.

"I'm afraid you'll have to refresh my memory. 28 November means nothing to me. Unfortunately, I don't have the time to rake over the past. I'm a busy man and I've things to attend to..."

"Kathy," Julian said, "you remember her, don't you? And if you don't, I have some things that may jog your memory, things that might interest you."

His heart was pumping. Once, John McKnight would not have tolerated this tone of disrespect. Julian imagined the man swivelling gently in his chair. There was more shuffling of papers at the other end of the line, and almost in a whisper McKnight said:

"What things?"

Julian stiffened. Something like a vibration had come with McKnight's voice. If the vibration held suggestions of tension and fear, it also held a hint of danger and it was ringing in Julian's ears like an alarm bell. He said:

"A photograph and my diaries."

"What photograph, Julian? What diaries?"

The voice had lost all pretence of friendliness. This was how Julian remembered him - hard and ruthless, and capable of anything. McKnight's tone did not make him less afraid, but he was comfortable with the familiar.

"A photograph of you and Kathy," Julian said. "And my diaries for November 1968."

There was a long silence. Looking up, Julian saw that although it was still early afternoon, the evening seemed to be settling over London. Colours were diluting quickly, and the sky had dropped low over the streets. Yellow lamps punctuated the outside world. Their light, shimmering pools on the wet pavement, swallowed up the crowd of early commuters as if it was a mirage.

"Why should I be interested in those things?" McKnight asked.

Julian breathed out slowly, giving himself the time to free his voice from any feelings. He was surprised when he heard scorn, tightly wrapped around his words:

"Aren't you interested? I'd better tell you then that someone else is. Actually, they broke into my hotel room to look for them and..."

He was interrupted by what he took to be a harsh intake of breath followed by a few words muttered so low that he was unable to catch them. After a long and uncomfortable silence, McKnight said:

"And you have these things with you? You have them here - in London, now?"

Julian took a deep breath. Lying had become so easy.

"Yes," he said.

"So," said John McKnight, "you can refresh my memory. But we'd better meet face to face. I'll give you ten minutes, but only ten minutes. Do you know Nick's cafe?"

"On the corner here?" Julian said. "The corner of Southampton Row and the Aldwych?"

"Meet you there in twenty minutes, boy," McKnight said.

Julian hung up, and the world, the distorted roofs and walls, the sound of traffic and police sirens came rushing back. He pushed at the door, stepped out into the street, and set off for Nick's cafe. He had twenty minutes in which to gather his wits, to rebuild the confidence he had found such a short time ago on the other side of Waterloo Bridge. The problem was that the other side of the bridge lay a long way off and almost in another time and place.

17

Nick's cafe had been a favourite meeting place for students and drop-outs when Julian had been at the university. In those days, the cafe had always been cheap and a place of great choice: beef, pork chop, veal and chicken, and a variety of curries. Julian remembered that whatever you ordered, you seemed to get veal. But it did not matter because it was always so good, and because it was served with a flourish by a man whose dark eyes seemed to burn with the revolutionary ardour that matched that of his young customers. Such was student politics in the late 60s, that Julian and his friends had little doubt that Nick was a refugee from some Latin American dictatorship, someone who had rubbed shoulders with Che Guevara. As far as Julian knew, nobody had ever produced evidence to confirm this.

Nick had, therefore, been part of the natural order of Julian's student days, a character actor who had unwittingly played an inspirational part on the stage of Julian's university life. Now completely white, slightly crooked in the back, and much shorter than Julian recalled, the man who had known Che Guevara was still flitting like a butterfly from table to table. For Nick, it was clear that Julian had been just one other forgettable petal in the audience. Julian could accept that, but when he saw the menu card, emblazoned with the logo of Knight and Day Catering Services, he failed to suppress an unreasonable sense of betrayal. Nick, whose dark eyes had fuelled such political passions, had obviously sold out to the capitalists.

The students had yet to return, so Julian had a choice of tables at which to sit. Deciding he wanted to see John McKnight coming, to take his measure before any confrontation, Julian chose a seat with an easy view of the street. Sliding the chair from under the table, he nodded a greeting at two men in blue reefer jackets, who were sitting nearby. They held hand-rolled cigarettes between their fingers, and mugs of tea hovered under their lips. They acknowledged Julian's presence and his greeting with almost imperceptible nods of their own.

Julian twisted his body towards Nick. His arm was hanging in the air, his fingers about to beckon when he was struck by a sensation rolling and fluttering inside him. The sensation was not new to him. It was one he had experienced going to the dentist, or waiting for the whistle to begin the one-hundred-yard sprint at school. He told himself that the sensation would pass, that something oppressive had not really entered the room at all. Perhaps he had simply noticed the flicker of a neighbour's eye, or his mind had registered the squeak of shoe leather on linoleum.

John McKnight was, at first, a blur in the corner of Julian's eye. Then, he was a heavy trench coat, stuffed with the idea of a man Julian had half-forgotten. McKnight's eyes briefly met his and then flicked away. Julian did not venture a smile of greeting, and McKnight kept his hands firmly in the pockets of his coat. Memories of confrontation rushed in to fill the space between the two men.

While these memories jostled for position, Julian found himself coming to terms with somebody new, another person emerging from the image he had harboured for over thirty years. It seemed to him that McKnight's lips had thinned and set in an expression of permanent hardness. What hair he still had was greased tightly down above the ears and it had taken on a yellowish film as if it were stained with cigar smoke. Julian reflected that this was a man who had risen from nothing, a man who had come from the streets of Belfast to London to create a life for himself, a life that was, perhaps, about to reach a pinnacle in its run for MP. That creation might be fragile, but McKnight was not going to give it all up by allowing Julian to destroy or change the mould of the person he had chosen to emulate. It was McKnight who eventually broke the silence.

"How nice to see you again."

He spoke with deliberation, careful, Julian noticed, not to let a consonant or a vowel pass his lips that might give away his Belfast origins.

"So very nice," McKnight continued, "to be able to do business with you again."

His hands showed no sign of movement. Julian's memory of McKnight had extracted itself from the coat and now hovered like a ghost to one side of the man so that Julian thought himself to be suffering from double vision. He realised that he and McKnight were both staring, both searching for the person they had once known until they became familiar with the new, comfortable with the image they were with.

"You'll excuse me, I'm sure," McKnight said. "I'm a busy man. You have ten minutes."

He pulled one hand from his coat pocket and, muttering to himself, he pressed his hand into the small of his back and pushed, as though he wanted to straighten his spine. He then slipped out of the coat and handed it with a smile and a flourish to Nick, who was waiting at his elbow. Julian had to admit that this expression of personal charm, power and authority was impressive, but he felt sorry that the man who had rubbed shoulders with Che Guevara should be reduced to such a cringing lackey. Still smiling, McKnight turned to face Julian and said:

"So, what exactly can I do for you, boy?"

He examined his chair, and brushed at it with irritable strokes of the wrist before taking a seat. He folded his hands in front of him as though he were about to chair a meeting. Julian noticed the initials JM on the chest pocket of McKnight's shirt. McKnight turned his wrist, glanced at his watch, and then looked briefly around the room as though to ensure he could not be overheard. The smile slipped from his face.

"And what's all this about 1968? And this photograph? Do you have it here?"

Julian was still troubled by double vision and rubbed at his eyes, but he saw no ripple of agitation on the calm surface of the man in front of him. McKnight's pale and high forehead betrayed no sheen of tension, and the shadow of the man's smile was still playing around his lips when he said:

"What's up, boy? Cat got your tongue?"

Watching the expression on McKnight's face pass from easy familiarity to rigid hostility, Julian reflected that John McKnight's ghost had had blue eyes. The eyes of the man in front of him had become darkly threatening. Julian's gaze shifted towards John's nose, thick and fleshy around the nostrils, cartilaginous above. Then, with calm deliberation, Julian spoke about his life in Italy, his return to the UK, and about Kathleen, reborn on the cliffs of Dover. He was looking forward to the punch line, to seeing McKnight's reaction, to shaking him from his disinterest. But if Julian could feel sweat sliding down his rib cage, John McKnight seemed to be as calm as the air. He raised his hand and said:

"Please get to the point. You mentioned 1968, so what exactly..."

He interrupted himself by rocking forward and resting a fist on the edge of the table. His head was low and his eyes were now cold and staring above the rims of his glasses.

"So, what about it?"

In that drowsy and almost empty room the only sounds were the faint rustle of a newspaper, the clink of cup on saucer, and the scraping of matches being struck. But Julian became distinctly aware of a faint tremor, a sort of vibration that came through McKnight's fist and seemed to shake the top of the table. Julian remained a long time without speaking. He was living over again those thirty years of uncertainty. Was this man, a man who was apparently going to run for MP, the person he had seen that night in 1968?

"You know," Julian said, "the police are interviewing JD, but they are interviewing the wrong person."

John McKnight looked back at Julian over the rims of his spectacles. Julian was not really sure whether he was listening to him, or whether he was simply following the mysterious thread of his own private agenda.

"Why do you say that, boy?"

Julian had been looking forward to this moment, the moment when he would confront McKnight with his misdeeds. He had seen it all in his daydreams. But now the time had come, he felt slightly disappointed. The words rose to his throat but he was loathe to let them go, wanted to savour every syllable before articulating them for the one and only time.

"Because," he said, "I saw you with Kathy on the night she disappeared."

John McKnight continued to stare with a calm and cool expression. Julian was trying to find there some trace of fear, some sense of recognition that might reinforce his own memory. What he saw was a flicker of irritation which barely disturbed John McKnight's passive features. McKnight half-turned and beckoned to Nick. While ordering coffee, McKnight lightly placed a hand on Nick's forearm and spoke quietly, his eyes glinting with a friendly familiarity. Then, he turned his face back to Julian's.

"Sorry," he said, "what was that you were saying?"

Julian thought it might be better to leave right then. His rib cage was now cold, and when he backed away from McKnight, he felt the skin under his armpits unpeeling like a plaster.

"I saw you with Kathy," he repeated.

He had attempted to invest these words with power and feeling, but it was futile. The words were just not made to be repeated twice. He watched McKnight's lips open, and the voice that came from between them was steeled, polite, as if he were talking to a complete stranger.

"You saw me, boy?" he said. "Where did you see me?"

"In her flat," Julian said very low.

John McKnight nodded several times but the movement was not one of agreement. He seemed to be saying, *so this is the sort of nonsense I have to tolerate, is it?*

"This is very interesting and very observant," he said. A smile spread across his face. "And what makes you think it was me? It may've been any one of several men, by God. Our Kathleen wasn't a one-man girl, as you know."

The ghost of the eighteen-year-old Julian flinched at this remark, and he opened his mouth to protest, but

John McKnight interrupted Julian's thoughts before he managed to utter a word.

"So, you think you saw me or someone like me," McKnight said slowly. "Then you admit being outside her flat. Tell me, what were you doing there? What were you doing there skulking in the shadows? Umm? Are you going to tell me? What, exactly, were you doing there?"

He seemed to have expanded, and he filled his chair like a Buddha. He glowered at Julian from behind his spectacles but remained absolutely still, and confronted by this stillness, Julian was powerless, enchained by impotence. McKnight said:

"Kathleen knew she was being followed. She even thought it was one of my men. Really, by God. As if I would ever have done such a thing. So - now we know."

He spoke slowly and thoughtfully and while he spoke, he seemed to get larger and larger, like a genie escaping from a lamp until he appeared to tower over the tables and chairs in the room, an almost mythical figure about to devour his prey. Julian knew that now this monster had escaped, it was going to be difficult to put it back. McKnight's enormous face suddenly darkened, and he pointed a thick finger at Julian's chest.

"I suppose it was you," he said, isolating each word. "It was you, wasn't it? You are the young pervert the police wanted - and still want - to talk to. Perhaps you are the one who made the phone calls. It was you, Julian, wasn't it? Eh?"

He shot forward again, and leaned over his hands, his eyes staring. He must have seen Julian hesitate because he leaned even further forward until his nose was almost tip to tip with Julian's.

"So, what did you do, boy?" he whispered. "Did you wait and watch her through the window? Did you wait and watch her undress? Did it give you a thrill? Pathetic.

Fucking pathetic. I suppose that was the nearest you ever got to her, wasn't it? Would you like to talk about it? Is this why you wanted to see me? To live again your finest hour?"

Through the glass frontage of the cafe, Julian saw the rain driving down in the beams of the car headlamps. Every now and then, a blast of wind carried water in ripples across the roads and pavements. Varying shades of people passed by the window, their heads bowed, the tails of their raincoats flapping in the wind. A faint sound of whooshing and splashing crept through the door. It was the reminder of something alive and vibrant from the world outside, and for some moments, Julian wanted to run out of the cafe and grab hold of it, stop himself from sinking. McKnight had pushed himself back in his chair and raised his voice to expose Julian's vulnerability.

"Well," he said, looking around the cafeteria, "did you go home and masturbate? Perhaps you masturbated there on the pavement. Tell us Julian, tell us do, but please spare us the gruesome details, boy."

He chuckled to himself, but Julian was strangely calm. The moment of humiliation came and went in an instant. Nothing changed. The two men in blue reefer jackets continued to sip at their tea, the rain continued to fall, and the world continued as normal, although something nasty had been unleashed. Much to his surprise, he found he was neither ashamed nor angry. More importantly, he had noticed something in the tone of McKnight's voice, something in his calm and commanding veneer that seemed false, as though there was another man, a frightened man, hiding beneath the skin. Nick arrived and placed two coffees on their table.

"Please put it on the bill, Nick," McKnight said with a pleasant smile.

Nick moved away without making a sound.

Following the man's back with his eyes, Julian watched him dance through the tables and glide away into the kitchen. A clock struck, the deep-toned vibrations filling the cafe. McKnight waited, his lips drawn tightly back over his teeth while Julian counted the strokes. On the stroke of three, McKnight said:

"She jilted you, didn't she, boy? Kathleen jilted you, and it was too much for you to take, is that it?"

A faint smile of satisfaction spread across his face, and then he said, almost to himself:

"You didn't like it, did you, boy? So, you stalked her, caused her such distress, such unhappiness, and then you felt guilty. Have you been brooding about it for thirty years? Is that it? And now you want redemption, right?"

Both men picked up their tea spoons and stirred their coffee simultaneously. John McKnight, with bowed head, was chuckling again.

"Fucking good job I got rid of you when I did before you could do any more harm..."

Suddenly, he dropped his tea spoon. It made a loud clatter as it hit the saucer and seemed to announce a revelation, which he decided to tell the world.

"It was you, boy, wasn't it? You couldn't face life without her, so you finished her off. You took away the body, threw it in the river... That's how it was, wasn't it? Well, fuck me..."

McKnight sucked in a breath and sat back in his chair looking at Julian with an expression of wonder. Nick reappeared from the kitchen and busied himself behind the counter. Julian wondered why Nick was tidying and rearranging the cups. Surely, he had found enough time to tidy them over the preceding thirty years.

"Who said she was dead?" Julian said. "The police still haven't identified the body they pulled from the river."

John McKnight shook his head and waved an

impatient hand.

"That won't do, Julian. There are techniques for finding out these days. You should know. You're the one with all the education. Judging by the look of you, it didn't do you much good."

The vibration that filled the top of the table was now stronger. It travelled down Julian's arm and into his legs. Both were shaking uncontrollably. McKnight lifted his cup to his lips and sipped from its contents before replacing it with a clatter on the saucer.

"Ever heard of DNA, Julian, or are you living in the past too? And dental records, if there are any, will tell forensics what they need to know."

"And if they prove it is her body?"

John McKnight shrugged.

"You tell me, boy. You seem to know it all, don't you?"

He suddenly lifted his hand and pointed at Julian's forehead.

"So, just for the sake of argument, let's suppose it is her body. What'll this sack of old bones tell them? And what'll you do? Go and tell them it was me who did for her?"

Julian looked up quickly. Trying to master the shakiness of his voice, he said:

"The bones might tell them that she was beaten about the head."

McKnight blinked, and his lips moved for some time, but he seemed to have lost his power of speech. Eventually, Julian followed up with:

"You did hit her across the head, didn't you?"

McKnight leaned back and stared. His composure had suddenly disappeared. He looked tired and jaded.

"You'd better leave the past alone," he said in a whisper. "You don't know who you're dealing with. Some things are better left as they are." He added in a detached but strangely conciliatory tone, "It would be better for both of us, boy."

He stared at Julian again, but Julian had nothing to say, had no idea what McKnight was referring to. There were just a few confused fragments of conversations wandering in his memory and pulling him back to 1968.

"I'm in trouble," Mrs C is saying. "I've been bound over again."

It is one week before the end of the season and Julian is in the bottle store with Paul. Both are listening to Mrs Croucher talking to the colonel. They are standing in the tourist thoroughfare outside the store. Through the gaps in the fencing, Mrs Croucher's silhouette is unmistakable. She is talking in a way that Julian has never before associated with the manageress.

"I'm to appear next month."

Her tone is secretive, confessional and frightened.

"I thought you'd been cured," the colonel says. "What was it this time?"

Mrs Croucher's voice is so low that Julian can hardly hear her reply.

"A pullover," she says. She wraps her arms around herself and seems to be shivering. "I won't do it again, promise."

"You said that last time. You don't need a pullover," the colonel says. "You need a shrink."

Julian can smell the colonel's sleeked back hair. He can smell Mrs Croucher's fear. It is in the air with the colonel's cigar smoke. Mrs Croucher says:

"I can't get involved in McKnight's little game. It'll be the end of me. I know what's going on. I can't turn a blind eye, but I can't get involved in his terrible plan..."

The memory is extinguished, obliterated by the sound of a wailing siren from somewhere in the streets of London. It gave Julian some comfort that someone, somewhere, needed help as much as he did. John

178

McKnight leaned towards Julian again and calmly clasped his hands together.

"At the end of the day," he said, "it's your word against mine. Do you have evidence?"

"Yes," Julian said. "I do have evidence. I kept diaries, you know. And there's the photo."

Holding his breath, Julian watched his adversary. Almost in a whisper, McKnight hissed out:

"Still your word against mine. And what'll the fucking diaries prove? Who'll believe them?"

Julian managed a nonchalant shrug. Then, he dropped the spoon into his coffee and slowly stirred. He tried to look as though he was considering the question.

"Well," he said, "someone believes them. Someone broke into my room to look for them. Someone has been following me..."

John McKnight's gaze rested on him.

"You're being followed?"

The gaze was almost expressionless but, in its persistence, there was now something which resembled fright. He said:

"Someone broke into your room? And you thought it was me, boy? You thought it was me? Let me tell you, by God, that until you phoned me, I'd forgotten your very existence. So, you've spoken to others about your evidence, haven't you, boy? So now the cat's well and truly out of the bag. By God what've you done...?"

If McKnight had started in an aggressive and provocative tone, he finished in a whisper as if the power of speech had left him and when he passed his hand over his forehead, it seemed to Julian to be a gesture of suffering or of despair.

"By God," he repeated to himself, "what have you done?"

Both men sat looking at each other without words for a considerable time. The conflicts and concerns from the past were now confused and complicated by things present. Julian no longer had double vision. John McKnight had come through a rapid transformation and the man who sat in front of him was in late middle age, with a bad back and, Julian wanted to believe, afraid. It never occurred to him to wonder what a frightened man might do.

"Look, boy," McKnight said, "it's been a pleasure talking with you. Your ten minutes are up, and I'm a busy man."

He lifted his hand and wagged his finger.

"I'll do you a favour. I did you a favour before and because I'm a generous man, I'll do you another. I'll refrain from going to the police and telling them that you are the little fucking pervert they have been longing to talk to..."

McKnight's words appeared to fade away. The word "police" was threatening to take Julian back again, back to that day in the bottle store but concern for his own position and a desire to break free from the tyranny of memory kept him in the present. McKnight was saying:

"I want you to forget it all and go back to Italy where you belong and leave the past alone. You're in great danger, boy, believe me. You've touched things that should be left in peace."

A dagger of doubt seemed to pierce Julian's stomach. His self-confidence vanished completely, and he was gripped by fear, by something bigger than him, something huge and frightening like the big man on the train.

McKnight stood up to go, and Nick was there, with coat in hand. McKnight slipped his arms into the sleeves. Settling the coat upon his shoulders, he pulled the belt tight around his stomach. He looked attentively at Julian's face as if he had seen something there, he had not before noticed. He sat down again but in a way that suggested his legs had given way beneath him.

"What do you want, boy? What is your interest in all this? Why do you want to rake over the past?"

His face suddenly lit up as though he had found the answer to some tormenting riddle.

"It's money you're after, is it, by God? You want money for that photo and the diaries, don't you?"

He nodded towards the briefcase. Instinctively, Julian covered it with his hand and drew it closer.

"So," McKnight said, "once a thief, always a thief. I'll give you one more piece of advice. Go and see a fucking shrink, boy. Do yourself and me a big favour and get some fucking help before it's too late for both of us."

Julian stared, deflated and open-mouthed. McKnight got to his feet and he added in a whisper:

"You don't mess around with them, boy. You're with them or you're against them and once you're with them there's no way out. Ask your old pal, Paul. He was with us and he wanted out, and the only road out was the road to hell. Too late for him. Maybe too late for us already."

He turned away. Without a further word, he lifted the collar of his trench coat and walked out into the pouring rain.

18

Julian finished his coffee, stared through the window and tried to connect with his thoughts. He half-closed his eyes. He wanted to think in confidence, ignore the two men in reefer jackets. Both were behaving strangely, but one of them was acting in a disturbing and threatening manner. He looked first at his companion, and then glared into Julian's face. Several times he seemed on the point of walking over to his table. Julian closed his eyes completely, shut the two men out of sight. Perhaps, he thought, they would go away. But his mind would not function properly, and his ideas were smothered in a blanket of anxiety before they had a chance to grow.

His eyes were opened by shouting from the world outside. He had not heard the two men leave, but they were arguing in front of the cafe. Their movements were agitated, and rough talk and aggressive language were flying between them. Then, one of the two darted away in the direction of Waterloo Bridge, and the other set off in pursuit.

With the men gone, Julian's thoughts emerged from

under their blanket. His conversation with McKnight returned, but he was unable to reflect on it. His mind wandered, his attention attracted by a paper menu pinned to the wall. He eyed the menu from his chair while Nick bustled about his domain. The paper seemed to be afflicted with some irritating nervous disorder and fluttered continuously. Julian shot out of his seat with the intention of ripping the menu from the wall. By the time he had taken a couple of strides across the cafe, good sense had pacified him, told him that he was reacting to the sort of fear and feelings of helplessness that corrupted everything and everyone, including paper menus and unknown men in reefer jackets. He was about to sit down again when the helplessness returned and neatly side-stepped the words of good sense. Fuelled by Blodwin's warning and McKnight's suggestions of powerful forces, that neither Julian nor he could control, the helplessness mutated into bewildered impotence.

Nick approached with a deference which suggested that some of McKnight's power and authority had rubbed off on his customer.

"Is there anything else I can do for you?"

Julian stared at Nick through a faint cloud of cigarette smoke and shook his head. He looked for the face of the Nick he had known thirty years previously. This futile attempt jolted Julian's mind into life, focused it on his own doubts and reinforced them. Perhaps this was not Nick at all. Perhaps it was his brother, his cousin or even his son. And perhaps, Julian thought, it was not McKnight he had seen thirty years before, but someone who looked like him. Apart from the gap of thirty years, it had been a dark, misty night, and he had seen the face at a distance of around twenty or thirty yards. It might well have been someone else he had seen striking Kathy. Maybe, Julian thought, he should take the man's advice and go back to Italy after all.

Searching for consolation, Julian stared through the window and tried to find something that could ease his worries and doubts. But the afternoon offered no solace. It was cold and damp, and the wind had strengthened, bringing thick and rolling clouds from all directions. The rain had let up, and a weak, watery sun had temporarily come out over London. For a moment, the windows in the buildings opposite picked up the sun's rays and reflected them as burning points of shattering light. There was an insistent voice at Julian's elbow.

"Can I bring you something more?"

Julian shuddered. This man had plotted with Che Guevara and fuelled Julian's revolutionary spirit. By selling out to the capitalists, Nick had betrayed his memories.

"No, nothing," he said.

Julian flung some coins onto the table, grabbed at his briefcase, and rushed out of the cafe. He emerged in the Aldwych and into a world of flat and lengthening shadows. Turning up his jacket collar, he shunned the shadows, and set off towards Southampton Row and the university.

The road which stretched before him appeared as a long and dark tunnel from which he could not escape. *You are in great danger boy*, McKnight had said. *You have touched things that should have been left in peace.* Julian walked quickly down the tunnel, and it seemed to him he was walking against a faceless crowd of rushing people. He saw them hurrying in and out of buildings and he imagined them doing this every day with the monotony of a thoughtless and unstoppable army of ants. He was now envious of their life, its repetitive normality, and its suggestion of safety.

He eventually reached the end of the road and emerged on the edge of Russell Square. He clenched his eyelids tightly shut, opened them again and shook his head, but he was feeling numb. A misty rain was falling and it came through the sunlight like a coloured curtain and settled on his clothes where it appeared to be glowing dust. The rain darkened the trees in the square and dripped from the leaves, but it also washed away Julian's black mood and replaced it with something altogether different. He experienced a sudden and clear vision of what had occurred in the cafe. Of course, McKnight would try and frighten him off with a faceless and nameless threat. What, Julian asked himself, was he expecting from him - a confession? And that nonsense about Paul. His old friend was simply a failure. There was nothing more to it.

His clear vision was followed immediately by a solution to his problem, and with it came such an intense feeling of excitement that he was forced to stop. He was standing at the entrance to Russell Square gardens when, very distinctly, he said to himself, "The man must be somehow removed."

He walked on through the misty rain with the jaunty step of a person who accepts that his decision is irrevocable. Desperate times required desperate measures. "Yes," Julian repeated to himself, "the man is simply too dangerous to me."

He was halfway across the square, heading towards the university buildings, when his excitement was flattened by a familiar and unwelcome sensation. He felt he was the focus of someone's attention. While he skirted the fountain that rose in the middle of Russell Square, his thoughts painted a picture of himself, and in this picture, he was at the centre of a telescopic sight. Somewhere a finger squeezed at the trigger, and he had moments to live. Instinctively ducking, he surveyed his surroundings. To his right was the cafe in the square. A handful of people, attempting to enjoy the weak and fitful autumnal sunshine, were sitting and reading papers under umbrellas on the terrace. Not one of them was looking in his direction. To his left, an elderly woman was going through a stretching routine, and there was a jogger on the perimeter track.

Julian's shoulders were hunched as he emerged from the square. Walking towards the School of Oriental and African Studies, he lowered his head as though expecting a cuff around the neck. He wanted to turn around, to seek out the eyes that followed him, but he was unable to decide how he should do it. A slow turn might give the watching person time to hide. A fast turn might mean a confrontation.

He drew to a halt, paused and then turned. There were a few bicyclists on the road between the Senate House and the School of Oriental and African Studies, and someone in a blue jacket was walking up the college steps. Julian took a deep breath, but the hand that grasped the briefcase was clammy. His heart was thumping against his ribs as he continued into Malet Street, past Birkbeck College, and towards Pritchard's, the university bookshop. It was four fifteen. Julian decided to browse in the shop before taking the tube to Waterloo. If he stayed for twenty minutes he could be on the tube before the rush hour started.

At the entrance to Pritchard's, Julian glanced back along Malet Street. Understanding dawned as he passed into the world of books. He had been watched in the square. He had been watched in the university precinct. It was reasonable to suppose that it was the same pair of eyes that were watching him as he entered the bookshop. He did not want to accept the word that had appeared in his thoughts. Followed. Being followed. He was being followed.

He was trying to reject the idea as he jogged up the stairs to the history section. He found a bookcase near the window. Looking through it, he was just in time to see a blue jacket disappearing through the doors of the University of London Union. Above the Union building, Julian saw that the sky was a mixture of grey and red. It was beautiful, but it all seemed so very far away.

He selected a book and scanned its pages. But the written words were strokes and lines that blurred and danced before his eyes. Every few seconds, he looked through the window at the entrance to the Union building. The sight of the blue jacket disappearing through its doors had disturbed him.

He returned his eyes to the book he was holding, but he remained at the window. A tingling sensation centred in his stomach, prompted him to look for a toilet. It was a sensation he had known since childhood. Libraries and bookshops had always stimulated this nervous excitement. That particular afternoon, there was a fundamental difference. It was not excitement he felt while he flicked through these books. It was fear.

He tried to concentrate, to convince himself that he was reading, taking in information, and deciding which books to buy. He was staring instead at the corrugated pages. They were billowing and vibrating in response to his shaking hands.

There was a man in a blue reefer jacket standing on the steps of the Union building. Julian stared at him. The man turned his eyes upwards and met Julian's gaze head on. There was no attempt to conceal it. Perhaps it had been the upturned eyes that jogged his memory, but he suddenly made the connection that had eluded him. The man outside the union was one of those he had seen in Nick's cafe. The revelation spread through his consciousness and settled in his stomach like a dead weight. Once the connection was made, everything slotted into place. Something John McKnight had said, something that Julian had filed away and sent on its journey out of memory, was snatched back. *You are in great danger.*

There was no doubt in Julian's mind that this danger was John McKnight, that the man in the blue reefer jacket was McKnight's man, and that he wanted the diaries. It could even have been the same man that Julian had met on the train earlier in the day. He could not say that he articulated these thoughts, but nonetheless, they were suddenly there and registering in his brain. And they were soon followed by another. Where was the other one? And there was something else, something that made his knees shake, something that made the dead weight in his stomach even heavier. While they had been out of sight, the men had not constituted a physical threat. The fact that they had felt the need to remain anonymous suggested that it was necessary to keep it that way. The man outside the Union building made no secret of seeking out Julian's eyes. He found the openness of it humiliated him. The man seemed to be daring him to do something, and this confronted him with the fact that he was incapable of doing anything. He was powerless.

Julian's heart was beating fast, and beads of moisture were forming under his hairline. He was surrounded by thousands of books. Together they contained the collective wisdom of centuries, but not one of them could help him. And the people, frittering away idle moments before taking the train, were anonymous faces made more faceless by being buried deep inside the pages of books. Julian had heard it said that birth and death were the only times in life when people knew the true meaning of the word "alone." He knew this was untrue. Nobody could have felt more alone and vulnerable than he did, standing in that shop.

It was a quarter to five. The man on the steps was looking up and down Malet Street as if he were looking for a bus. His hands were buried in the pockets of his reefer jacket, and he was kicking his heels on the concrete. Occasionally, he looked at the bookshop window in a way which suggested he was intent on catching Julian's eye. Julian turned away from the man and from a feeling that was taking hold, was sliding snakelike through his veins. The feeling was embarrassment that he and his pursuer were forming a relationship. It was the relationship of the hunter and the hunted, the lover and the beloved.

He suddenly felt he was about to keel over. The ground seemed on its way up to meet him and he had to grab on to the shelf for support. This is what he had done to Kathy. At that moment, time and place became suddenly dislocated, and Julian experienced the first stirrings of what could become panic. He closed his eyes and forced himself to concentrate, to get a grip. Glancing through the window, he saw there were now two reefer jackets on the steps. For reasons that escaped him, he found he had dubbed them Laurel and Hardy. There was nothing funny about them. They did not make him laugh or rock on his heels with merriment. His knees were shaking, and the movement was spreading to his thighs. Laurel was standing on the bottom step. He was brandishing a newspaper and pointing at something inside it. Hardy was nodding his head. They could have been talking about the next race at Ascot. The normality of it was terrifying.

For a moment Julian thought there had been a power surge. The electric light in Pritchard's somehow seemed stronger. A high-sided vehicle had been attempting the corner into Torrington Place and had stopped, blocking out the daylight. The driver must have miscalculated, and the trailer had crossed the pavement. The Union building was obscured from view.

Julian dropped the book he had been pretending to read, and took the stairs to the ground floor two at a time. He ignored the protests of people who received blows from the swinging briefcase. He was beyond caring. He rushed into the street and, using the stranded vehicle as cover, he ran off towards Russell Square.

He was sure he heard a shout from behind. He did not look back. If he did not see the two men, then perhaps they were not there. He kept on running. He could not run fast enough. The briefcase disturbed his natural balance, and his legs felt heavy as if stolen from a bad dream. He did not turn until he had reached the Russell Hotel. He stopped to catch his breath, spun round and looked behind him. There was no immediate sign of his pursuers. Breathing heavily, he took the last fifty metres to Russell Square tube station at a jog.

For once, Julian was thankful it was rush hour. He joined the throng of people milling around the entrance to the lift, bent his knees so that he might not be seen. He was thinking that he may have lost the two men when, with a hiss of compressed air, the lift arrived. He moved with the crowd into the lift, and standing with his legs bent, he waited impatiently. *Stand clear of the doors*, intoned the speaker system. S*tand clear please*. There was the sound of someone running, and the lift vibrated as two flying feet crashed down on the lift floor. The pressure of people on Julian's chest increased as he heard the doors close with a thump. A few seconds later the lift dropped.

He kept his eyes firmly fixed on the floor. He scanned the feet, the legs, and the umbrellas that surrounded him. If he could not see them, Julian thought, then maybe they could not see him. He knew this was ridiculous, but the idea persisted, and he grabbed at it in the same way that a drowning man might grab at a straw.

The lift halted with a thud, and everyone tumbled out into a headwind. A busker was singing: *"If you go to San Francisco, be sure to wear some flowers in your*

190

hair..."

Through the soot-smelling murk, Julian saw that the platform was filling with passengers. They spread out like a lava flow, a never-ending stream of people. He moved up to the end of the platform and, with his legs still bent, he waited for the train. The people hustled around him, but he was intent on keeping his space.

The pressure behind him increased. He felt heavy body parts pressing into his back, his knees and ankles. He heard the rustling of newspapers and raincoats and the faraway clackety-clack of the approaching train. The wind tugged at his trousers and roared in his ears.

He thought it was these sounds that prompted the people behind him to lean forward in anticipation of the train's arrival. At that moment, he felt a twitch of irritation that they should be so impatient. He pushed back in response, just to let them know that they should let up. They did not let up. The pressure increased. Inch by inch, he was edging towards the tracks.

There was a moment when he could have turned and roundly cursed the person or persons pushing him. There was another point when the threshold of irritation was crossed. He was so close to falling over that he spent all his energy attempting to stay upright. Suddenly it was too late for words of remonstration. It was a time to act, a time to survive. Spreading his arms, he felt his briefcase smash against someone's legs. He was like a police officer trying to control a crowd. He might just as well have been holding back the sea. Then there came the moment, he could not say when, but there was a moment on the platform that evening when he knew he was going to die. The normal world collapsed. Usually the word "train" meant swaying and sleep-inducing warmth and comfort. At some point, the association changed. The word "train" meant bone-smashing horror. Julian knew he was going to die under this train.

It first appeared as a light in the black tunnel. Then the horror itself materialised rolling down the track towards him. He saw the driver. He saw the driver's face staring blankly through the cab window. Julian was falling forward. A series of still images, flashbacks on his life, flickered in front of his eyes. He is the little boy on the platform waiting for the Bournemouth Belle. Clickety clack, the Bournemouth Belle, this beautiful thing. It comes for an instant. It comes from one place. It rushes to another. Faster and faster came the tube train. Faster and faster came the images. Julian's world was a jumble of bodies, a confusion of cries. Shouts hung in the air. A medley of past and present, of memories and photographs, is trapped inside his head. Here came the death train. It was useless to struggle. Here came the train that would crush him, smash him, cut him open like a jagged knife would cut him open. His shoes were scraping on the concrete floor. Someone shouted. He pushed, shoved and scrambled to get away, tried to fight through an undergrowth of arms legs and flaying elbows. He was losing his balance, was toppling forward when someone from behind pulled him back from the precipice. A huge and blue shape pulled him roughly and threw him against the wall. Julian fixed his eyes on the green tiles and saw the inscription, *Kilroy was here.* The tube doors banged and there was that peculiar whine that meant the train was departing. Someone struck him across the face with a newspaper, and the briefcase was snatched from his hand.

"You got away the first time didn't you, son," said a voice. "I'll take it now."

The newspaper was pushed under Julian's nose.

"And read this."

The newspaper had been folded to a quarter of its usual size, and the article Julian was to read was impossible to miss. He scanned it with vacant eyes. The girl from the river had been identified. Kathleen's body had been found.

"Now," said the voice roughly. "Leave it alone, you hear? Leave it alone."

Julian nodded weakly as the voice continued:

"We'll be watching you, son. We'll be watching your every move, hear me? If you don't want to end up like this fucking stiff in the paper here, just leave it alone and fucking back off."

There was an explosion in Julian's head, a flash in front of his eyes, and his knees crumpled under him. Sliding to the floor, he recognised the huge, blue back he saw disappearing in front of his eyes. The first time he had seen it disappearing towards the ticket barrier on the platform of Vauxhall Station. This time it was disappearing up the stairs towards the elevator.

19

He did not dare take the elevator up to street level. The idea that he might share the lift with the huge man in blue prompted fear of embarrassment rather than fear itself. The breathless intensity of their relationship evoked the after-the-orgasm discomfort of the prostitute's bedroom. With no purpose for further conversation, no more space for further action, only the memory of recent intimacy hung between them. Being together with such people in the confined space of a lift would have been mortifying.

Julian hovered at the bottom of the steps. Everyone appeared to be looking at him. His flirtation with death made him feel special and marked out in some way. He suspected that there was something about him that told the commuters jostling around him: *This man was nearly smashed to pieces.* The looks of the passers-by were piercing, penetrated to his very core, and played with the shame conjured up by his experience. Julian wanted to ask them what they were looking at, but he remained open-mouthed and silent, and wondering at the sensitivity which had taken control of his being. He even let his mind loiter over the unaskable. What if the two men in reefer jackets and the big man in blue were not working together?

Cold sweat was running from under his arms and forming dribbling pools at his waist. An image of himself flashed across his consciousness. He was a broken, ripped, and bloody mass spread out over the tracks. Julian rushed at the stairs and took them two at a time. Arriving breathless in the ticket hall, he tried to take in his surroundings, but he realised that, back on the stairs, he had dropped a part of himself.

His body was stiff and clammy, and his insides were vibrating as if they had been shaken. He wondered if he would start frothing at the neck like a bottle of cola. It was so shocking to see people going about their business and living their lives as normal. It seemed blasphemous after what had happened to him.

He wandered into the street and found himself at the door of the Friend at Hand. The saloon bar was a blur of dark suits and pale faces. Loud and raucous laughter was forced louder by a jukebox thumping in the corner. Julian stood and listened to an old classic. For what seemed an eternity, he tried to come to terms with the feeling that he was not there. He was entirely oblivious to his body parts and apparently floating in space.

He heard someone asking for a double whisky. It was a surprise to recognise his voice. He looked down at his feet to reassure himself that he was connected to some physical entity. His thoughts drifted to what lay beneath him in the tube network. Something terrible had happened, but he was incapable of remembering exactly what. His mind was wrapped in a thick and protective blanket. And something odd had happened to his hearing. People appeared to be laughing and talking, but to him, there was just a distorted babble of voices, rising and falling in waves. Through it all, the old classic continued: *"I just heard her say goodbye."*

Julian gulped down the whisky and left the pub. Passing the Russell Hotel and intent on walking to Waterloo Station, he was restless and irritated that his breathing was coming in short and uncomfortable gasps. A double whisky had probably been a bad idea. Perhaps he was drunk. Everything was happening in slow motion, and sounds merged into one prolonged and muted roar. Julian tugged at the collar of his shirt and said out loud, "Get control before it's too late," but the only response was the occasional contemptuous or pitying glance thrown at him from the crowd of passers-by.

He was then standing at the beginning of Waterloo Bridge, and without any recollection of how he had arrived there. The bridge seemed to stretch before him on its way into an apparent eternity. Setting off towards it, Julian seriously wondered whether he was moving out of time. It seemed for a moment that perhaps he was. It was indifferent to him whether he looked forwards or backwards. At one and the same time he was the person he had been, and the person he would become. While in this state, Julian was sure that someone called his name. The voice was familiar, and it came at a moment of stillness, a second's pause while the city held its breath. Julian cocked his head and listened, but all he heard was the sound of water rushing under his feet. And yet, looking down at the river, Julian saw that its surface was glassy, smooth and unruffled, and reflected in it, parts of London were lying like some identical but separate underwater city.

A rustling made Julian spin round. He was expecting to see someone, but there were only leaves tumbling along and brushing the pavement. Peering along the bridge, Julian thought he recognised a figure hurrying through the crowds. He could not mistake this figure, or the clothes he wore. It was the person Julian had seen in the Tiltyard gardens. In a disinterested daze, Julian knew that it was himself he was looking at, his own ghost following Kathy across the river. He shook his head, told himself he was suffering from shock, that he should get help.

In an attempt to place himself in the perspective of time, he turned his thoughts to the events of the afternoon. He saw a platform and a train. He put out his mind to touch them but it recoiled in horror. Then he wondered whether he was asleep and walking around in his own dreams.

Somehow, he crossed that eternally long bridge, and he was standing on the main concourse of Waterloo Station. His hands were covering his ears in protection from shrill and intermittent whistle blasts. The trains and the crowds reminded him of something unpleasant. He tried to grasp the memory, but he was groping in darkness while he walked away from the concourse and into a black hole.

He was sitting on a train, and with a clamour of shouts and whistles, it pulled away from the platform. He searched for a thought but he found only an emotional response to some incident in the past. The event itself was beyond recall, but the terror it had evoked was still there and wandering in his memory. He rested his head on the window and watched the rain lashing against the glass. He felt a drop on his hand, and he realised with a shock that his hair was wet and dripping. He looked up at the window, into another black hole, and darkness descended.

When he awoke, the train was stationary at Hampton Court. He glanced at his watch. It was half past six. Julian first pinched himself to see if he was awake, and then, tentatively, he sent his mind out to search for recollections of the afternoon. He decided to put the memory into the spoken word.

"Someone in London," he murmured, "tried to kill me."

He held his breath, wondering if he was strong enough to accept this awful reality. Something stirred in his stomach. Perhaps it was the residue of fear, but he did not turn to stone or fall to the floor. With renewed confidence, he decided to ask himself another question. He whispered it to himself.

"Will they come again?"

Before he could answer the question, he was obliged to hurry off the train. Piercing whistles, angry cries from the guard, and the sound of running feet announced that the train was about to depart. Julian bought a copy of the Evening News from the station kiosk and, without glancing at the headline, folded the paper and tucked it safely away under his arm.

His whispered question, however, was not so pliable and each word of it returned like a hammer blow. "Will they come again?" Searching in vain for a comforting answer, one that would offer him a way out, he saw that he was unable to delude himself. There was only one answer, and its urgency required immediate attention. Yes, he thought, while he had the diaries and the photo, they would come again.

He loitered outside the station wondering what to do next. Before he was fully aware of any decision, he found himself walking in the direction of Strudwick's yard. He fingered the newspaper while he made his way along the Hampton Court bypass, but it remained firmly under his arm while he turned off the main road and headed towards the breaker's yard to collect his diary.

*

When Julian arrived at the George and Dragon, he

198

ordered some food, but he merely poked at it with his fork. Near death experiences, he realised too late, did not inspire hunger. Aware that he could no longer postpone the inevitable, he went up to his room, threw off his clothes and wrapped himself in a blanket. He wanted to feel physically free and unfettered when he read the article and faced the final chapter of a story which had begun so many years previously. He switched on a side lamp, removed his watch and, sitting on the edge of his bed, he opened the newspaper.

Face Reconstructed in Clay
Police can confirm that the remains of a woman's body dredged up from the riverbed late last month are those of Kathleen McCullagh, who disappeared in November 1968. Dental records and a clay reconstruction of the face of the woman helped solve her identity. The remains were found under Kingston Bridge on 29 August 1998. A post-mortem may help to establish cause of death. Police are appealing to anyone who believes they may have information to contact the incident room at Kingston police station, or if you wish to remain anonymous, you can call Crimestoppers on 0800 555 222.

He put the paper to one side. It lay open on the bed and, while he sat looking at it, he sensed a change in the weather outside. There was a gust of wind, and he heard the rustle of trees as they swayed in response. Julian sat and mourned in silence. Nothing moved in the room. He held out his hand and pressed it upon the cover of his diary as if this touch would put him in contact with Kathy. He wanted to travel back in time, revitalise those empty days and speak to her. She held pieces of the past in her hands, but these pieces could contaminate the present, could combine to destroy him. He hardly recognised his own voice when it muttered in the semi-darkness, "Why didn't you stay where you were?"

He did not know how long he sat there or what time it was. His thoughts were eventually truncated by a mournful sound from somewhere far away. A dog had let out a howl and it continued for about a minute before finally ceasing. A lamp threw a sickly light throughout his room. He gazed at the shape and colour of the walls, and the arrangement of furniture around the room. In that light, it seemed to him that he was looking at it all for the first time. This novelty heightened his bewilderment, and memories of 1968 rushed in to whirl in his head.

Julian is back in the King's Arms. He is sitting with JD, the man who has walked away with his dreams.

"What brings our scholar and gent here at this early hour?" he asks.

"I've been sent away for nicking cafeteria funds," Julian says.

"You don't mess around with people like McKnight," JD says. "He lets nobody stand in his way. He stops at nothing to get what he wants."

Julian is listening to the pain and anguish in his heart. He is not listening to JD. He is not listening when JD says:

"McKnight's already putting the screws on me and Kath..."

"Is McKnight seeing Kathy?" Julian asks.

"Ask yourself," JD says. "If you think she is, then she is. Don't ask me. I'm just the cook."

Julian let the blanket fall to the ground and he made his way into the bathroom. Taking a shower, he considered packing up and rushing back to Italy. Even as the thought appeared, he was consumed with hate for the man who had put his hands on Kathy, and had effectively tainted his first marriage. The same man tried to take his life by having him pushed under the wheels of a train. Worst of all, he might well try it again.

While he dried himself, he calmly listened to the voice of truth speaking within him. Impatiently, he picked up the words and spoke them aloud. He wanted to hear them live and breathe in the real world and in the real world he would deal with them. In a matter-of-fact tone, he said, "While you are in possession of the diary, you will be in constant danger. It is only a matter of time before McKnight's men come again."

Making his way back into the bedroom, Julian recognised the bones of a plan moving in his head. His mind was already overcrowded with thoughts and feelings, and the plan was disjointed and lacking direction. He concentrated, tried to listen to his inner voices, but all he heard were the shouts coming up from the bar below along with noises of plates and chairs being shifted around. These sounds were real and so very different from the leftovers of thought and memory of a traumatic afternoon.

He placed his hands on the edge of the 1968 diary and leaned forward, his head bowed. What he really needed, he thought, was more information, but he was aware that most of the information he might need would be unattainable, buried in the grave with the people who had harboured it. Mrs C and the colonel had almost certainly drunk themselves to death. Dick Duncan-Smith seemed to be as much in the dark as he was, and Paul was so far gone that he could not even remember, apparently, who Kathy was.

Julian moved aimlessly around the room, at least, as aimlessly as the size of the room allowed. Four steps towards the door, turn left, three steps towards the wardrobe, turn left, four steps towards the wall. As he walked towards the wardrobe, he caught sight of the diary in the high mirror. He saw it appearing at his back on the corner of his bed and next to the open newspaper. He swung round, and bending forward, he peered at the diary. He took a step towards it, then another. He sat down on the edge of the bed, opened the diary at random and began to read of long-forgotten days.

*

15 October 1968
Why's the middle of the afternoon such a depressing time? It seems to me that around three o'clock, and especially in the autumn, the day begins to die and the evening's yet to be born. Anyway, in this dreary interval today, I made a decision.

I was in the JCR and discussing history with Robert Morton. I said we should get in touch with the past in order to understand the present. Robert seems to think there is, perhaps, no past to get in touch with. He said that all the chronicles and the resources we have are only interpretations. He maintained that historical facts are only the interpretations of the chroniclers. Is he right? Is there only a permanent present, and is the past a simple succession of empty days? What about people who remember? Are their memories simply part of the present? Do they simply interpret their past to suit their here and now?

Robert said that I'd better get some advice when I write my CV. He said that if I don't interpret my past to suit a potential employer, I'll have problems getting a job. I said that was unfair and telling lies. He said it was just life. Classes were cancelled. There was a debate in the lecture theatre. Americans out of Viet Nam!!

I don't recall making the decision. I simply wandered out of the college building and into the brightness of a late autumn day. The sunlight was filtering through the thinning trees, and from the cafeteria in Russell Square came the clinking of crockery and the smell of tea and cakes. These penetrating sounds and scents disturbed my present with memories of Hampton Court and the Tiltyard. Only six weeks have passed since I vomited outside the pub, but I'm sure I was happy there. Happiness gleams through the trees with the sunlight.

"Ah love, such happy days, such days as these." Where now is the friendly touch of hand upon shoulder, the intimate sound of voices from the King's Arms?

I didn't know where I was heading. I wandered around for a while and I found myself in the Aldwych. The sun had gone down by the time I arrived. I was surprised to see that I was trembling in anticipation. It must've been about half past five when I saw her. I realise now that for six weeks I've been deprived of something I can only describe as an endless and aching need. How have I managed to live for so long without her presence? No imaginative expectation could match the reality of Kathy strolling along the Strand.

She didn't see me of course. My head span, and I was filled with such desire and longing, I didn't want to let her go. I watched as she turned to begin the long walk over Waterloo Bridge. I let a couple of minutes pass, and then I crossed the road and stared along the bridge that stretched before me. Somewhere amongst the jostling commuters was Kathy. Her presence on the bridge invested it with a special beauty. A group of tourists were taking photos of St Paul's and Big Ben. How could they take such delight in dead things when real happiness lay in the people on whom they had turned their shoulders?

I feel my mind's in pieces. I walked back to hall in darkness.

18 October 1968
Skipped lectures today so as not to miss her. Took up a

position between the Wellington pub and the public toilets. You never came. Are you ill? Do you need my help? I shall come tomorrow. Tomorrow will never come, but I'm already looking forward to it. Tomorrow, and tomorrow, and tomorrow. There's always hope, but, "Shalt thou not wonder that it liveth yet, the useless hope, the useless craving pain."

20 October 1968
Followed you across the bridge again. What a dream you are, and you're all the more perfect for it. But why did you turn around on the bridge and give me such a shock? When you stopped dead in your tracks and turned to look behind you, there was nowhere for me to hide. I spun round and leaned over the parapet with my head in the direction of Charing Cross. Is there something wrong with me? Should I be doing this? But then, why not? I'm not harming anyone. And I can stop any time I want. I will stop at some time in the future. But not now.

It was already dark when I walked back through Russell Square. Senate House and the Russell Hotel seemed to confront each other like Titans. The evening isn't a good time to walk through the square. Dark and muttering shapes loomed before me in the night shadows, and the bushes shook, swayed and rustled as unseen bodies moved amongst them. Am I as bad as these people - these perverts? Surely not!

When I got back to the college bar, Robert stopped me and asked why I'd been "absconding from lectures." Burrell told him to tell me that lectures are compulsory and that my non-attendance has been noted. I'd better be careful in future.

23 October 1968
For two days I've stuck to the promise I made to myself. I've tried to concentrate on my work. I've been to

lectures but I think only of you. I write nothing except the date at the top of my notepaper. Most of the time, I've daydreamed. Me the hero - you the woman who loves me. "Shalt thou not hope for joy new born again, Since no grief ever born can ever die through changeless change of seasons passing by?"

And beauty born of things that must die! It torments me that you will grow old! Every day you'll change a little, and I must miss the changing you. In a very real sense, every day that passes can never return. Every day means I'll never see you again, for the you of today is not the same as the you of the day before.

What if you are with another man? No not you! You're perfect and your perfection will not be tarnished in the arms of another. I know this, but please forgive my weakness. The image of you in the embrace of another man torments me. I want to see you again - to reinforce what I know already. So, tomorrow, it'll do no harm to break my promise - just for one day.

25 October 1968

Monday. It was a long weekend of waiting. Two days that would never end. At last I could see you again, but I took great care as I followed you. Oh bliss! The trains were delayed so I could watch you for an extra half-hour while you waited outside the barrier with the other passengers. I was so far away with my dreams that I had neither the strength nor the desire to let you out of my sight. I bought a ticket to Kingston and followed you home - your home and such a wonderful house because it holds you in its four walls.

27 October 1968

My friends at college think I have taken up photography as a hobby. If only they knew the truth! The truth is this. I can't live without a vision of you. I took a photograph of you while you were standing under the clock. You weren't looking. You don't mind, do you? Please say you don't mind. But why were you speaking to McKnight? Why was McKnight there with you on the station platform? Does he take the train every day too?

Funny, but I don't feel very comfortable. Someone is watching over me. Sometimes I get the strong feeling that others can see me as I see myself. I think I've developed the ability to step outside myself and see as others see. Today, on my way back from the station, a complete stranger stopped me to ask the time. I'm sure there was a suspicious look in his eye. Or was it my own eye observing myself?

Last night I lay in bed, listening to the hum of silence. I know there's nobody out there to protect me. I'm sick, I should see a doctor. Perhaps I should just help myself. Oh God, help me. My thoughts are just shadows, and I can only go on and think and dream in my empty room.

30 October 1968

YOU HAVE BETRAYED ME! DOUBLE-CROSSER - SHE-DEVIL - FIEND. Oh, how could you do that after all the things we've done together? All the things we've been through and all the evenings we've spent together. How could you? HOW COULD YOU?

Maybe I was mistaken. Perhaps I'm not being fair to you, my dear.

I'll tell you how it happened. I got up at six today. Saturday morning. Only a few students, with shoulders hunched against the world, were prowling the corridors. Funny, isn't it? Still warm from sleep, the girls clutched at themselves with arms that wrapped their bodies like creepers.

Left the hall at six thirty. The suspicious look in the porter's eye must've been my imagination or was I, perhaps, looking at a reflection of my own guilt? Felt more comfortable with the tramps and drunks I met in the square and on my way to the station. The train to Kingston held night-shift workers.

Dawn was breaking when I arrived outside your house, and a thick mist was hanging low over the river. I still don't believe what I've seen. And I don't want to believe it. There were shadows moving about – IN YOUR FLAT - shadows. I leaned over and retched. Bloody woman and her dog. She asked me if I was all right! What could I say to her? How could I explain my presence outside your house at that hour? I just ran. I remember nothing except my arms and legs whirling in front of me. What was I running from? Was it my self-loathing? Was it my guilt or was it the pear-shaped head I had seen in your flat? Did I really see this person, or was it my imagination? Why would JD be in your flat at that hour?

I knew you wouldn't mind. I had to check. I found a phone box and rang you. Oh, how wonderful it was to hear you. There was no man's voice in the background. I must've been mistaken about JD. I held the phone to my ear for ages. I listened to your voice. I listened to the sound of your breathing. Then, there was just a silence. I was mistaken, wasn't I? Please tell me I was mistaken and that you need me still, that you love me just a bit, that there is some secret you won't tell me, please PLEASE.

*

Rubbing his fingers over this last entry, Julian felt his doubts and pain oozing from the written words and infecting his fingers. He snapped the diary shut, got to his feet and rushed to the window. He threw it up and put his head out. At the touch of fresh air, a face leaped out of his imagination and floated in front of his eyes. Julian drew his head in, made a few steps and stumbled against a chair. He pulled on some clothes, threw the door open and dashed down the stairs and into the telephone booth. Flicking through the phone book, he experienced a staggering sense of the absurd that he should be looking for help from a person he had once hated. But necessity swept away any need to justify the idea or the actions that might result from it. He wrote down the number he was given. He dialled. There was a click at the end of the line and a voice crackled into his ear.

"Justin King?"

20

King's Arms. 7 September

JD turned to the bar and drew his glass towards him. Settling his elbows on the armrests, he nestled his beer between his hands. Words emerged brokenly between his thin and cracked lips.

"You're keeping something from me."

His watchful eyes were watery and tired, and Julian looked back at him in complete surrender, careful not to reveal any expression that might show his delight at his old adversary's appearance. His skin was sallow, and spittle glistened on his chin. His movements were clumsy, and his hands were shaking.

"There's no more to tell," Julian said. "I've come to you because I've nowhere else to go, nobody else to speak to."

He had confessed almost everything and carefully watched each line and wrinkle on JD's face for any movement that might betray his thoughts or feelings. JD placed his beer on the table and leaned forward. One elbow was cupped in the palm of his hand while the other hand held a smoking cigarette at his ear.

"OK - so what makes you think you were the last person to see Kath alive? What makes you sure McKnight had anything to do with it? You'd better have some evidence; yes, evidence..."

After a second of stillness, JD's head began a series of rolling nods, each one bringing Julian a moment of pleasure. He nodded along in order to make JD feel at ease and stifled a smile when he saw the collar of his old rival's shirt. It was threadbare, and flecks of white cotton marked the spots where the top buttons used to be. Looking towards the floor he said in a hesitant tone:

"So, can you help me?"

JD crossed his legs and, tipping his head to one side, he looked beyond Julian's shoulder and towards the entrance to the bar. Silence swelled between the two men. Julian lifted his head, sought out JD's eyes with his and opened his face to invite comment.

"I want to know what'll happen if I go to the police. I'll have to tell them I was the so-called mysterious prowler."

He was monitoring his words, touching them with regret and shame and he finished with a well-practised tone of fatality.

"And I'll have to tell them I was the person who made those calls, the man they've been waiting to interview for thirty years."

JD dragged on his cigarette. He uncrossed and then crossed his thin legs before intertwining them as if they were pipe cleaners. He picked up his beer and sucked off the foam.

"So? What do you think'll happen then?"

Julian shrugged, surprised at how easy it was to manipulate.

"Can they put you in prison for withholding vital information?"

JD shook his head.

"Unless you're a principal you won't find yourself at risk of prosecution when you do come forward, even if it is much later."

Julian remained outwardly calm.

"You seem very sure of yourself."

"Oh, I am," said JD. "When you've had the law on your back for thirty years, you do your homework."

Julian listened for tones of regret in JDs voice, but it was in the trembling jaw that he found relics of anger and bitterness. JD said:

"And the fact that you would've been suspected of the murder is usually considered sufficient reason for keeping quiet - at the time."

He licked his lips but traces of foam remained in the lines that radiated from the corners of his mouth.

"You still haven't told me why you think you were the last person to see Kath alive? And what makes you think McKnight was responsible for any of this?"

Julian shuddered inwardly at these familiar words. They touched and stirred the nagging doubts which taunted him.

"I saw John McKnight hit her," he said. "What if Kathy fell? What if she hit her head?"

"What if, Julian? Too many what ifs. What if it wasn't him you saw? What if you saw someone who looked like him? What if thirty years have clouded your memory? What if you were asked to put your hand on the bible and swear it was him? Would you?"

JD wrapped his fingers round his glass and raised it to his lips. His eyes, staring over the rim, were soft but mocking.

"And a slap in the face," he said, placing his glass on the counter, "doesn't usually kill people, you know?"

His cigarette glowed. He squinted through the smoke in a way that suggested he enjoyed seeing Julian wrestle

211

with his doubts.

"You, such a scholar and a gent, you should know that we..."

Julian interrupted with a short breath of imminent protest, and JD allowed his voice to trail off. He rotated his glass between his palms while he waited for Julian to say something. Eventually, he flicked ash from his cigarette towards the table. He said:

"We don't even know that someone killed her at all. Maybe it was suicide. She was here one day and gone the next. That is what we know."

Julian watched the ash slowly crumble in a pool of beer and made a bet with himself that the ash would dissolve by the time JD ordered more beer.

"Do you really believe," JD said, "that telling the police everything you think you saw that night will be enough to arrest the man?"

His eyes searched Julian's before moving away and settling on a point over Julian's shoulder.

"What is the evidence? Thirty-year-old silhouettes at the window and faded shadows on the wall?"

He inserted a fingernail between two teeth and removed a piece of tobacco.

"No, Julian."

He paused while he stubbed out his cigarette.

"They need more evidence than that. They even need a motive, you know?"

He reached for the drinks, his shoulder brushing a photograph that hung on the wall above his head. The photo, a relic from the Second World War, slid sideways, teetered for a second and then dropped towards the ground. Julian just managed to reach it before it hit the floor.

"Then why would he want to push me off the station platform?"

Julian replaced the photograph. Smiling faces peered

at him from its frame. Thirty years previously, some of these faces had returned to the King's Arms for a reunion. He wondered where they were now, those people who had danced to the music of Glen Miller, and who had sung "Lilli Marlene," and "Those Were the Days."

JD leaned sideways and pulled a tobacco tin from his jacket pocket.

"Excuse me," he replied, prising open the tin's lid, "but you don't really know who tried to push you, do you?"

He spread tobacco over a rolling paper and added:

"But whoever that man was, if he had meant to kill you, you wouldn't be here now. Someone wanted to silence you, to scare the shit out of you. And my guess is that, whoever that someone is, he succeeded, right?"

He brought the cigarette to his lips, licked the glued side and waited. Julian was concentrated on the ash. It was slowly and irritatingly crumbling away in the pool of beer.

"Partly," Julian said.

He placed both hands on his thighs and leaned forward. He had intended to raise his voice, but he found himself whispering in a monotone.

"The photograph I took thirty years ago shows Kathy and McKnight on Waterloo station together. And in my diary, I've recorded everything. John McKnight's man tried to take it from me."

With the tip of his tongue, JD moistened his lips and placed the newly rolled cigarette between them.

"Tell me again. Why would McKnight be frightened of some diary?"

"Everything I saw that night in 1968 is recorded there," Julian replied. "I could show the diary to the police, have McKnight taken in and questioned."

At first, Julian noticed nothing but the silence which

followed his words. But the silence had a quality of expectation, of something in the air before a storm. And into the silence he said:

"And if he denies being with her, I can show them the photo."

JD's jaw was twitching again. He shook his head and said:

"No, Julian, no. A chance meeting on Waterloo Station? The jealous imagination of a young boy? Interesting, but hardly enough to put the man away."

"McKnight doesn't know that," Julian said.

JD patted at his pockets for his box of matches. His head was still shaking, his eyes glistening like those of a drunk. When he parted his lips to speak, they were joined together by a piece of saliva, thick and heavy like a matchstick.

"Unfortunately for you, that's right. So, let's suppose it was McKnight's man who took the case. What do you think he'll do when he sees it's empty? What are you going to do about that?"

"I haven't decided," Julian said.

"Then you'd better decide. I told you once that you don't mess around with people like John McKnight." As an afterthought, he said: "I told Kath too."

He took a box from a pocket, opened it and selected a match. He held the match in front of him. The match flared, and in its light, the lines around JD's mouth danced like stick men.

"But she didn't listen," he said, "and she paid for it."

His shoulders lifted as though to protect himself from a terrible memory, and then he added: "She paid more than just a slap in the face."

"Sorry," Julian said, "you've lost me. What do you mean?"

JD's jaw quivered again.

"John McKnight put the screws on her, tried to

frighten her. He had her followed. Maybe the same type of men that followed you, assuming it was..."

"But I don't understand why...?"

"Hold on a minute and listen."

As if suddenly overcome by a painful memory, JD emitted a brief cry of emotion before continuing with:

"You told me just now that you followed her, right?"

Julian nodded.

"So, you didn't realise, did you?"

While Julian stared, JD slowly blew a cloud of smoke towards the ceiling.

"Didn't you ever stop to think she knew you were there?"

Julian had not prepared himself for this, but he lived through all those days and evenings when he had followed her home. He felt them all in a second, and those feelings appeared in his eyes as gathering tears.

"No, I..."

"Listen to what I have to say."

There followed a period of silence. Both Julian and JD exchanged glances but neither spoke. Eventually, JD took a last drag on his cigarette and stubbed it out. Lowering his voice to a whisper he said:

"She thought you might be protecting her."

He paused and searched Julian's eyes with his.

"Did you know she found your presence comforting?"

He raised his eyebrows. It was a signal that he wanted a response. Julian hesitated, was carried away by the thought that even after thirty years, Kathleen was deceiving him. He forgot himself so far as to say with anger:

"Yes, I did follow her. And I told you, I telephoned her too."

"And what did you say to her?"

"Nothing. I just wanted to hear her voice, to hear the

phone ringing inside her flat."

"You really were in love with her, weren't you?"

"Oh no," Julian said, "I never really knew her. How can you love someone you never know?"

"Easy," said JD, and with a movement of his thumb he indicated the photo behind him. "You put someone on a wall like this one here, or you put someone on a pedestal and that someone remains perfect and unstained forever. You know how it is."

JD wiped at his eyes, recovered his balance and looked at Julian reflectively.

"Kath told me about the calls," he said, "but not your calls. She told me about the obscene calls. That was almost certainly John McKnight's doing as well."

"Obscene calls?" Julian said, genuinely puzzled. "What sort of obscene calls?"

"There is only one sort. Things most of us might only think about. They talked about it."

"Sorry, but why would he do that to her? Why would he have her followed? Why would he order someone to make obscene calls? Was he in love with her, obsessed or something?"

In the silence that followed, JD picked up a beer mat and slowly tore it to pieces.

"In love with her? I don't think so, Julian. She was threatening to expose him."

"Expose him? Expose him for what?"

Julian thought he saw a suggestion of contempt in JD's eyes, a suggestion which tried Julian's patience. The effort he was forced to make, the effort to remain calm, the effort not to take a step forward, to wrap his hands around that scrawny neck and throttle the life out of the man, was almost unbearable.

"So," JD said, "you never knew then?"

"Knew what? What didn't I know?"

JD slapped the pieces of beer mat down on the table.

"That our under manager, the man who now heads Knight and Day Catering, the man who says he's going to run for MP, was running a little racket. Not so little actually. Probably amounted to tens of thousands a year."

Julian was, at first, unable to interpret the words he was hearing. Struggling with astonishment, all he could say was:

"And?"

"And he needed the support and compliance of everyone in the restaurant. The waiters were happy. They received a small cut. I was involved, and so was Kath."

Julian nodded, but astonishment was transforming itself into comfortable, inner warmth.

"Those who didn't go along with him got the screws put on them. Maybe you know I was already in trouble with the law and so was Mrs Croucher. Remember Mrs Croucher?"

"Yes, but what...?"

"Mrs Croucher was a woman of many virtues, but she had one major weakness. She got her kicks out of men in uniform. During the sixties she was done several times for shoplifting. It was not that she couldn't afford anything. She did it for the thrill of being arrested by men in authority, our friends in blue. The last time, they put her away for six months. When she came out, she went on a drinking binge and never looked back. She died in '73."

Julian was genuinely absorbed. He stared into JD's eyes and wondered how easy it was to misunderstand people. JD was nodding again and he continued in the triumphant tone of one who has the power of knowledge, the power of the secret.

"But Kath? She was made of stronger stuff."

"And she worked at the head office of Park Merchant

Catering in the Strand, didn't she?"

"Clever boy," said JD. "Accounts clerk actually. She found out what John McKnight was up to and she was threatening to tell the management. In the end, she was even threatening to tell the police."

Julian was stunned. But he was proud too. Proud that someone to whom he had given so much should refuse to buckle. And then, across a chasm of thirty years, Kathy reached out to him. He saw her raise her hand as she had raised it when he had seen her at the window in November '68. He wondered whether it had been a greeting or a sign of farewell, whether that had been her way of saying goodbye.

"And did she tell the police?"

JD shrugged.

"I don't know. Nobody knows what she did. I do know that after Kath's disappearance, McKnight stopped his racket altogether. As far as I know, he has never since stepped on the wrong side of the law, has led the life of a model citizen."

"What was he doing?"

"Not sophisticated, but very effective," said JD. "Spirit measures and pints in the bar were doctored, and the meals I served up were not quite as they should've been. A little less meat here, fewer potatoes there. Alcohol, food and cigarettes were ordered and then sold to one of John McKnight's contacts. He had to be careful though and he ran a tight ship."

This information hit Julian like a thunderbolt. A series of emotions and thoughts bubbled up inside him so that for a moment, he floundered in them. His lips were trembling with an expression of joy, but he closed his eyes and stayed silent.

"You know," JD said, "I've thought about this for the past thirty years and I've reached some conclusions. Do you want to know what I think?"

Julian nodded. He allowed his eyes to wander over JD's complexion, his shirt collar and to the ash, still sitting in its pool of beer.

"Can we really be sure," JD said, "that McKnight was the top man?"

It was not a question and it received no reply. JD was busy rolling another cigarette.

"Why else would he have been scared shitless when he found out about you, Julian? Imagine. Someone else in the Tiltyard was meddling with the stock, threatening to sink McKnight's tight ship. And that was why you were fired so quickly. Have you never thought about it? There must've been someone else."

"Like who? Organised crime?"

JD looked down at his feet and then back up at Julian. The silence was like an invitation for Julian to voice his own conclusions. JD lit his cigarette and blew out a stream of smoke.

"I've no idea," he said. "But let's go back to motive. Why would McKnight want Kath out of the way? You'd better ask yourself because the police will. After all, his crime was no greater than yours. You wouldn't kill someone just to cover up a small crime like pilfering, would you?"

Julian shook his head, but the words he was hearing were having a magical effect. JD said:

"But what if Kath had stumbled on something bigger? What if McKnight was told to remove her?"

Julian watched JD's eyes recede and narrow as they probed for the memory of some special moments or feelings. He smoked for a while in silence before stubbing out his cigarette with a finality that suggested he had no more opinions on the topic.

"You know," he said, "Kath and I spent a lot of time together during her difficult period. Nothing ever happened between us but that's not to say I didn't want something to happen."

Julian detected a quaver in JD's voice, the echo of a deeply buried or barely acknowledged feeling.

"I liked her too," JD continued. "I never told her, but then perhaps she knew. She knew everything did Kath."

His eyes gleamed, and his legs tightened round themselves.

"She often talked about you."

Julian felt a tingling in the stomach but he set his face in an expression of interest, of curiosity, a cover for the grim reality that possessed him, the reality of a feeling that had never fully left.

"About me?"

"Yes you, Julian. She liked you. She liked you a lot, but she knew you were living in different worlds. She was proud of you, proud that such a scholar and a gent was off to university. The evening she spent with you in London was an oasis of normality in her life then. Gone with the Wind? Well maybe. It made her feel sorry sometimes that she was mixed up in something so dirty that she was unable to tell you about it."

At that point Julian sensed her presence in the bar, and she took him to the edge of history. He smelled her perfume and he heard her foot falling on the carpet. For a second, he wanted to touch her, to speak to her and to tell her to leave him alone. But it was too late, thirty years too late. Julian said:

"Tell me about what?"

JD sat tense and still.

"She knew you wouldn't understand. I guess you don't understand now. But she knew it would hurt you. She was deeply ashamed, and she didn't know what to do. She needed help."

Julian was overcome by a variety of thoughts and feelings that he had believed to be buried for thirty years. But they had refused to lie still and now emerged to taunt him. Eventually, he muttered:

"You think I could've helped her?"

JD was quivering, and his head was nodding and rolling again. He said:

"Who knows? Who knows what happened? Maybe McKnight had something to do with her disappearance. The fact is Julian, she's gone. She's been gone for thirty years. Nobody knows how she went. Does it make a difference?"

Julian was about to shake his head when his attention wandered. There was a rustling in the air of someone who had come, stood with them in the bar and who had then moved on. Kathy had vanished again. Julian wondered why she had not turned her head, why she had not said a final good bye.

"Thank God," he whispered.

"What was that?"

"Oh, nothing," Julian said.

JD relaxed. He reached into his pocket and took out the tobacco tin.

"Maybe that man who tried to frighten you was right," he said. "Maybe we should leave the past alone."

Julian nodded. Inside he was chuckling. Kathy's passing had broken the knot that tied him with this man. They had raked over the past but they would never meet again, had no future together. Above all, there was no more need to listen to the ramblings of a broken man. The two exchanged pleasantries.

"When are you going back to Italy?" JD asked.

"Couple of days."

"To pick up the pieces?"

"That's right."

"Another drink?"

"I must be going. Things to do. Things to think about."

JD looked at Julian with concern on his face.

"Don't wait too long. If it was McKnight who wanted the photo and the diaries, he'll come looking for you again. He knows where you are staying, doesn't he?"

"Oh yes, but there's nothing for him there."

JD held out his hand. As Julian took it, JD looked him in the eye.

"Italy's the best place for a scholar and a gent like you."

Julian smiled his lop-sided smile and stared at JD in silence. It was a normal silence, a silence filled with the ease of a conversation completed and, for Julian, a job done. Released from his role of passivity, Julian allowed his contempt to penetrate his next words.

"If I were you, I might keep a low profile for a few days."

He watched an expression of concern pass over JD's face, and in that instant, Julian's contempt became an almost irresistible power. In a completely changed voice, he added:

"There's going to be a lot of shit flying around."

JD looked searchingly into Julian's eyes. For his part, Julian was aware of a rage that now consumed him. He spat out:

"Suppose I tell the police it was some other bastard I saw that night, someone with a pear-shaped fucking head and long fucking hair. A fucking weirdo...?"

"What..., you wouldn't..., you..."

Julian interrupted him. At first speaking steadily, he allowed his tone to reflect what he was feeling. The tone was ferocious.

"Ask yourself. Don't ask me, I'm only the fucking teacher, the fucking pervert."

Julian realised his teeth were set hard and his hand was ready to snatch a glass, to push it into JD's face. It was with a huge effort that he pulled himself back from the brink of this wild place. He spun round, walked out of the pub and slammed the door behind him. The sound of the door was an explosion which called him back to his senses. With the residue of rage settling inside him, Julian let his mind wander back to that useless individual, to a victim who was unable to get a grip on life and give it a direction of his own choosing. JD was right about one thing, Julian thought, and he allowed himself to drift away to the medieval streets of Verona and its beautiful squares. Italy was the best place for him, but Italy could wait until he had redrafted the last chapter, until he had re-written history.

21

Julian passed through the Lion Gate and into the palace grounds. Making his way towards an avenue of trees, he allowed his mind to find peace. His aggressive feelings and wicked thoughts drained away, and he was left cool and focused, soothed by the conviction that the information he now possessed put him in control of his destiny.

Still pondering, he passed the maze and wandered into the Wilderness gardens. Tired shadows spread in net-like patterns over the path in front of him, and Julian vaguely noted that the sun was about to go down. Behind the trees, the sun was the heart of a firework burning through the autumn leaves, and it bathed the palace in warmth. The glowing walls were punctuated by yellow lights weakly blinking through windows. Julian barely noticed the two gardeners who emerged from the door of a hut. They straddled their bicycles and pedalled noiselessly and needlessly beside him, made him feel increasingly uncomfortable before they accelerated and disappeared into the gathering darkness.

By the time he passed through the main gate of the

palace he had forgotten both the cyclists and his discomfort, and the sun had vanished. Setting off in the direction of Thames Ditton, Julian was oblivious even of the night settling around him. He was restless, unable to decide on the details of his next move. Fixing his eyes firmly on the pavement, he probed for possibilities, but access to his thought processes was hindered by a wrapping of fog. Nonetheless, through this fog, ideas and voices shifted, moved closer to his inner eye and presented themselves for inspection.

He knew that nobody would care if he simply left things as they were, went back to Paola, disappeared once more in Italy. He checked this possibility with a slight shake of his head and he walked on through Long Ditton, experiencing nothing but a momentary tightening of his stomach. He looked around him, as if searching for someone to whom he could turn for advice. Seeing nothing, not even his own shadow, he told himself there had to be a better way forward than an immediate return to Italy.

Julian lingered for a while at the entrance to a pedestrian walkway which stretched before him. Turning into it, he knew that he was not afraid of indecision, but he was aware of the dangerous instability of his whims and he also knew that the business of making up his mind did not rest with himself alone. The past, he thought, also had its responsibility. He hurried on.

The houses on either side of him seemed to crouch under the darkness of the night, but it was only when he passed a street light that he recognised the place in which he was walking. At first, he saw only his shadow spreading from under his feet in the lamplight. He followed the shadow with his gaze until it broke over the mesh fencing. He raised his eyes to the hidden sky and, in the moment of recognition, closed them tightly. He heard again a sound which has a quality all of its own. It was the sound of the school playground - no matter which school and no matter which time. He heard again that echoing mixture of laughter, shouts of surprise and of excitement. It exploded high into the air and hung over his head as bright as a Roman candle. There were no such sounds now. It was night, and there was a hollow silence hanging over the world, but Julian knew he was standing outside his old school in Watery Lane.

He peered over the fence. The Victorian schoolhouse was still there, but grafted on to it was a modern building, and it jutted out into what had been the playground. The nooks and crannies, that had served their purposes for he and his friends, slowly materialised from the darkness, but Julian saw no cricket stumps painted on the walls. He allowed his thoughts to wander to the children with whom he had played, with whom he had fought Custer's last stand and with whom he had once played marbles and cards. Break times had been a short while, but to him and his friends, they had seemed to stretch out for hours and hours, an infinity of time. He wondered what had happened to all of those children, to those minds that dreamed and wondered what they would be when they grew up. It saddened him when he realised that he was standing outside the school in darkness, lost in the world of his own childhood dreams.

Forty years had passed. Things had happened to them all, small influential things; conversations here, events and relationships there, perhaps unimportant in themselves, but gradually and imperceptibly moulding them all, so that the finished product barely resembled the raw material that still haunted this old playground.

He touched his chest and proudly reflected that the Julian who had played in this schoolyard would surely have approved of what he had become. He was, he admitted, indecisive, but he was proactive, willing and able to shape his own life, to refuse to be the victim. He knew that the past was dead, and the present was an insecure and dangerous place. He now had the power to shape both to his own satisfaction.

He turned his back on his old school and, making his way back to the pub, he was aware that each step was a step away from his own history. He thought that if he span round, he might catch the little boy who had been living inside him. He might see the boy watching his back disappearing down Watery Lane. The boy would be weeping, his hands would be linked between his thighs, and his knees would be bent. Julian was not sure whether it was the cry of the new-born he would hear or the rattle of a being in its death throes.

He hurried on, determined to shape his own memories, and his face betrayed nothing, expressed nothing but bone structure and an arrangement of features. Only the cold air, stirred by a strengthening breeze reminded him that he was still there. So, what, Julian thought, was special about that evening? What would give this moment a meaning? He was forty-eight, and it was the middle of September 1998, and he knew it was time to let go of the past, time to say his own goodbye.

He finally acted later that evening when he was alone in his room. He grabbed the phone directory, found the number he was looking for and marched down the stairs to the telephone kiosk. It was eight o'clock. He was listening to the purring of the phone. There was a click.

"John McKnight."

Julian had been expecting a secretary. He gathered his wits together.

"You sent some men to get my diary," he said. "But all they got was an empty case, wasn't it?"

At the other end of the line there was a heavy silence, and for some time Julian made no effort to break it. Then he said:

"So now you have a choice. Either you pay for it or I give it to the police. What do you say?"

He heard McKnight snigger.

"I say the leopard doesn't change its spots, by God. As I said, once a fucking thief, always a fucking thief, right, boy?"

"You should fucking know," Julian said. "And so should the police when they investigate Kathy's disappearance again."

Silence.

"Your case was stolen, you say?"

"Why yes," Julian said, "as you well..."

Mcknight interrupted sharply.

"I've never seen this case."

Julian was expecting a denial. In a mocking but irritated tone he began:

"Come off it, John. You're still trying to frighten me off with some other vague and mysterious..."

McKnight interrupted again but, in a voice, which had dropped to a tone so deep and low, that it sounded like wind in the pipes of an organ.

"Who said they were vague? Who...?"

His voice trailed off to a whisper before abruptly returning in a more business-like tone.

"We'd better meet, boy."

"Where?"

"In the Tiltyard tearoom. Tomorrow at eleven o'clock."

Julian was surprised by this capitulation, so surprised that he was unable to articulate anything more than that which what he had rehearsed, that which was now redundant.

"And leave your men behind you."

There was another silence, and then McKnight said:

"Just watch your back, boy. By God you'd better watch your back."

The line went dead. Slowly, Julian tried to put the receiver down. His hand was shaking so badly that it took him three attempts to return it to the holder. He stared at the receiver for some time before snatching at it again. He dialled. First, there was the faint sound of his breathing, and then a voice crackled on the other end of the line.

"Crimestoppers?"

He opened his mouth to speak and let out a sort of croak. There was so much to say that he did not know where to start.

"I have some information that you may be interested in," he said. "It concerns a woman's disappearance..."

He wanted to say more, but for a moment, he faltered. Julian Everet covered the mouthpiece and shook with an uncontrollable burst of shivering.

22

Julian awoke from a dreamless sleep. A clear and strong light was coming through the curtains that he had failed to close properly the evening before. But it was not the light that made him wake up, it was a surge of joyous impatience to get on with his new life that stirred him from sleep. A voice whispered at him: *From this day on, you will be more respectful of yourself, more sensitive to your own existence.*

When he opened his eyes, he was ready to face the challenge. Self-respect demanded the world's approval, and he was loath to allow even the next hour to join the thousands of others that had been ignored, had become part of lost time and empty days. He jumped out of bed and strode into the bathroom. Cold water woke him up completely, and he went back to the bedroom and dressed at a rush. Then, he picked up the 1968 diary and clattered down the stairs. He ate a quick breakfast and strode towards the exit of the George and Dragon.

Coming out of the doorway, he was enveloped in a

light so bright that he had to close his eyes to the day. The sun's rays touched even the most hidden places, and the air was light and delicate. The village clock struck the hours, and he hurried off towards Hampton Court.

Although the sunlight was intense, it was a changeable sort of day. At one moment, everything would be clear and bright, and cumulus clouds danced across the tree tops. Then, in an instant, the light would dim, and the world turned grey and cold while a breeze brought a taste of winter to his tongue and the smell of snow to his nostrils.

It was in one such wintry moment that Julian dived into a stationer's and bought a large, brown envelope. Emerging into the street, he flicked open the diary cover and the paper sprung to life. He grabbed two pages between thumb and forefinger and, pulling them away from their binding, he slid them into the envelope. Grasping the diary tightly, he looked up. He was expecting to see brown and crisp leaves flying about, but instead, the morning turned bright as the sun appeared again and brought life to his surroundings. The day itself was alive, beating like his heart as he set off through Long Ditton and towards his rendezvous with John McKnight.

Julian had told the police that he would leave the envelope with the porter at his lodge near the main entrance to the palace. Having deposited it, he made for the river path at the west front. A light, autumnal mist was hanging over the Thames, and the dipping of oars was clearly audible. There were vague outlines of boats scattered over the water's surface, and he saw ripples lapping against the river bank. He sat down on a bench and opened the diary. He thumbed through the pages until he reached 29 November. Then, he looked skywards and, with fumbling fingers, he ripped the page out. Julian scratched around for a large stone. When he had found one, he wrapped the paper around it. He imagined himself throwing the stone with all his energy towards the river's surface. He imagined the page as a whirling blur, flying towards the river, splashing through the surface and sinking to the bottom. In his mind's eye, he saw the 29 November slowly swaying with the current towards the riverbed. He wondered how long it would take for the page to erode. Perhaps, one day, it would be dredged up from the riverbed, but the written word would have dissolved in the water and flowed away with the current to the sea.

"Can't do that," said a voice.

Julian looked round in alarm. A palace gardener, a strong, stocky man, all belt and braces, was standing behind and above him on the towpath. With one hand the gardener was holding a bicycle. The other hand was lifted, and a finger was pointing in Julian's direction.

"Can't throw your rubbish away," the gardener insisted, "not in the river."

Julian was shocked and disappointed. It was the world's approval he was aiming for, and in this world, he was an object of concern, his presence was noted, his views and needs attended to. Instead, he was faced with a persistent and rebuking finger, a finger that oscillated like a windscreen wiper.

"There's a law about throwing rubbish in the river," the gardener went on. He was evidently not going to treat Julian's anti-social behaviour with indulgence. For one terrible moment, Julian faltered in his good intentions and he allowed the bad voice from without to smother the good voice from within.

"It's not rubbish," he snapped.

The gardener showed no sign of moving. He seemed enormous, rose like a mighty oak from the river bank. His mouth was set in determination.

"There are litter bins for rubbish," he said firmly,

"please use them."

He took a small step forward, seemed on the point of dropping his bicycle and coming down for a serious argument.

"Please," he said, the finger still oscillating.

Both men were now still, contemplating one another with eyes that wondered how they had reached this point of confrontation. Julian told himself that he could not allow the gardener to damage the developing fragility of his own self-worth. Collecting his senses, he rose to his feet and stuffed the paper into his back pocket. Attempting to master the shakiness of his voice, he mumbled an apology - anything to make this idiotic and absurd man go away. The gardener made an almost imperceptible nod of the head and, swinging his leg over the bicycle crossbar, he pedalled slowly along the river. After a few moments, he turned his head and said:

"Don't forget, son. We'll be watching you, making sure you don't get into any more trouble."

Anxious that the gardener might change his mind, come back and confront him again, Julian hurried off towards the Tiltyard. A breeze pushed at his back and helped him through the gate to the west front. Walking through the rose garden, he saw his surroundings as a child might see them for the first time. There were no associations, no ghosts. He told himself that he was, at last, alive in his own time, and there were no stones to weigh him down and tie him to the past. His head was confidently poised when he pushed open the door of the Tiltyard Restaurant and marched inside.

He stood at the sign which bade him wait, and he took in his surroundings with a sweeping glance. The restrained and dignified din bore witness to the fact that the restaurant was doing a brisk business. Susan approached with a synthetic look of welcome. She asked him to wait while she consulted her book and returned a few minutes later. As if her charge were blind, Susan stayed close to Julian's shoulder while she led him to a window-table in a far corner. It was a table for two, and it had been partly shut off from the rest of the restaurant by a curtain. Julian reckoned that McKnight wanted their meeting to be held in secrecy. Susan waved Julian to a chair.

"Mr McKnight knows you are here," she said.

He smiled his thanks and, sitting down, he tossed the diary onto the table. He settled himself in his chair and gazed at the customers.

There were four people grouped around the table to his right. An elderly man was helping a young girl through the menu. The girl hung affectionately on to his arm. The person Julian took to be the girl's mother was conversing in whispers to a man next to her. She caught Julian staring and stopped talking in mid-sentence. She looked indignant, and Julian looked away. To the left of the elderly man, three men and a woman, all about Julian's age, sat nursing a pot of tea. Beyond them, he saw that all the other tables were occupied, and waiters in striped, silk waistcoats and waitresses in black were bending like new and loving parents over their charges. Through the window, he saw gatherings of tourists wandering across the Tiltyard lawn. Others were grouped under the cedar tree. There were two gardeners by the flower beds. Their heads were bowed, and their elbows moved rhythmically while they clipped at the borders.

John McKnight materialised in the doorway that led from the kitchen. His dark suit might have been the suit he had worn thirty years previously. He scanned the tables and pulled at the cuffs of his shirt. The clinking of china and the rattle of cutlery from the kitchen followed him like a vapour trail. There were occasional and muted shouts, and each time Julian heard them, he thought the

234

sounds could so easily have been echoes from 1968, wandering around Hampton Court with other restless spirits of times past.

McKnight slowly made his way to Julian's table. He was moving in time to the piped music that weaved its way through the ebb and flow of conversation. A sudden lull in the hubbub greeted a perennial favourite - an orchestral version of *Unchained Melody*. McKnight pulled at his cuffs and occasionally stopped to bow politely to guests. This towering figure seemed to get bigger as he approached. When he eventually appeared between the curtains, the shadow of his welcoming smile lingered, but the eyes that stared at Julian were those of a sleepwalker. He was about to draw the curtains when Julian opened his attack.

"You've left your hired thugs behind?"

McKnight dropped into a chair, and the two men shared an exchange of silent insults. It briefly occurred to Julian that he and McKnight must have looked like two antagonistic chess players. A huge chasm lay between them, and from his side of the pit he heard McKnight say:

"You're a complete fool, boy. It's not my men you have to worry about."

A shiver of anxiety spread from Julian's feet to his stomach. McKnight continued with:

"But they're out there, boy; they're out there..."

Julian interrupted with a dismissive movement of the wrist.

"Those mystery men again..."

"No mystery," said McKnight quickly "and they're sure to be watching us down the barrel of a rifle now, by God. How does it feel, boy, your head in the centre of a telescopic sight, your life literally blown away at the pull of a trigger?"

Julian allowed his attention to wander while he

disconnected himself from this unwelcome image. In front of him, the young girl had twisted herself round and stood smiling at him. She did not seem put off by any imaginary danger. She looked as though she wanted to make friends. Julian felt better, re-associated himself with normality. Of course, there were no mystery men. McKnight was simply trying to frighten him.

"Give me the diary and you'll be safe," McKnight added. "Believe me, boy; if you value your miserable life, it'd be better for you."

Contemplating his response, Julian looked through the window. Formations of cumulus were passing rapidly across the sky, their shadows appearing and disappearing on the Tiltyard lawn. The world was calm with itself. The tourists were still standing and chatting under the cedar, and the sound of clipping sheers was now nearer, reassuring with its suggestion of domestic tranquillity. With words that he filled with dismissive contempt, Julian said:

"You must think I'm a fool."

Behind his steel-rimmed spectacles, McKnight's eyes opened as wide as saucers. Then he crossed his hands in front of him. Julian saw him glance at his watch.

"What do you want, boy?" he snapped. "Whatever it is, make it fucking quick. I'm a busy man."

"What do I want?" Julian said. "Isn't it you who wants something? You or your men broke into my hotel room to find something you want. Then your men took something from me on a London underground station, remember? They took a briefcase. They thought it contained a diary - a 1968 diary in fact. You know what happened in 1968, don't you, John? A woman disappeared. She worked here, didn't she? And she worked in your London office. And you know what happened a week ago? The same woman was dragged off the riverbed. And in this diary, it says it was you I saw her with that night. In this diary..."

"Diaries prove nothing," McKnight snapped. "Your word against mine."

"Then why send your men to get it?"

He looked away from John's unblinking eyes and stared through the window. The cumulus clouds had temporarily disappeared. The sunlight, shining through the window, covered the two of them like a mantle. McKnight took a deep breath.

"You really are walking around with your eyes shut, aren't you? Do you really think I'd be afraid of some diaries written thirty years ago? Do you honestly think that these would be enough to convict me of something I never did? Do you, by God? You must be an imbecile, boy."

Outside, the light dimmed, and the cloud shadow appeared again on the lawn. The spaces between the shadows were fascinating. To Julian, they seemed almost like the entrance to another and better world. This was his world, and it was a place soon to be freed from the constraints of the past.

"Yes, please," said a woman's voice.

A black-and-white uniform was poised at Julian's elbow. It was the present, now casting its own shadow over the table.

"Pot of tea - for two please, Susan," said McKnight with a charming smile.

"With milk or...?"

"With milk, Susan."

Susan noted down the order, offered a sort of curtsey and hurried away towards the kitchen.

Turning his attention back to Julian, McKnight bared his teeth in an imitation smile and stared until he was sure Susan was well out of earshot. His eyes, intense and unblinking, remained focused on Julian's, and they held his attention as surely as if he was hypnotised.

"You don't listen, do you, boy?" McKnight said. "How many times do I have to tell you it was not my men who broke into your room? Think boy, for the love of God. I tell you, I'd forgotten your miserable existence, knew nothing about these diaries until you phoned me. How could I have possibly known about you then?"

Julian shook his head, tried to look blank and vaguely helpful. He parted his lips to speak. He intended to say that he had used Dick, had given him the information that might be passed on. But McKnight interrupted before Julian could enjoy the pleasure of telling him he had been set up.

"I know who broke in to your room. I expect you want to know too, don't you, boy?"

From somewhere in the tea-room a phone rang. In this short interruption, Julian was aware of a huge wave of uncertainty that had risen up in front of him. He kept his hand firmly on the diary and inhaled deeply. He somehow knew that if he just kept breathing in and out slowly, he would be all right. McKnight said:

"You can answer that one yourself, boy. Think, for the love of God. Who knew about your damned diaries before I did? Think. Who was it?"

Julian leaned back and tried to relax, but the wave of uncertainty had now broken over him. It had never before occurred to him that Dick himself would break in to his hotel, and for the moment Julian refused to entertain the idea. That Dick and Blodwin were somehow responsible for searching his room was so absurd that Julian easily dismissed it as another of McKnight's attempts to throw him off the track.

On Julian's left, the three men and the woman were ordering another pot of tea. Through the din, he recognised a familiar tune. It was the tune he had taken from the air, the same tune, unknown and unnamed, that had been tracking him since his return to England. The music was faint, an echo of some past life, and it came and went with the babble of voices in the tea-room. Occasionally, it went out of earshot but it always came back - an association with some point in the past that Julian could put in neither place nor time.

"If you won't tell me, perhaps you'll find that you can tell the police then," Julian said. "They'll also want to know why I wrote in my diary that you struck Kathy on the night she disappeared. The papers said she was last seen leaving the office in London on the night of 28 November. This is untrue. *You* saw her and so did I. The only difference is that *you* struck her and *I* didn't. Why did you strike her, John?"

Even as he asked the question, Julian felt his head draw back in alarm, and heard his voice falling into the bottomless pit that lay between them. A sudden lull in the conversation from the tea-room allowed Julian to hear other voices; the dark and seductive voices that lived in his own brain. Perhaps the idea that Dick had tried to steal the diary was not so absurd. Why had Blodwin kept him talking on the lawn in front of her house? These voices of doubt were speaking so loudly that he could only hear McKnight's voice as if from far away.

"My feeling is that the police've better things to do than bother about a disappearance that happened thirty years ago."

"Don't you believe it," Julian said. "If they're given a lead, then I'm sure they'll follow it up extremely thoroughly."

"So, you want money for the diary, do you, boy? Is that it? Yes, yes, of course it is. I know, I know. Indeed, boy, you're a sad case, by God. I've listened to your crazy and sick stories. Now let me tell you a story of my own. Maybe you'll realise what you've been dealing with."

Julian became aware of a soft tapping somewhere close at hand, but he did not want to look away from McKnight's face. Their eyes were locked together like the antlers of rutting deer. McKnight leaned forward, placed his elbows on the table and folded his hands under his chin.

"How much do you know about Northern Ireland, boy? How much do you know about being born a second-class citizen? How would you feel if you were considered a danger to the state, of being less deserving of a job than others, of being deliberately excluded from any position of power and influence?"

Julian shook his head. The conversation was going into areas over which he had no real understanding and no real control. Worse still, the soft tapping continued. He became aware that the noise was coming from under the table. His leg was shaking uncontrollably, and his heel was tapping against the carpet.

"We formed a group, back in the sixties," McKnight was saying. "We were impatient with our representatives, people who resorted to the politics of ineffectual complaint, monotonous repetition of familiar grievances. We wanted more than the civil rights movement, more than Bernadette bloody Devlin and those ridiculous peace marches. What we wanted was hard action, by God, and we wanted it now."

As if to add urgency to his words, McKnight accompanied them by rapping his knuckles on the table.

"Yes, we were extreme," McKnight said. "If you weren't for us you were against us, it was as simple as that. Most of us are still out there, boy, out there sleeping, as it were. Sleeping or not, they won't let a little prick like you get in their way, let me tell you."

"And who," Julian asked, "do you mean by we?"

"In 1968? All of us who were unhappy with the

vacillations and inactivity of the IRA, all of us who wanted battle and were ready for it. But even as we were preparing, events were developing by themselves. There were so many disparate elements among us; Republicans, Socialists, and Marxists, trade unionists, students...plenty of young but hard-line students. You remember how it was?"

Julian nodded but he doubted whether he had ever really understood those words, often spoken by Dick, *If you aren't with us, you're against us*. Worse, a memory resurfaced. It was the memory of McKnight and Dick behaving furtively in the shadows of the cedar tree on the Tiltyard lawn. McKnight's revelations were now casting their own shadow on the path Julian had planned for himself.

"We soon realised," McKnight said, "that we'd be better fighting together, fighting behind one banner."

"Which was?"

"The Provisionals, boy, the Provisionals. But all that happened a little later."

McKnight paused but his eyes, which never left Julian's face, appeared to be evaluating the effect of his story. Apparently satisfied that this had been absorbed, its full meaning digested, McKnight picked up the threads of history.

"In 1968, we needed money and we needed to make it ourselves. What I did, my little game here, was part of something much bigger, a bigger movement, a swell of activity that has since outgrown either of us, boy. At least we were there at the beginning..."

McKnight's proudly shining eyes seemed to imply a condemnation of all those who had not been part of this bigger movement, a movement which clearly ennobled him, enriched his memories. Julian felt ill with a kind of angry faintness.

"And Kathy's mistake," he muttered, "was that she

found out about it."

"Kathy's mistake was that she wouldn't listen to reason. We tried to convince her that she should back off, but what a good southern girl she was, boy. Had no time for extremists of any colour."

Suddenly exhausted, Julian had the distinct impression of being in the presence of something evil. The faintness had given way to a dreamlike state of insecurity, a state he had never before experienced and in which even the strongest part of him seemed ineffectual. This was the moment when everything slipped out of his grasp. He heard himself say in a pained voice:

"So, you had her followed..., made threatening calls to her..."

"She didn't back off and so I paid her a visit."

Julian suffered a moment of dizziness. He grasped the diary between his fingers, never took his hand from it. It was the only way he knew to hide from McKnight the fact that his hand was shaking in time to his leg.

"We argued," McKnight said. "And not for the first time, let me tell you. She was a strong woman, boy; and much too good for a little English prick like you."

McKnight's tone contrasted so strongly with the sweet smile which accompanied these words that Julian was left floundering, unsure how to react.

"I wanted to know," McKnight continued, "what she'd told the police. I had to know if she'd given them any names. She just laughed at me, and I slapped her, too hard. I knocked her unconscious and I left."

"So, you did kill her," Julian whispered.

"No, boy," McKnight said with finality. "I needed her alive, don't you see? I had to find out what she told the police, you understand? Had she given them any names? I had to know, and so I went back. It must've been a couple of hours later. I climbed in through her

242

window but someone had got there before me, had left a bunch of roses; but she had gone, forever as it turned out."

His staring eyes faltered and their gaze momentarily dropped to the table top. For one brief moment, Julian thought that McKnight was going to burst into tears. His tone then changed from the dictatorial to the confessional.

"We all thought she'd gone into hiding. So, we never knew what she had told the police, never knew which of us was in danger. It was a difficult time, I can tell you, boy. At that point, sleeper cells were being set up all over the UK. When the Provos took over I was removed, told to lead a life cleaner than a whistle, keep out of trouble and away from the law. But they are still there, boy, still there. They broke into your hotel room. They followed you to London, and they are watching us - now."

At this point, Julian felt his convictions fade away to nothing. Not even the shadow of a plan remained to prevent the fear from vibrating inside him.

"We thought we were safe," McKnight said, "but then, Kathy's body was found, threatening to rake up the whole business. These sleepers could not allow this to happen. Many of them have spent years establishing themselves in positions of power, of respectability in English society, just waiting to be woken up as it were. To make matters worse, along comes a little prick and his diary, threatening to stir things up even further. Your diary must be destroyed. But you have the opportunity now. Give it to me, boy, and we will let you go back to Italy. Of course, you can refuse. If you do, you are a dead man."

The statement was so preposterous that Julian backed away from McKnight, put as much distance as he could from the man and his suggestions. Julian's mind was in a whirl. Everything had disappeared, everything except his strong sense of life and the need to preserve it. McKnight himself remained silent for a while and then with a polite smile and a movement of his head towards the diary, he said:

"Just give me the diary, boy."

These words were spoken in such a gentle, almost tender tone that Julian found himself too weak, too sick and faint to do anything other than what he was told. He pushed at the carpet with his heels, forgetting himself and the diary. McKnight calmly reached over the table and picked it up. For some moments, his face became as still as a mask while he flicked impatiently through the pages.

"You really should mind your own fucking business, boy," he muttered. "And if I were you, I would go back..."

McKnight interrupted himself. His mouth dropped open; he surged to his feet and bent over the table.

"Where are they?" he whispered.

Julian sat and watched him. Every instinct screamed for him to run while he had the chance. He had no strength left, no strength to get up, and no strength even to think. He vaguely heard a terrible groan come from McKnight's lips.

"You have lied to me," he said between clenched teeth. "I won't let you fucking lie to me..."

He put out a hand to grab Julian. Julian jumped to his feet but McKnight thrust him back into the chair. He loomed over Julian, his body rigid.

"Shit," he spat out, "where the fuck are they? What've you done with them?"

From the corner of his eye, Julian saw the three men and the woman rise quickly from their seats. There was a rustle as the curtain drew back. One of the men was holding a brown envelope and two pages in his hand.

"Are you looking for these, sir?"

McKnight spun round. His face had gone a sort of purple colour. Then, he put a fist into the small of his back and screwed up his eyes. Julian heard a soft explosion of pain come from between his lips. The man at the curtain took a step closer and put the pages on the table.

"These must be the pages you're looking for sir," he said, "28 November, 1968. Am I right?"

The new arrival slipped his hand into an inside pocket and drew out a card.

"Detective Inspector Luff, sir. Metropolitan Police."

At that moment, the waitress arrived with the tea. She bustled through the curtain with the busyness of a black bird. Lowering the tray on the table, she arranged the pot, the cups, and the saucers neatly in front of the group. McKnight had lowered his head. He was whispering to himself and loosening the top button of his shirt. The inspector had a hand on McKnight's elbow and was smiling warmly as the waitress finished her routine. With a clink of tea-spoons, she made a sound of satisfaction, curtseyed, and bustled away again. Luff took an audible breath.

"So, sir," he said, "we'd like you to accompany us to the station. We would warn you that you are not under arrest, but we'd like to ask you questions concerning the disappearance of Kathleen McCullagh on 28 November 1968."

McKnight had regained some composure. He was slowly shaking his head. Then he pointed a finger at Julian's chest.

"This man was trying to blackmail me," he said. "He's had a grudge against me for years."

Then, looking directly at Julian, McKnight whispered:

"You've just signed my death sentence."

Luff tugged at McKnight's arm.

"We'll see to all that, sir."

Then, Luff indicated his colleagues for the first time.

"If you could just go with these officers, sir. We would appreciate it."

With something approaching anger, McKnight said:

"And I want to bring charges against this man. He was blackmailing me."

Luff tugged at McKnight's arm. When the Detective Inspector spoke again, his voice was edged with hardness.

"I said we'll see to that."

McKnight massaged his forehead with his fingers. Julian noticed the well-manicured nails, but the finger joints were crooked and swollen. He vaguely registered that McKnight must have been suffering from arthritis. The pain in his back had somehow deflated him. His face was ashen, and he looked beaten and tired. A strand of his yellow hair had peeled itself from his head and now hung untidily over the ear. It was absurd but Julian realised he felt sorry for him. McKnight opened his lips as though he wanted to speak, but his eyes just stared out towards the Tiltyard lawns. For a few seconds, there was silence.

The next thing Julian noticed was the gardener, close up to the window. Julian thought that he might be urinating against the glass or that he was a pervert, showing himself off to the nice little girl sitting with her grandfather. He then noted a ripple of agitation from inside the restaurant, and then there was a heave, a collective intake of fearful breath, and someone cried out:

"Oh my God, he's got a gun.... Oh my God..."

The voice belonged to an American woman. She was upright and rigid. Her hands were covering her face, and her eyes were as round as moons. But what startled

Julian was that these moons appeared to be staring at him. From the surrounding tables, other customers had raised their heads from the confines of their private worlds and were looking in his direction. He was about to mutter something to the effect that he did not have a gun when there was a flash and two muted thumps.

At this point, the little girl broke free from her grandfather, leaned forward and let out a continuous and ear-splitting scream. It seemed to Julian that the scream released the restaurant clientele from civil restraint, and they appeared gripped by a sort of collective madness. The ripple of agitation had developed first into a confused swell, followed by a rapid descent into uproar. Some people had already thrown themselves flat on the floor while others were cowering under tables, their arms wrapped over their heads. Several other people screamed.

Julian span round towards the flash. The glass window of the restaurant appeared to have shattered, and the urinating man had disintegrated, his body unclear and fragile behind an infinity of web-like cracks in the glass. Only his head was clearly visible, apparently precariously balanced on a splintered cobweb of glass. Julian closed his eyes, squeezed them as though to clear them of a film of tears. When he opened his eyes, the balanced head had gone, and McKnight was staggering in his direction, seemed to be on the point of lunging at him again. Julian was bracing himself for the impact, when McKnight fell to his knees, his chin smashing the edge of the table. He remained still for several seconds and then he slowly tipped towards the floor. It was then that Julian saw the two, red holes neatly drilled beside the initialled pocket of McKnight's shirt. His dead weight appeared to lose balance and fell sideways, its head striking the corner tiles with a sickening crack.

23

"Now," said Inspector Luff, "we'd like you to start from the beginning again, if you don't mind, sir. Just tell us what happened - one more time."

"The beginning? Again?"

"Yes, sir, the beginning again. That's easy enough, isn't it? Just start from the beginning again."

"It was on 3 September that I..."

Luff interrupted with a languid gesture of dismissal, shook his head and leaned over the table that separated him from Julian. Luff's ears were attached to his head at different levels, but the most remarkable feature of the face was the long forehead, and the two parallel folds of skin that divided it.

"No, no, the beginning," Luff said, "right from the beginning - 28 November, 1968. You know, the beginning, for the sake of our friend here."

Our friend was a sinister figure, who had never been introduced. He was little more than a grey suit, pulled and pinned into shape for the purpose of window display. This impression of stasis was disturbed by the man's head, which fell continuously forward and back so that he seemed to be on the point of dropping off to sleep. Only when Julian looked closely did he notice that the upturned eyes, shining balls of intelligent light, were staring straight at him.

Julian shifted and stabilised his backside. The seat was made of brown, lacquered wood, and it creaked and groaned under his constant fidgeting. Luff said:

"We just need to establish the facts, Mr Everet, sir. For our friends from the anti-terrorist squad. You understand, don't you, sir? The connection with the IRA is of the utmost importance to them."

Julian looked around the interview room. It matched the new man's suit. The walls had been glossed dark grey to shoulder height, with a lighter grey above it. At first sight, the surfaces were as smooth as the gloss suggested, but on closer inspection, he saw that they were rough and pitted. Apart from the table and chairs, the only other notable object in the room was a dim light hanging from the high, arched ceiling. There were no windows in the walls, and Julian imagined that the dim light burned dimly for twenty-four hours, indifferent to whether it was night or day.

"You might begin by telling us," Luff said, "what you saw that night in 1968."

From where Julian sat, the light from the lamp threw the lower half of Luff's face into shadow. Julian was unable to clearly see the movement of the man's mouth, and he wondered whether it was Luff who spoke or whether he was a ventriloquist's dummy.

"It is a long time ago, Mr Everet, but tell us what you saw on the night of 28 November."

It was a long time ago. But since the moment he stepped into the interview room, Julian had been in a timeless zone where past, present and future were bound together. From outside in the corridor came the sound of knocking. Julian thought it might be brooms or mops

249

banging against the walls, but he did not know whether it was time to go home, or time to start the day.

"I remember seeing McKnight," he said. "I remember that he struck her."

"And you were standing in the street?"

"Yes."

"How far away from the window?"

"About twenty yards."

"And it was dark, Mr Everet, wasn't it?"

"Yes."

Luff pulled some papers from a folder and suspended them over the desk, his long fingers pinching the papers at the top.

"And we have the testimony of one witness. The lady who saw you, Mr Everet, the lady with the dog. She said it was a foggy night."

Luff scanned the page in front of him.

"She told the investigating officer at the time that the night of 28 November was a real pea-souper."

He looked at Julian reflectively for some seconds. Then, he leaned back in his chair and, holding the page at arm's length, he contemplated the contents.

"And apparently the river was dangerously high."

Short and sharp memories jostled for space in Julian's consciousness. He drew in his breath so quickly that Luff turned his eyes from the page and looked straight at him.

"A lot of rain that year," Luff said. "That's what it says here. But we'll come back to that."

The inspector was running his finger from his nose, up his long forehead and down again. He rested his finger on his lips. It looked as if he had come to a decision.

"The point is this, Julian. Thirty years ago, on a dark and foggy night, you think you saw someone strike Miss McCullagh. And you say you saw all this at a distance of thirty yards. You say you saw it through a closed window - silhouettes on the wall, in fact. Did you think that this would be enough to convince a jury? Did you think this would be enough to convict the man?"

"Twenty yards actually," Julian said.

Luff steepled his hands and rested his chin on the point where his fingers met. Thirty seconds passed - maybe a minute. The silence between the two men was broken only by the tapping of the mops or brooms against the walls outside. When Luff spoke again, his tone was absent minded, but not unsympathetic.

"Look, Julian. I'd like to help you and I'd like to get to the bottom of all this. But what I want personally is unimportant. In the final analysis, there's something at stake much bigger than whether it was twenty yards or thirty."

Luff glanced at the terrorist man and then lowered his hands. He spread them on the desk in front of him. He appeared to be studying them.

"To be brutally frank, I'm sure your story would never have stood a cat in hell's chance in a court of law. Sorry."

Julian looked expectantly at the inspector and saw the two folds of skin draw together.

"Look at it from the point of view of a juror," Luff said. "Foggy, dark and a long time ago, but the most relevant thing is that we can't establish the cause of death. Maybe she was struck, maybe not, but the fact is, Julian, the bones are too far gone to produce anything valuable. We just don't know *what* killed her. And if we don't know *what* killed her, we'll have a rare old job finding out *who* killed her - supposing she was killed. Understand?"

Julian nodded weakly.

"Yes, but..."

Luff lifted his hand, dipped it into the top pocket of

his jacket and extracted a pen. He flipped it back and forth in his fingers.

"No buts, Julian," he said. "It could've been an accident. As I told you, the river was high and flowing fast and dangerous. Perhaps she went for a walk and slipped. Perhaps she decided to take her own life. We just don't know. Frankly, we'll never know. Apart from you, nobody's ever reported seeing her that night. For all practical purposes, when she left work that evening, she could've just vanished into thin air."

Julian sighed and then made a clicking noise with his mouth.

"But McKnight was there and he had a motive," Julian said with all the incredulity he could muster. "She was threatening to expose him. He could've..."

Luff waved a deprecatory hand.

"Yes, yes. We know all about that too. Mr King has always kept to that aspect of his story. He told us McKnight had his hand in the till. But did he? We need witnesses, Julian. We need witnesses who are prepared to come forward and swear, after thirty years, that McKnight was a thief. The problem is, Julian, that it's all history."

"But history was recorded in my diary," Julian burst out, "and he tried to take it from..."

He was interrupted by a loud clatter. Luff had allowed the pen to slip from his fingers and fall to the table.

"And you don't have any evidence of this either, do you?" Luff said. "Where are your witnesses? Someone mugged you on a London underground station. It happens all the time. And who can say that this person was in the pay of John McKnight or of anybody else for that matter?"

Luff paused for several seconds. Then he raised his eyebrows and said:

"This is the problem. There's nobody around now to accuse McKnight of anything he might've done in 1968. Most of the waiters are dead and the ones that aren't? Well, even if we managed to find them, the chances that they would admit to anything are nil. Don't forget, they were - apparently - involved too. The only person who could really help is Mrs Croucher, but she died twenty-five years ago." He let out a long sigh. "Time does move on, Julian - for most of us."

Julian leaned forward and put his head in his hands.

"I suppose so," he mumbled. "Have we reached an age when our friends fall away as readily as old teeth?"

"That," said Luff, "might not have been the case, had you come to us earlier."

Julian looked up and, watching the policeman's face, he tried to read what was behind it. The inspector's eyes had a distinct glint but Julian guessed that the man's words and expression were sympathetic rather than accusatory. He shuffled on the chair and tried to find a comfortable spot for his backside. Shrugging his shoulders, he felt the shirt peel away from the sweat that was rolling down from his armpits. When he spoke again, he was surprised to hear the slow pace - the calm.

"So, there's no evidence McKnight had a motive for any misdeeds. There's no proof that it was him I saw. In fact, if I understand everything correctly, there's no evidence to suggest he was involved in anything at all."

"That," said Luff, "is a pretty accurate summary."

"So why was he shot, then?"

Luff shook his head and then put his hands together and clasped them as if he was praying.

"We'll probably never know. We can only speculate. All the evidence we have is circumstantial - impossible to prove in a court. Let my friend here fill you in."

The terrorist man raised his head and then let it drop again. He leaned forward.

"All we know for certain, Mr Everet," he said, "is that there is indeed someone out there as McKnight told you. And they were efficient enough to arrange for a hit man, to have him removed. Why did they do this?"

Expecting the man to answer his own question, Julian stared stupidly until an uncomfortably extended silence suggested that the terrorist man was waiting for him to say something.

"He did mention the IRA. I already explained..."

"Exactly," the terrorist man said. "Let's look at the facts before we begin our speculations, shall we? There's certainly some credence to what he told you. Let's look first at the civil rights movement in Northern Ireland in 1968. What do we know about it?"

The terrorist man raised his eyebrows and started anew and with deliberation.

"This was not a party but a group wide enough to embrace every anti-Unionist element in the land. You'd be wrong in thinking that the IRA were the dominant force in this movement. It was just one component amongst many. At this point the IRA was essentially Marxist and led from the south of Ireland. Yes, there were plenty of young extremists at that time and they were strongly wedded to the idealistic notion that working-class links could be forged across sectarian lines. Do you know any Marxists, Mr Everet?"

Before Julian could answer, the man said:

"Of course, you do. If you are not for them you are against them, as you know. But let's move on, shall we?"

The terrorist man paused with a smile that seemed to involve Julian in a conspiracy of some kind. He continued:

"Many of these extremists were unhappy with this direction of fanciful reconciliation. They eventually dismissed what they saw as unrealistic notions and prepared themselves for battle. Among these were the young and idealistic students we already know about, don't we, Mr Everet? These are facts, and you can find them in any history book. And this is where McKnight and Duncan-Smith might come into the picture. This is where we begin speculating."

At the mention of these familiar names, Julian's face twitched grimly and he was moved to whisper:

"McKnight and Dick were in the IRA?"

"We know that disenchanted Catholics like McKnight and hard-line Marxists like Duncan-Smith were sent to England to help in the setting up of sleeper cells, terrorist groups who were willing and able to help the Catholic cause. At that stage, they were mere pawns, forced to resort to petty crime in order to finance a fledgling organisation. Hence McKnight's hypothetical little game in the restaurant - hypothetical you understand, Mr Everet. We can only assume he was part of this movement, only assume he was one of the pawns and acting on orders..."

A thump, perhaps of mop against door, temporarily silenced the man. He continued in a changed tone:

"These activities were merely a prelude to the fateful split in 1969 when the Provisional IRA came into being. But for about one year, there were many groups like McKnight's hypothetical group and they were loosely united in a common cause. We also know that when the Provisionals cut their links with the Official IRA, most of these small groups and their prominent members cast in their lot with the Provisionals. But let's be clear. If McKnight was involved in any of this, he was not a big fish, not one of the leaders."

"So, what did Kathy have to do with it all?" Julian interrupted.

"Let's look at the facts again, shall we? In the summer of 1968, the police received a complaint from

Miss McCullagh that she was being followed by persons unknown. She later told police that she was receiving telephone calls, obscene calls actually, from unknown people. On investigating these complaints, the police at that time discovered that she had stumbled on certain illegal activities. Before she could give any details at all, she disappeared. And this, Mr Everet, is where facts end, and speculations begin."

As if to emphasise the point, the terrorist man leaned forward and brought the flat of his hand hard down on the table.

"And," he continued, "this is where you come into the picture. The reappearance of Miss McCullagh and your return to England at this time shuffled the cards again, so to speak, and brought the whole business back to the present. McKnight must've been terrified. He would've known that under no circumstances would the leaders of the Provisionals in England allow him to be interrogated. The slightest possibility that, under pressure, he would've exposed them was unthinkable. In this very real sense, McKnight had been living with a death sentence for thirty years. But I repeat, we are only speculating, Mr Everet, just hypothesising."

The terrorist man allowed himself a melancholy smile.

"A most frightful situation to be in," he said, and then, with the air of one who was prepared to hear a lie, he added, "don't you think so, Mr Everet?"

Julian was about to say that McKnight deserved his fate, that a thirty-year sentence was too good for him, but the terrorist man was still busy building his speculations.

"We suppose that Miss McCullagh warned McKnight to stop his activities. We suppose that he tried to frighten her off by various means. She refused. McKnight visited her and killed her. He probably didn't mean to kill her, but McKnight must've gone back to the flat, and found he had a dead body to deal with. A most unfortunate situation for him because there was this burning question for him and his leaders that would forever remain unanswered. That question was, how much information had Kathleen given to the police? Had she given the police any names?"

The almost playful tone of the words contrasted strongly with the man's serious expression. Then he opened his arms and turned his palms upwards in the manner of a Buddha.

"With Miss McCullagh dead, they would never know."

He closed his arms and let his palms return slowly to the table, and his head followed as though it was connected to his hands by a piece of string.

"But let's go back to that fateful night in 1968," he said. "McKnight had a dead body on his hands - another frightful dilemma for him, don't you agree, Mr Everet?"

Julian blinked, stared dumbly and lightly shook his head.

"Well," said the terrorist man, "look at it from his point of view. The presence of a dead body would've meant a murder investigation. A murder investigation would, sooner or later, have involved McKnight. This, in turn, would've led to our questioning of him, and questioning of him would've led to the bigger fish - a situation which these fish, the leaders of the Provisionals in England, could never and can never permit. McKnight was the man who knew too much, you see? Disappearance for Miss McCullagh was the only real solution for him. So, what do you think he did next? What would you have done, Mr Everet?"

Julian's eyes were now as dry as his mouth but blinked and blinked again.

"I'd have tied weights to her body and thrown it in

the river, wouldn't you? With no body, no apparent motive, and no murder weapon, there could never be any suspects. Miss McCullagh would've taken her secrets to the bottom of the river. But I can only repeat that this is just hypothesis, you understand? Just hypothesis, Mr Everet."

Julian nodded weakly.

"And do you believe that this is what happened?"

"As I said," the terrorist man went on, "we can only speculate. So, shall we continue?"

He leaned back in his chair and settled himself comfortably before going on.

"In order to keep an eye on their own ticking time-bomb, the Provisionals had to keep an even more watchful eye on McKnight. Of course, they wanted your diaries. Any evidence, however flimsy, that might've brought McKnight to the attention of the police, would put their own position in danger. Under no circumstances could they allow McKnight to be interrogated. They had you constantly followed as you're probably aware. McKnight knew this, and the thought must've frightened the wits out of him. And the irony, the blessed irony is that your diaries are useless as evidence. Nobody would've been convicted of anything on the basis of the ravings of a lovesick youth with a grudge against his employer. And the photograph? The photograph proves nothing. Why shouldn't Miss McCullagh and McKnight have conversed on the concourse of Waterloo Station? But it was the idea of the diaries that put McKnight in danger. Implication in her disappearance was enough to have him killed, and he knew it. They must've been watching events closely. They must've been following the both of you. When you had your meeting yesterday, McKnight's fate was in the balance, but when the police appeared on the scene, his fate was sealed. But all this is only speculation. There is no solid evidence. The hit man escaped. We can prove nothing."

"So," Julian said, prompted back into life, "perhaps McKnight was telling me the truth when he said he didn't break in to my room?"

"Absolutely. Enter your idealistic Marxist friend, Richard Duncan-Smith. We've had him checked out. It seems that, until now, he has led a life of complete respectability. We wanted to bring him in for questioning, but unfortunately, my men tell me that Duncan-Smith's disappeared as completely as Miss McCullagh. If we don't find him, the Provisionals will kill him. It's a simple as that. We'll almost certainly never see him again. He's a danger to them in the same way that McKnight was a danger. It's highly likely that Duncan-Smith was responsible for the break-in at your hotel. He arranged to have you followed. The man on the train was certainly one of his. Duncan-Smith wanted to see the diary too. He had to know whether or not its contents would involve McKnight in a murder enquiry. Above all, Duncan-Smith had to know whether he too was in danger."

"What about his wife? Was she a party to all this?"

"Highly unlikely. She was part of his cover, part of his role as a respected and respectable family man. I expect she guessed what was going on, who she was married to, but what could she do? It must've been a hell on earth for her."

"So why," Julian asked, "didn't Dick just finish me off?"

"Too dangerous. Dead bodies are difficult to ignore. Dead bodies mean an investigation, the very thing he wanted to avoid."

At this point Detective Inspector Luff decided to break in to the conversation.

"Of course, much of all this could've been avoided

too, had you come to us earlier. We'd like to know why you waited thirty years before contacting us. And we'd like to know why you didn't come forward at the time."

Sweat was now rolling down Julian's back. It was icy-cold to the skin. He tried to speak slowly, to hide the tremor that lived in his voice.

"Because," he said, "I felt that I would've been under suspicion."

"Of what?"

"Oh, I don't know. I was seen outside her house."

"Acting strangely, apparently," Luff said.

"Umm."

"But what was there to be afraid of? Nobody ever said you were implicated in any way. It was just a line of inquiry we wanted to eliminate at the time."

To Julian, it seemed to be getting hot in the room, excessively hot and airless. He struggled to keep calm. He let his hands slide along the seat of the chair, trying desperately not to grip at it. His palms were hot and clammy, and his shoulders were pressing against the chair back as if he was escaping from a punch.

"I was ashamed," Julian said, "of my obsession, that I was unable to speak to her, ashamed that I couldn't be a man."

"You were only eighteen," Luff said.

Beads of perspiration burst out on Julian's forehead.

"I was infatuated. I followed her sometimes. And I called her too."

"Yes, we know about the calls…"

"No," Julian snapped, "not the obscene calls. That wasn't me. I just rang her. It gave me satisfaction to hear her - just breathing."

"I see," Luff said, directing his words at the door behind Julian. "And what did you do after you were seen that night. You thought you saw McKnight striking her. And then?"

"I just ran away."

"You went back to London?"

"Yes."

"And?"

"When I found out that Kathy was missing and I realised I was the so-called mysterious prowler, I was terrified that I might be connected in some way with her disappearance."

"So, you decided to keep quiet all these years," Luff said. "You were in Italy, you say?"

"Yes."

"So, what made you come back at this time?"

"I needed to think things through."

"What things?"

"My wife left me. I wanted time to myself to think about my next move."

"And you came back two days after the remains were pulled from the river."

"Yes."

"Why didn't you come to us immediately?"

"Same reasons as before," Julian said. "Guilt, and fear that I might be in trouble."

"So why the phone call yesterday? Why did you arrange this rather elaborate set-up?"

"Change of heart," Julian said. "And the conviction - yes, the certainty that I knew who was responsible for Kathy's disappearance."

The room felt suddenly claustrophobic. Julian's heart was racing, and his face was hot and felt impossibly flushed. The grey walls made him feel nauseous. From somewhere far away a telephone rang.

"The point is," Julian said, "that McKnight wanted the diary. He nearly killed me, for God's sake. I knew I'd never be safe while I had it. I wanted you to see for yourself how important it was for him. I wanted to provide you with evidence that he was desperate to get

261

his hands on it."

Luff turned the pages he was holding and placed them on the table.

"The diaries are interesting," he said, "but, as our friend here told you, they'd hardly constitute evidence in a court of law. It's impossible to ascertain on exactly what day they were written. And they could so easily be the fabrications of a man with a grudge against his employer. McKnight humiliated you, didn't he?"

Luff cocked his head and looked at Julian quizzically. Julian resisted the temptation to wipe at his forehead. He could feel a bead of sweat rolling down his right temple.

"Tell us," Luff continued, "why exactly did he kick you out of the cafeteria?"

"I was making a bit of money on the side."

Luff let out a long sigh and shook his head.

"Doesn't do to get caught with your hand in the till," he said. "Getting caught is the crime, Julian."

Luff replaced the papers in the folder. He leaned forward and placed his hands on his knees.

"But your biggest crime is that you've been living in an enclosed world with your eyes closed. It's time you woke up, Mr Everet, sir. Time to start living again, if I may say so."

Julian stared at him. The realisation came at a slow, leisurely pace, and with a strange sort of peace. Perhaps, he thought, it was a peace born from tiredness. His eyes felt sore, and his head was singing. But the truth was there. The police were going to let him go. Luff got slowly to his feet.

"Just make sure we have your details, sir. In case we need to contact you."

Julian stretched his legs in front of him and pushed himself to his feet. He stood awkwardly in front of the inspector, unsure whether it was the "done thing" to shake a policeman's hand.

"There's one other thing, if you don't mind, Mr Everet, sir..."

Luff put out an arm, palm downwards, and he waved Julian back in his seat as though patting an imaginary child on the head.

"Obstructing the police with their enquiries is a very serious business."

He paused when the door clicked and another blue uniform appeared from the world outside. He was wearing white plastic gloves, and Julian wondered whether this was the cleaner, the owner of the mop that had been constantly banging the walls.

"We may take action," Luff said, "and we may not. But the fact remains that had you contacted us before, you may've prevented the murder of McKnight, and we may've been able to interrogate him. Just let this officer know where you are in case we change our minds."

Luff indicated the man with the gloves. He had moved a couple of steps towards Julian and he had produced something from his jacket pocket, was holding it tightly in his palm.

"And there's one last thing, Mr Everet."

There was the bare outline of a smile on Luff's face. The terrorist man had been examining his fingernails He looked up and those pin pricks of light were suddenly like spotlights trained on Julian's face.

"We need a swab if you don't mind," Luff said. "Your saliva, sir. Nothing to worry about. We're doing DNA tests, you understand?"

The man with the white gloves took one step nearer, opened his palm to reveal a small glass container.

"It's those roses," Luff said. "We've always been concerned about those roses. The person who put them there must have pricked his finger and left a blood stain on one of Miss McCullagh's record. One of my favourites actually, by Davy Cohen. Perhaps you know it, sir?"

Julian raised his head as a shadow closed over him. Against the shadow the surgical gloves and the swab were white and threatening.

"Relax, sir. It's not a poison," Luff said. "It's just another line of enquiry we want to eliminate, you understand? So, if you don't mind, Julian…"

24

10 September

It was in the afternoon of 10 September 1998 that Kathy said goodbye for the last time. She simply blew away in the wind while he was enjoying the view from the cliff. He had left Dover town centre, had climbed up the cliff to read again the story in the newspaper. The headline read: *Prominent businessman in double murder mystery*. There were no revelations in the article. There was talk of old enmities, business feuds and love, and tentative connections were made to the dredging up of Kathleen McCullagh's bones from the riverbed. Kathy's face was there with McKnight's on the front page. There was no mention of Julian but he knew they would be coming for him.

He set off down the cliff and let the paper go on the way. One minute it was in his hand, and the next minute it was gone. It was while he was walking past the gun emplacement that he saw the three men trudging up the cliff towards him. He had been expecting visitors for the past two days. At last, there they were. He recognised

Luff by his long forehead and ears. Even at a distance of a hundred yards, they gave his face an odd and unbalanced quality. One hundred yards was all that remained of life, Julian thought, a tiny stretch of chalky path between him, his past, his crime, and his punishment. Nothing else mattered now. History had never really gone away.

Julian fumbled in the back pocket of his jeans, collected the remains of the diary-page he had stuffed there when confronted by the gardener. It was time to let it go.

Julian had gradually and efficiently reduced the page to tiny bits of torn paper and he extracted it when Luff and his men were about fifty yards away. Julian sidled closer to the edge of the cliff, turned and threw the paper into the wind. For a moment, the paper hung in the air like confetti before dispersing and disappearing from view.

Julian glanced over his shoulder. Luff was closer and he was holding one arm in front of him as though he was calming the traffic. Julian edged sideways, his foot sliding on the loose chalk. He heard Luff cry out but his words were carried off by the wind that was blowing from the south.

Julian turned his face to the sea and to the mist that was now thickening. He received the odd notion that it was his own vapour trail, thirty years of it that was now gathering to engulf him. He moved towards it, felt his foot step into the emptiness. At precisely that moment, he recalled the song which had been following him for seven days. It was the melody that came first. He apparently plucked it from the mist itself. As the sun began to set over the channel, Julian started to whistle the tune. Then he whispered the words into the twilight wind.

"I just heard her say goodbye, goodbye,"

What was the year of the song?

"I'll never know your reasons why,"

This song from empty days.

"My tears can't drown those blows,"

It was 1968, and it was Kathy's favourite song.

"It's just the way life goes,"

He, the poor singer, had played and sung it to her…

"It's just the way life goes,"

On the night she died.

"I know we'll meet again on high,"

The title? He sang it out loud and stepped into the strengthening breeze.

"But I just heard her say goodbye, goodbye."

25

6.00 a.m. I see it all so clearly now. Yesterday evening was meant to be. I was blessed with one hour of complete happiness. One hour of happiness is better than a lifetime alone. He had left the window open, and I returned to look after you. I had you to myself. You were mine, all mine! You were so still and peaceful. You lay there, next to my roses, on the floor. You were like a sleeping child. Hardly a breath came from you to disturb the stillness of the night. I simply stared at you. How could he have raised his hand - the hand that dealt such a cruel blow?

I could see you were calm with me there beside you. I knew all the time you were waiting for me. We are meant for each other. I played your song for you - the one by Davy Cohen. His singing will never be done. You and this night will last forever. Such perfection should never be ruined by the passing of time. You will never grow old. There was no other way but death for you, painless death. I wrapped my fingers around your neck and squeezed, but

gently, so as not to hurt you. I squeezed until you breathed no more. Now, you will wait for me and I'll wait for you until my days are done.

I said: "Come with me my love."

I held your lifeless body in my arms. I carried you down there to the garden that dips to the river, the river that flows to the sea.

I said: "Draw closer my sweet."

You came to death with me - down there to forever, down there to the sea. Now we are lover and lover and on your last night, you were given to me. I kissed your cold and lifeless lips and I laid you on the water.

Goodbye, goodbye my love until the day I die. Goodbye.

Now I must put it all away - one hour of bliss that can never be repeated but will never be forgotten.

Printed in Great Britain
by Amazon